THE FINAL WINTER

AN APOCALYPTIC HORROR NOVEL

IAIN ROB WRIGHT

SALGAD PUBLISHING GROUP

Now this was the sin of Sodom: She and her daughters were arrogant, overfed and unconcerned; they did not help the poor and needy. They were haughty and did detestable things before me. Therefore I did away with them as you have seen.

— **Ezekiel 16:49-50**

The first fall of snow is not only an event, it is a magical event

— **J. B. Priestley**

What He really hates is the shit that gets carried out in his name. Wars. Bigotry. Televangelism

—**Rufus, *Dogma*; View Askew Productions, 1999**

1

Harry sipped his latest beer as more news updates flashed up on the pub's dusty television. A female reporter, enveloped by a bulbous pink ski-jacket and covered in snow, began her report. "Good evening," she said, a shiver in her voice. "I'm Jane Hamilton with Midland-UK News. As you can clearly see, the nineteen-inches of snow Britain has witnessed in the last forty-eight hours has left the nation's transportation networks in disarray."

The camera panned to overlook a deserted motorway. A sky-blue transit van lay overturned and abandoned in its centre; its mystery cargo strewn across, and half-buried by, the snow.

The reporter let out a breath, which steamed in

the air, and then continued. "Major roads are closed and rail services have been terminated until further notice. Schools and many business are temporarily suspended, while hospitals and other vital services are doing their best to remain open. The current death toll has reached twenty-seven and is feared to rise. Emergency services have set up a helpline in order to assist those in most need, and to offer advice on how best to survive the current freezing temperatures. That number is being displayed at the bottom of the screen now."

Harry shook his head. He was never one for fretting about bad weather. The freeze had come suddenly and would leave the same way.

"Even more concerning," the reporter continued, "is the fact that it is currently snowing throughout numerous other areas of the world." A multi-coloured map of the earth superimposed itself at the top-right of the screen and then slowly turned white, representing the recent snowfall. "From barren deserts to areas of dense rainforest, all have been subjected to unprecedented cold spikes. Never before in recorded history has such a widespread cold weather system been known to become so widespread. Certain religious leaders are calling this-"

"Rubbish!" Old Graham, the oldest regular of

The Trumpet and resident of the one-bedroom flat above the pub, threw his hands up in disgust. "A little snow and the country falls apart. Every time. It's a shambles."

Harry lifted his head away from his half-finished pint and glanced over at Old Graham. The grumbling pensioner was pointing to the television screen.

Harry shrugged his shoulders. "No need to get wound up about it."

Old Graham huffed and pouted toothlessly. "Your generation can't cope with anything unless there's a video on that *Your Tube* or *My Face* to tell you about it."

Harry glanced at the television. Scenes of heavy snowfall. Locations from around the globe had become half-buried in blankets of slush and snow. The Pyramids of Giza, ice-capped like Himalayan Mountains; the canals of Venice frozen over like elaborate ice rinks; and Big Ben rising above a snow-covered Westminster like a giant stalagmite.

The television began flickering with interference.

Harry returned his gaze to Old Graham. "I agree it's much ado about nothing. People just enjoy a good panic from time to time. No point in letting it bother you."

The old man huffed again, the sound was wet and wheezy. "You think Canada, Norway, Switzerland are panicking about the snow? This is a heat wave to a bloody Eskimo! All this climate-change, ozone-layer hogwash they're harping on about is just to scare us, you mark my words, lad."

Harry thought about it. According to the news, it was categorically denied that climate-change could cause such unprecedented weather. The various meteorologists and talking heads all maintained that the snow was being caused by something else.

Harry swallowed another mouthful of crisp lager and kept his attention on the flickering television screen. Old Graham continued to gawp at him. Eventually the pensioner's persistent staring irked Harry into speaking again. "Bet everything will be back to normal this time next week, huh, Graham?"

"You bet your balls it will." He slid along the bar towards Harry, arthritic knees clicking with every step. "I've lived through worse times than this, lad!"

"Really?"

"Yeah," he said. "I used to be married." With that, Old Graham howled with laughter, until his worn vocal cords seized up in complaint and caused him to hack yellow-green phlegm bubbles over the bar. "Best go shift the crap off me chest, lad," were his parting words before he tottered off toward the pub's toilets.

Harry shook his head and turned to face the opposite side of the bar. Steph, the pub's only barmaid, was smiling at him while clutching a cardboard box of *Malt 'N' Salt* crisps against her chest. She placed the box down on the bar and pulled an old dishrag from the waistband of her jeans. She wiped down the area where Old Graham had coughed. "He bothering you again, Harry?"

Harry ran a hand through his hair, threading his fingers through the knots and trying to neaten the scruffiness. He sighed. "Graham's okay. Just had too much to drink."

Steph snorted. "You're one to talk. What time did you get here today?"

"Noon."

"Exactly, and it's now..." She glanced at her watch. "Nine in the evening."

Harry blushed. "At least I have the decency to pass out when I'm drunk, instead of talking people's heads off like Old Graham."

Steph rolled her eyes and smirked. "I'll give you that, but I'd like to remind you that you left a puke stain on my knee-highs on Sunday. I had to throw them out"

Harry stared down at the hissing liquid in his

glass and, for a split-second, felt ashamed enough that he contemplated not drinking it and going home instead. Instead, he downed what was left of it, dregs and all. "I must have been a pathetic sight," he admitted.

Steph shrugged. "You're not pathetic, Harry. Just a bit tragic. Things will look up for you one day, but you got to get a hold of yourself. I know life's been pretty damn shitty to you, but you only turned forty a couple months ago, right? Plenty of time to get back on your feet and start a new life." She stopped and looked over at the large plate-glass window that lined one side of the pub. "As long as this wretched snow don't freeze us all to death first, you'll be fine. You just gotta get a grip."

"You really think so?" he asked her with a sigh.

"You better hope so, matey, because I'm not putting up with you spewing on me again. Don't matter how handsome you are!"

They both chuckled and Harry felt his mood lighten a little. It wasn't often he heard such things from a younger woman. Not when the mirror showed him a man that looked closer to fifty than his actual age. Grief had been hard on his face.

Harry pushed his empty pint towards Steph and she refilled it diligently. The overflow from the glass slid down over the black *Foo Fighters* tattoo on her wrist and made her pale skin glisten. Harry was ashamed to feel a stirring in his loins as he looked at her.

Harry's wife, Julie, had been gone a long time now, but he never stopped considering himself a husband. Never once forgot his vow to love her forever.

Harry moved away from the bar, and away from Steph. The tattered padding of the bar stool he'd occupied for the last several hours had sent his backside numb and he craved the relief of a cushion. He headed towards the bench by the pub's front window. At the same time, Old Graham returned from the toilets. There was a small urine stain on the pensioner's crotch and Harry was relieved when the old man headed back to the bar instead of coming over to join him.

Harry eased down onto the worn bench and sighed pleasurably. He placed his pint down on the chipped wooden table in front of him and picked up the nearest beer mat. There was a picture of a crown on it, along with the slogan: *Crown Ales, fit for kings.* Without pause, Harry began to peel the printed face away from the cardboard. It was a habit Steph was always scolding him for, but for some reason it seemed to halt his thoughts for a while and kept back some of the demons in his head.

Relaxing further into the creaking backrest, Harry observed the room he knew so well. The lounge area of The Trumpet was long and slender, with a grimy pair of piss-soaked toilets stinking up an exit corridor at one end and a stone fireplace crisping the air at the other. A dilapidated oak-wood bar took up the centre of the pub, probably older than he was. Several rickety tables and faded patterned chairs made up the rest of the floor space.

In the pub's backroom, a small, seldom-used dance floor collected dust. Harry had only seen it once, at New Year's.

The Trumpet was a quiet, rundown pub in a quiet, rundown housing estate – both welcoming and threatening at the same time. Much like the people that drank there.

Tonight the pub was low on drinkers, as it typically was on a Tuesday. Harry wasn't a big fan of company and preferred the quiet nights. Of course it helped that the snow had confined most people to within a hundred yards of their homes, clogging the main roads with abandoned snowbound vehicles.

Somehow Steph had made it in, holding down the fort as she did most evenings. Harry often wondered why she needed all the overtime she worked. She seemed to enjoy her work, but it could've just been the barmaid's code to be bubbly and polite at all times to all people. Maybe, deep down, Steph really counted each second until she could kick everybody's drunken arses out. Whatever the truth, Steph was a good barmaid and she kept control of the place.

Even Damien Banks behaved on her watch. Weekdays were usually free of his slimy presence, but tonight was an unfortunate exception. The local thug was sat with his Rockports up on the armrest of the sofa beside the fire, iPhone fastened to his ear.

Harry had heard – from sources he no longer remembered – that the young thug pushed his gear on the local estate like some wannabe drug lord. No one in the pub liked Damien, not even his so called friends – or *entourage* as Old Graham would often call them in secret. Rumour had it that the shaven-headed bully once stomped a rival dealer into a coma, taunting the family afterwards by revelling in the grief he'd caused.

Harry shook his head in silent derision. He hated the way Damien lounged around like he owned the place.

There was one other person in the bar tonight. A greasy-haired hulk named Nigel. A lorry driver, from what Harry had gathered over time, the man spent a lot of time on the road. The poor guy would probably have to sleep in his cab tonight.

Just the five of them. Tuesday was a quiet night.

Harry pulled his right knee up onto the bench and peered out of the pub's main window behind him. The Trumpet sat upon a hill overlooking a small row of dingy shops and a mini-supermarket with steel shutters over the windows. Steph once told Harry the pub just about survived on the wafer-thin profits brought in by the lunchtime traffic of the nearby factories, but if it were to rely on its evening drinkers alone, the place would have closed its doors long ago – even before the public smoking ban had come in and crippled local pubs across the land.

On a normal night, Harry could see the shops and supermarket from the pub's window, but tonight his vision faltered at several feet, the view swallowed up by swirling snow. Thick condensation hugged the glass and made everything foggy. For all Harry knew, the darkness outside could have stretched on forever, engulfing the world in its clammy embrace and leaving the pub floating in an inky abyss. The image was unsettling. Like something from the *Outer Limits* TV show.

Snow continued to fall as it had done nonstop for the past day and night. Fat, sparkling wisps that passed through the velvet background of the night, making the gloom itself seem alive with movement. Harry shivered; the pub's archaic heating inadequate in defeating the chill. Even the warmth of the fireplace was losing its battle against the encroaching freeze.

God only knows how I'll manage the journey home tonight without any taxis running. Maybe Steph will let me bed down till morning? I hope so.

Harry reached for his pint and pulled it close, resting it on his thigh as he remained sideways on the bench. He traced a finger over his wedding ring and thought about the day Julie first placed it on his finger. He smiled and felt the warmth of nostalgia wash over him, but then his eyes fell upon the thick, jagged scar that ran across the back of that same hand and the joyful sensation evaporated. The old wound was shaped like a star and brought back memories far darker than Harry's wedding day. It was something he dared not think about.

He took another swig of his beer and almost spat it out. In only two minutes since he'd last tasted it, the lager had gone utterly flat, as if something had literally drained the life from it. Before Harry could consider what that meant, a stranger entered the pub.

A second later, the lights went out.

2

"**B**ugger it!" Kath cursed aloud and slapped her palms down on the supermarket's checkout desk. She'd been two minutes away from finishing the 9pm cash-up and the building's power blinked out like somebody had flipped a switch. "Peter!" she hollered into the darkness. "Check the damned fuse box, will you!"

A muffled voice from the nearby stockroom let Kath know her order had been received. She sighed and waited for her vision to adjust, wondering where she could find a torch or some candles (*Doesn't Aisle 6 have some?*). The *Fire Exit* sign above the supermarket's entrance gave off a faint green glow too weak to even highlight her acrylic fingernails in front of her face.

Kath heard footsteps echoing down the Bread & Pastries aisle.

"Who's there?" she called out.

The unexpected proximity of the voice made Kath flinch. "It's *me*," said the voice. "Jess."

"Jess? You stupid girl! You gave me a fright."

"Sorry, Kathleen. Didn't mean to. You know why the lights are out?"

"No. I've told Peter to check the fuse box."

"Good idea. You reckon it's just us, or the whole area?"

Kath shrugged in the dark. "How should *I* know? Walk out the front and see for yourself."

"Okay," said Jess cheerily, before wandering towards the store's main entrance with a skipping hop. Her complexion became ghostly as she entered the pulsing green glow of the Fire Exit sign.

Kath cleared her throat. "Well? What are you waiting for?"

Jess pushed open the door. A howling chill entered the supermarket, rushing to all corners like a horde of squealing rats. The weather outside was so bad that it was like opening the gates to hell.

Kath waited impatiently while Jess gingerly poked her head out of the door and looked left and right, then left and right again. Finally, she leant back inside and closed the door. When she turned back to Kath, the girl's work fleece was peppered with snow.

"The weather out there is craaaay-zee!" said Jess. "With a capitol zee"

Kath sighed. "What about the lights? Are anybody else's on? What about The Trumpet?" The dingy pub was set opposite, up the hill.

"I can't even see the pub," said Jess. "I can't make out Blue Rays or any of the other shops either. The snow is coming down like it's the end of the world."

"Wonderful!" Kath shook her head and felt a migraine coming on. If the whole area was out then she would be forced to sit and wait for the electricity company to get off their overpaid behinds and do something about it.

...and God knew how long that would take. Two minutes? Two hours?

Kath couldn't set the alarms and go home until she cashed up the tills, and she couldn't do that without power. She breathed in deep, before letting the cold air out through her nostrils. *What a wretched waste of intellect*, she thought, *being stuck in this wretched place ten hours a day.*

"It'll be back on in a jiffy," said Jess, still standing by the fire exit. "It never takes long, Kathleen. Tell you what, I'll take a little walk over to the pub and see if anyone knows anything, okay?" Without pausing for an answer, Jess slid out through the exit and was immediately swallowed by the shifting snow and darkness outside.

A second later it was as if the girl had never even been there.

Kath sighed, leant back into the torn-padding of the cashier's stool, and rubbed at her aching forehead. Shivers ran up and down her spine and made her clutch at herself. It was Britain's worst winter in history and she was stuck in a building with no power. Before long the place would become freezing.

"Screw this," Kath decided. She'd give Mr Campbell a call and see if there was any chance he'd allow her to cash up in the morning. He should have been thanking her for even turning up at all in this weather. She slid her fingertips along the icy surface of the cashier's desk and groped for the phone. At first she found only a stapler and some biros, but eventually the side of her hand found what it was looking for and knocked the receiver from its cradle. It fell from the desk swung by its cord. After a couple of half-blind swipes, Kath caught the receiver and pulled it up to her ear. She tapped at the buttons on the phone's cradle, waited a beat, then tapped them again.

No dial tone.

Perturbed, Kath placed the handset back down onto its cradle, before picking it up and trying to ring out once more.

Nothing.

"Please, for the love of God!" Kath patted down the pockets of her work shirt and located her mobile phone. She plucked it out and slid up the illuminated screen to expose the keypad. She selected Mr Campbell's number from the phone's memory and pressed the green CALL button, before putting the phone to her ear and waiting.

Ten seconds passed and Kath pulled the phone away from her head to look at the display. She could barely contain her frustration when she saw NO NETWORK COVERAGE scrolled across the top of the screen.

"For crying out loud!"

Before Kath could put her thoughts in order, a male voice echoed in the darkness. "Ms Hollister?"

The voice had a Polish twang.

"Peter," Kath said, more calmly than she felt. "Have you checked the fuses?"

"Yes, Ms Hollister. I need show you something. Come."

Kath rolled her eyes. Speak properly, for God's sake. If you're going to come here, at least learn the language.

Reluctantly, she followed the boy down to the back of the store, ducking through the strips of clear plastic that separated the cramped warehouse from the shop floor. "So, what is it that's so important, Peter?" she asked.

"I will show to you."

Peter turned a corner in the cramped warehouse. Kath stayed close behind, lighting her way with her mobile phone. It didn't work particularly well, but it at least illuminated any over-stacked boxes she would otherwise bump into.

Kath was getting impatient. "Come on now, Peter, I need to find a way to call Mr Campbell, so we can all go home tonight. Unless you want to spend the night sleeping in the staff room?"

Peter stopped at the far wall and pointed upwards, just above the height of his shoulder. Kath glanced at the area a few inches away from the boy's outstretched finger. She didn't understand and felt her patience thin even more. "What exactly am I supposed to be looking at?"

Peter rolled his eyes in the faint glow of her phone display and then pointed more emphatically at what he wanted her to see.

"The fuse box? Yes, very impressive."

Peter rolled his eyes again and she was about to scold him for it when she spotted what he wanted her to see. It was the fuse box alright – at least it had been in a former life – but now it was a black, melted decay of wires and bubbling plastic. The green metal box that housed the circuits was untouched, but inside it looked like it'd been subjected to a hellish blaze. The acrid stench of singed rubber lingered in the cold, crisp air, but it wasn't as strong as she would expect after an electrical fire. "I don't understand. What could cause this?"

Peter shrugged. "I no sure. Fire maybe?"

"Obviously not, Peter. There hasn't been a fire because the alarms would've gone off. Not to mention it would have spread. This place is full of cardboard and paper."

"Vandalism?"

Kath considered Peter's wild suggestion, her thoughts wandering off into the dark, insidious alleyways of her mind. Could someone have really taken a welder's torch to the fuses or doused them in petrol? Was someone lurking in the shadows intending to have their way with her in the dark? Had some hairy beast of a man been watching her for months, planning something just like this? It was certainly an opportune time. The police would never make it in this weather, even if she managed to call them. It seemed ridiculous but, for a moment, so plausible in her anxious state of mind that Kath actually started to believe that someone was intending to murder her. It was like something straight out of that Richard Laymon novel she once read by mistake, thinking it was something milder. *Horrible, disgusting book full of rapists and monsters.*

"Ridiculous," Kath made herself say. "They have no power at the pub either. Same with Blue Rays on the corner."

Pete shrugged his shoulders and walked off. Nothing ever seemed to concern the boy from Poland.

Suddenly alone, Kath tried to make sense of the situation. Was some deranged madman really stalking the neighbourhood, cutting off everyone's electricity? Or was her biggest threat freezing to death on the coldest night of the year? Neither outcome was appealing. All Kath knew for sure was that the fuse box hadn't destroyed itself and that the real cause was yet to make itself known.

She shivered, the chill in the air thickening suddenly and constricting the gristle on her bones. There was no way she could stay there any longer. Not without power. Not in the dark. She made a decision. "Right! Peter, where are you?"

A scuffling sound from the far corner of the warehouse. "I'm here, by the beer crates."

"Well, make sure you're careful. You break anything, you pay for it."

Peter didn't respond, but Kath was certain she heard the boy sigh. She enjoyed getting under people's skin and let loose a smile as crude as the oil-slick darkness that surrounded her. Suddenly she felt more in charge, more like herself. "Peter," she shouted. "Place some pallets against the back shutter. We're going to call it a night, but we need to secure the building as best we can before we leave."

"Okay, I will do, but where is Jess? She help me."

"She's wandered off somewhere." Kath snorted. "Least of my worries right now, so go do as I've said – and make sure you're careful."

Peter scurried away, mumbling something in Polish. At least Kath imagined it was Polish. Could be Russian or Hungarian, or whatever it is all these Eastern Europeans spoke – ugly, primitive language that hurt her ears to listen to. How had Britain become so weak? There was a time when it had invaded third-rate nations, but now it seemed more interested in letting them all in and keeping them fed and warm. It made her stomach turn to think her government cared more about benefit-seeking immigrants than educated citizens like her. Where was *her* assistance?

Kath left the warehouse and re-entered the supermarket, listening to the loud scraping noises of Peter struggling to shift the pallets in the warehouse. The thought of him blindly bumping around on his own made her smirk as she marched towards the building's exit.

When she reached the glass fire door, she opened it up and glanced outside. There was little she could do to secure the building tonight – not without the electric shutter – but she could at least lock up with her keys. She didn't expect anyone would be desperate enough to brave the current weather just to steal a few groceries anyway. At least she hoped so...

3

"B'jaysus, it's nice to be in the warm again. Cold as a nun's pussy out there, so it is."

Harry gazed in the direction of the stranger's voice, over by the pub's entrance, and found himself at a loss. The cheery Irish accent was not what he'd been expecting. In fact, when Harry had first realised the presence of the stranger in the darkness, he'd felt something else, something...ominous. That seemed silly now.

"Hey, who is that?" asked Steph from behind the bar. "Anyone we know?"

A hearty chuckle floated over from the doorway. "No Lass, I do not believe we've had the pleasure. The name's Lucas Fergus and I am on a vital quest to get some beer down me neck."

Steph laughed and Harry found himself amused too. It wasn't often the pub was graced with such colour beyond old men and their tall tales of the past.

"Well," said Steph, "I can only offer you bottles and shots at the moment. As you can see the power is off, and that means the electric pumps are dry. Cash only, too, no tabs"

"Cash is the only way an honourable man pays for anything in my mind, so there be no worries there, and I don't care whether the beer comes from bottle or tap neither. It all ends up in the same place."

"No arguments there," said a voice Harry recognised as Old Graham's.

Over by the fireplace the flickering silhouette of Damien shifted and stirred. Damien didn't like strangers. People he didn't know were usually unaware of his reputation, and he did not appreciate that at all. Several months back, Harry had witnessed Damien carve his initials into some poor lad's forehead with a nasty-looking blade, just so people would know he was to be respected. The young man had screamed the entire time and nobody was able to do a thing as Damien's cronies took up guard.

The police never came. No one even called them.

Thankfully, Damien had been uncharacteristically quiet tonight, almost as if he was dealing with some internal issue, but Harry worried that might be something bad.

"Can we bear some light in here, you reckon?" Lucas asked, flicking open a glinting, metal lighter and illuminating his face with the flame. He looked about Harry's age, yet boyishly handsome with a cheeky grin to match. Wild tussles of mousy brown hair crept beneath his ears and halfway down his neck. Harry thought the guy looked like a handsome traveller from the front cover of one of the trashy *Mills and Boon* novels his wife used to buy at the car boots they went to.

"In weather like this I'm surprised you're not all round that lovely fireplace." Lucas moved toward the bar, his flame-lit face a disembodied ghost as it crossed the room. "Or does that wee fella on the sofa not play well with others?"

"The less said about that the better," warned Steph in a hushed voice.

Harry cringed, worried about the response the newcomer's comment could elicit from Damien, and was thankful, if a little surprised, when the young thug merely turned away and returned to whatever he was doing. It really wasn't like Damien to be so reserved. He was preoccupied with something. But what?

Confident that no trouble was going to occur, at least for the time-being, Harry decided he would join the newcomer at the bar. Sitting alone in the dark wasn't awfully appealing and he needed a refill anyway. His current beer smelt like bad eggs.

"So, Lucas?" Harry said, arriving at the bar and propping his elbows against its gnarled surface. "Where have you come in from?"

Lucas turned to Harry, the lighter still illuminating his face. "I've come in from the bloody cold fella, but before that I come from down south."

Harry raised an eyebrow. "South?"

"That's what I said now, ain't it? Been here-there-and-everywhere in my time – up and down, upside down – but originally I hail from the North. Been spending a lot of time in the South more recently though, after a falling out with me father. Suits me just fine, warmer climate, you know?"

"You mean Southern Ireland?"

"Where is that drink I heard a rumour about," Lucas said, ignoring the question. "This is a pub, is it not?"

Steph shouted from the backroom behind the bar. "Hold your horses! For a complete stranger you're pretty demanding."

"I'm a growing lad, and if ye make me wait I may just fade away. Or, worse than that, I may sober up."

Steph came back through to the bar holding a wooden tray full of mismatched candles. The flames danced around her breasts and Harry tried not to stare at them. Carefully, she placed the candles evenly along the bar and the heady smell of burning wax wafted into the air. The first candle she had placed in front of Old Graham, whilst the last went in front of Nigel. In between, Harry and Lucas got candles too.

"That's better," said Steph. "Now, who wants a beer besides our new friend here?"

"I'm ready for one," said Harry. "This one has gone bad."

"Mine too," said Old Graham, pushing his own pint forward. "I'm going to have to have a dozen more just to make up for it."

Steph scrunched up her face. "Strange... Maybe there's a problem with the pumps. Not surprised, the amount you lot drink. They probably couldn't take the strain."

Lucas chuckled. "Looks like I've come to the

right place. You're men after me own heart, and now that I can see a little bit better, I can also admire what a fine young wench we have ourselves behind the bar."

"Hey, less of the wench!" Steph objected. They all laughed and she got to work handing them their bottled beers, each of them swigging deeply as though it was their first of the night. Perhaps for Lucas it was.

The Irishman pointed a finger. "So, who's the beefy fella down the end of the bar?"

"My name is Nigel."

"Well, Big Man, come and suck ale with the rest of us."

"Maybe later."

"What's wrong with you, man? There a gal down there with you?"

"Huh, I wish."

"Get your mardy britches down here then! A fella shouldn't be lonesome on a night like this. The cold out there could kill a man stone dead, no word of a lie."

"Okay, okay," Nigel conceded. He slid down the bar and joined the rest of them, dumping his heavy mass down onto a creaking stool beside Lucas. Harry nodded hello. Lucas certainly had a knack for bringing people together. *Magnetic personality* was the phrase that came to mind.

Lucas spoke again. "You know something, fellas? I don't think that snow is gonna let up any time soon."

"Great," said Steph. "We've all got to try and get home tonight somehow."

Lucas put down his beer with a *clink!* "What? Are you drunk, lass? Ain't no man getting anywhere in that winter blanket."

Steph's face dropped slightly, the dull candle-light making her expression seem grim. "How did you get here then?"

Lucas smiled knowingly. "I was nearby and re-alised things were bad, so I thought to meself: 'where's the best place to be stuck on a night like this?' Well of course there was only one answer, wasn't there?"

"The boozer!" Old Graham shouted gleefully, clearly delighted by the Irishman's philosophy. "Anyway," the pensioner added, "don't you worry, young Stephanie, there's always room upstairs at my place to keep warm."

Cheeky sod, thought Harry. Wonder if the old guy even has enough lead in his pencil to get it up these days?

Steph laughed defiantly, the air from her nostrils slanting the flames of the nearby candles. "The only way you'll get me up there, old man, is if you're sleeping on the roof."

Everyone cackled and swigged their beers merrily in the dark. Everyone except Damien, who remained alone, staring into the fire like he was looking for answers.

4

"Dude, just sit the hell down! If you break something my Dad will freak." Ben didn't need this from Jerry tonight. Not with the power going out and such shitty weather. It was like a dozen winters rolled into one and he was stuck in his father's video store not knowing what to do for the best.

"Chill out, B-Dog!" said Jerry, shining his key ring torch into his own face and contorting his skeletal features into a ghoulish grimace. The DVD cases on the cluttered shelves behind him shone with every movement of the light. "You need to stop worrying about your old man. It's not like he ever does anything for *you*. I can't believe he made you come in today. As if anyone is going to come out and rent a movie in this weather. This place is the Video Store of the Damned even on a good day."

Ben frowned, though it was too dark in the store's dusty back-office for Jerry to see it. "Stop calling it that! The place is doing just fine. It's not every day that Dad trusts me to look after Blue Rays on my own, so the last thing I need is you making my life difficult, okay? Just behave and don't mess anything up."

"Okay, okay," Jerry conceded. "What would you like me to do with myself, oh wise Gandalf?"

Ben threw his head back and cursed. "I told you to stop calling me that!"

"Get rid of that gay beard and I will. Either that or I'll get some hairy-assed Hobbits in here so you can feel more at home."

"Just..." Ben took a deep breath and let it out slowly. "Sit down will you, while I try to get the power back on."

Thankfully, Jerry complied, hoisting his stick-like figure up onto the service desk and remaining quiet. Ben could still hear him fidgeting away for anything to get his spindly fingers on, but at least for now he was rooted in one place; his area of reck-lessness limited.

Sometimes Ben didn't know why he put up with his friend. They'd known each other since they were peeing in pre-school sandpits, but for some reason his friend had never seemed to mature like he had. Ben had gone to college, whilst Jerry sponged off his mom and stepdad. Ben started dating girls, whilst Jerry bought an Xbox. Eventually, Ben had started to shoulder some of his dad's business responsibilities, ready to one day take them on as his own, and Jerry...? Well now Jerry spent most his days hanging around Blue Rays Rentals bothering him and making fun of his beard or his 'jelly-belly'. Still, they were best friends and Ben knew that if it ever came down to it, Jerry would do anything for him. There was something comforting about that. *Not like anybody else cares.* Besides, deep down, Ben liked having Jerry around. Despite the odd annoyances, they had a lot of fun together. Even the *Ben and Jerry* jokes didn't really bother him too much anymore. Tonight however, Jerry was stretching his patience paper-thin.

"When you gunna get the lights on again?" Jerry asked. "It's like *Saturday Night Fever* in here." He swept his penlight around the room, illuminating the low-hung, suspended ceiling like a disco ball. A movie poster of a disgruntled De Niro and an awkward looking Ben Stiller lit up and disappeared as the light passed over it.

"If it is," said Ben, "then you're no John Travol-

ta!" He walked across to the far side of the office, behind the IKEA computer desk and towards the fuse
box. He didn't know anything about electrics and he
was hoping to flick a switch and be done with it.
Likely, it would be more complicated than that.

Before the power went off, Ben had been
watching the news with Jerry – well, to be more
honest, Jerry was waiting for a re-run of *The Matrix*
to come on. The reports had said that the country's
infrastructure was expected to be affected by the
snow for several more days and that blackouts were
likely as people's heating usages rose to monu-
mental levels. It didn't bother Ben too much, so long
as nothing happened to his father's store whilst he
was in charge of it. Business came first.

Before anything else.

Before silly little friendships with that imbecile,
Jerry.

Ben shook his father's words out of his head and
pulled out his keys from his pocket, sifting through
them one by one. Earlier, he and Jerry had become
concerned by the amount of snowfall – and more
than a little anxious that the bad weather was
spread throughout most of the globe. Having
watched so many disaster movies, Ben couldn't help
but get the *heebie jeebies* about how the snow
seemed to be falling so endlessly. When it had piled

knee-deep, Ben and Jerry had hurried to the supermarket on the corner, to stock up on snacks and beers in case they got stranded in the store. They were willing to wait things out if they had to. Ben just hoped Jerry kept his exuberance under control during. His best friend had a knack for breaking things. Ben called it the *Jerry effect.*

Ben swung open the fuse cabinet and flicked open his monogrammed lighter. He'd stopped smoking months ago but it had been a present from his father – and they were too few and far between to discard. His eyes glazed for a second as they adjusted to the light, and once they did he was confused by what he saw. The fuse box appeared to have burned and melted.

It made no sense. Wasn't the whole point of having fuse boxes to prevent electrical fires?

There wasn't anything Ben could think of that could cause such severe heat damage on the fuses, while leaving the surrounding cabinet completely untouched. Ben plucked at his scruffy brown beard rhythmically as he tried to find a thought that fit, a thought that didn't worry him. But all that came to mind was...

Das is going to blow a fuse of his own when he finds out about this.

At that moment, Jerry shouted out from the

shop floor. "What's happening, Gandalf? You stroking the salami back there?"

Ben shook his head and rolled his eyes. "Dude, I swear, not now, okay!"

"Okay, okay," Jerry said. "Don't get your beard in a twist. It's not like it's the end of the world – although we *are* missing *The Matrix*."

5

Kath wasn't prepared to stay there all night in the dark. She tried her mobile phone again and hissed when it still refused to dial out.

Everyone else in the country had been skiving off and throwing sickies since the snow started; why hadn't she? It would have made life a lot easier. *Because I have integrity*, she told herself. *Unlike most people these days.* Luckily, Peter and Jess lived within walking distance of the store and had had no excuses not to come in. They knew she wouldn't stand for any absence.

Kath glanced toward the fire exit. The doors were closed, but she could see the drifting snow outside, piling up against the glass.

It was beginning to feel more like the North Pole than the West Midlands.

Shivering, Kath pulled her arms away from her sides and groped around the cashier desk for the phone again. The thought that someone may have been responsible for the power going off still worried her and all she wanted to do was talk to someone in authority. Mr Campbell. The power company. The police. Anyone.

Peter stood nearby, she'd insisted on it, and the intermittent glow of his mobile phone made her feel a little safer, but it was only enough to take a slight edge off her nerves. She plucked the phone from its cradle and prodded the keypad.

Still no dial tone.

Kath slammed the handset back down.

"Is okay?" Peter asked in his horrible broken English.

"Everything is fine. I just dropped the phone. Do you know where Jessica is yet? I need to close up, but not before I've done a staff search. Its night's like tonight when things go missing."

There was silence for a moment and Kath's heart rate rose. A few seconds later Peter made himself known again. "I not know where she is. Do you?"

Kath sighed. "Would I have asked you, if I did?

Last I knew she was out front checking if anyone knew why the power was off. I don't think she's come back."

"Should I go look for her?"

The thought of being alone made Kath shout out. "No! Stay here. The last thing I need is you both getting lost."

Pete began walking back toward the counter. "You think she is lost?"

"That girl would lose her head if it wasn't sewn on. I'm sure whatever she's doing out there, she's managed to find her way into trouble. Just lea-"

Kath's body was suddenly wracked with shivers, cutting her words off mid-sentence. It hadn't seemed anywhere near as chilly just an hour ago when the power had first gone off. Without the heating things were going to become freezing. She glanced at the fire exit again. The snow outside swirled intently. The wind picked up and started to howl.

Kath wrapped her arms around herself and shivered. "For God sake, Peter, will you hurry up? We need to leave."

We need to leave right now.

~

JESS COULD BARELY SEE an inch in front of the freckles on her nose. The snow whipped her face relentlessly, filling her nostrils and blurring her eyes. It felt like she was going to suffocate, yet she had no choice but to persevere and find her way back to the supermarket. It was embarrassing that she'd managed to get herself so disorientated – it could only have been been ten feet before she'd found herself turned around and lost - but every direction led to a white, blossom background that seemed to creep on endlessly. She shivered, partly from anxiety but mostly from the fact she was freezing.

Really smart, Jessica. A+ for common sense.

She cried out for help and was unsurprised when she was met with near silence – the only other sound being the shrill whistle of the increasing wind. Despite the lack of reply, Jess called out again, lacking other ideas. Still silence. Jess paused to gather her thoughts. The biting cold was worse when standing still.

Jess fumbled amongst her loose change and pulled out her mobile phone. It was slender and metallic, painted pink with silver sequins. Her intention was to use it to call Peter at the supermarket and get him to shout out of the doorway. She'd follow his voice, feeling like a fool, but as long as it was only Peter she wouldn't mind too much. He would keep things to himself and not tell the super-bitch, *Kathleen*.

The phone lit up as soon as she pressed its key-pad, but it became immediately apparent that something was wrong with it. It still had power, but the display was garbled, distorted by vertical lines and random squiggles. She tried making a call but was unsuccessful. She put the phone away and re-sumed her directionless searching.

As a child, Jess had loved winter and wished for snow every Christmas – her favourite time of year – but this worldwide inclement weather made her nervous. There was a sense of foreboding in the howling wind that made Jess wonder if it would ever stop snowing at all. She'd heard on the radio that people had already begun to perish from the crushing cold, and it had only become worse since then. Now that her mobile phone wasn't working, it left Jess even more uncertain.

Of course her phone could have been faulty. "Yeah, that's it," she said to herself, hoping it would calm her nerves to hear a voice, even if it was just her own. "It's just faulty."

Somehow, she didn't believe it.

❦

IT WAS ALMOST thirty minutes before Peter had finished. Kath heard his footsteps coming from the BOOZE & SPIRITS aisle. "Is everything secure?" she asked him.

"Yes, Ms Hollister."

"Let's get going then."

"Where is Jess?"

Kath grunted. "She's responsible for her own well-being. I can't afford to wait around any longer. If you're so concerned, you go wandering around in the snow for her yourself."

"Thank you, Ms Hollister. I go now."

"Peter, wait!" she shouted after him. "Perhaps, you're right. We shouldn't just leave Jess to her own devices."

Peter's footsteps halted. "Okay, Ms Hollister. Please, hurry!"

The fact that she was being given orders by a staff member made Kath furious, but the increasing howl of the wind made her feel uncharacteristically subdued. "Coming," she said.

6

Harry shivered as he started his next beer. It was getting colder and the scar on the back of his hand started to ache in response. He swigged deeply from his beer bottle and tried not to think.

The Irishman, Lucas, turned his attention to Old Graham at the end of the bar. "So, Father Time, you must have been around a fair few turns of the world? You ever see snow like this before?"

"Well," Old Graham began, visibly delighted at being the centre of attention. "There was a time in the sixties where things got a little chilly as I recall; and me old man told tales of winter in the Ardennes that sounded a might more hellish than this."

"That's the Ardennes," said Nigel. "It's normal to

have snow there. The amount we've had here the past couple days isn't natural. Not to mention it's snowing everywhere. All over the world. In every country. Maybe it's because of the ozone layer or something?"

Lucas chuckled. "Give over, man! You think a couple of cow farts has the ability to change the weather?"

Harry smirked. "What do you put the snow down to then, Lucas? I mean I haven't known it to snow like this before. It certainly seems like something has narked Mother Nature."

"The world is a gazillion years old," said Lucas, putting his beer bottle down on the bar as if to make a point. "I bet there's been weather like this before, just not in your lifetime. It's a tad unusual, no doubt, but I don't buy all that ozone layer nonsense."

Nigel bristled in the light of his candle, maybe even turning angry. "That's just your opinion," he said. "Don't mean I'm not right. We've been abusing this planet for decades and it can't go on forever."

Lucas put up his hands. "Calm down there, fella, no need to get your hackles up. It's just the beer talking, you know? Makes me feel a thousand times older and wiser than I should ever admit to. You're probably right, though, humanity *has* been abusing the earth, and it can't go on forever. Right now, my only concern is having a good time with a tipple to keep me warm." He looked at Steph and winked. "And maybe a good woman wouldn't go amiss either."

"You're a letch," said Nigel, but the candlelight lit a good-natured smile on his face.

"Again, I've come to the right place, then." Lucas laughed out loud, hoisted his bottle up into the air and said *"cheers!"* The others joined him in the toast.

Harry took another swig from his bottle and sighed at the burning satisfaction it left in his chest. When he pulled it away from his lips it was two-thirds empty. It seemed he'd been taking larger and larger swigs lately.

"So what's *your* story, fella?" Lucas asked Harry. "What's the meaning of your life?"

Harry swigged the last of his beer then pushed the bottle toward Steph, who was already on the case with a replacement. "My life," he said, "has no meaning. Not anymore."

Lucas frowned. "Come now, everybody's life has meaning. We all have a purpose."

"Really? Then why don't you tell me what *mine* is, because I sure as hell don't know."

"I can't tell you that." Lucas smiled. "Every man has to find his own path and his own destination.

Who knows though, maybe you'll find yours tonight."

Harry started on his next beer with a hearty swig, gasping for breath afterwards. He looked Lucas square in the face. He knew he was getting drunk, but couldn't stop himself, as usual. "Sorry, but I find that hard to believe."

Lucas stared back, his face unflinching, like a slab of sculpted granite. He patted Harry on the back. "Well, Harry boy, perhaps what you need is a little more faith."

"Faith? You think I should believe that there's some almighty-being up there responsible for everything that happens?"

Lucas shook his head. "Like hell I do! Everything that happens down here is because of us. The good Lord's not here to babysit us. We can only blame ourselves for the things that happen in our lives. Well, we can blame ourselves or other people. Seems most people prefer to do the latter before they even consider introspection."

Harry felt his blood heat up, fighting back against the chill in his veins. He took offence to a stranger offering him life advice. No one could understand what he'd been through. Harry looked down at the star shaped scar on his hand and thought about the events which had led to it. Julie and Toby twisted and shattered in the remains of his bright red Mercedes, the car he'd been so proud to buy. That night Harry discovered cars, houses, and material possessions meant nothing at all, as the only truly important things in his life slowly bled away from him onto the asphalt. So much damage that Harry couldn't even tell where his wife and child's broken bodies began and the crumpled metal of the Mercedes ended. It looked like some abominable piece of modern art.

Harry had emerged from the crash with nothing more than a deep gash on his forehead. He was completely lucid as he watched his family die in front of him, one laboured breath at a time. Where had the justice been in that?

"Whoever is to blame for my life," Harry told Lucas, "can go fuck themselves."

Lucas moved a half-step back from Harry. "Easy fella, not looking for an argument. You just seem like a bit of a lost soul, and I like to take an interest."

"An interest in lost souls?"

"Absolutely. There's an endless wisdom in the agonies of man. Sometimes we don't understand what humanity really is until we have our hearts and flesh torn."

Harry put down his beer. "Sorry to let you down, but I don't feel anything. Not anymore."

Lucas continued smiling, as though he had the secrets of the world in his back pocket and was about to share them. "You can lie to *me*, Harry boy, but it would be a tragedy to lie to *yourself*. Men who say they feel nothing, usually feel the most. Denial only leads to trouble. That, my friend, I can promise you."

Harry sighed and moved away from Lucas before he said something he regretted.

THE TRUMPET WAS an old pub with a long history. A baby boy had once been born in its claustrophobic toilets; the England Cricket team had once rented the place after a win at nearby Edgbaston; and even a murder had once occurred on its oak floors. It was a place with both history and colour. A proud relic of working men's pubs, full of 'proper blokes' clocking off from a hard day's graft for a fag and a pint. But, like all relics, its day had come and gone. Now, the fag smoking was ostracised, the over-taxed beer was expensive and weak, and the colour had all faded along with the bleak wallpaper. All the pub had left now was its history.

Things hadn't turned out the way Damien's father had led him to expect. The golden years of smoke-filled boozers, loose women, and high-grade drugs had been extinguished. Drugs were getting harder and harder to push and women were getting harder and harder to fuck – feminist shows like *Sex and the City* convincing them to have self-respect. It had taken all the fun out of being a gangster.

Screw it! He'd been born in the wrong time. There was no tradition anymore. Damien's father and Grandfather had drunk in The Trumpet and had pretty much run the place in their days. Now you had people like this fuckface Irishman waltzing in and acting like they owned the joint after just five minutes. He needed to be taught a lesson about respect.

Damien stood from the sofa and turned towards the bar. He had enough to deal with tonight without loud-mouthed strangers giving him a headache.

WHEN HARRY SAW Damien rise up from the sofa and start making his way toward the bar, he cringed.

"Shit, incoming." Harry whispered in Steph's direction, hopeful that her authority behind the bar would be enough to stem any bad behaviour. He'd seen Damien's lack of hospitality towards strangers before and it was something he could go without seeing again.

Damien stomped towards the middle of the bar, halting half-a-foot away from Lucas. Lucas behaved as if he hadn't noticed, facing forward and sipping from his bottle calmly. Damien glared at him, eyeballs bulged like two squids.

Lucas leant over the bar towards Steph and spoke in a very clear voice. "Darling, you want to tell this young fella to wind his neck in before his peepers fall out on my shoes?"

Everyone at the bar sucked in their lungs.

Lucas turned his head to Damien, who looked like he was about to go off like a firework. "Listen, lad, I'm not a work of art, so take your beady little eyes off me and find something better to do."

Damien's features contorted like a broken whiskey bottle, full of crags and sharp edges. One wiry arm drew back as his young body tensed up, ready to attack.

In a move that seemed both casual and urgent at the same time, Lucas stepped back from the bar and slinked past his stool. At the precise moment Damien's fist began its arcing descent towards him, Lucas threw a punch of his own. It was quick, it was vicious, and it connected perfectly with Damien's incoming fist. There was a loud crack as the two men's knuckles collided at full force.

"Fuck!" Damien howled, clutching his withered hand against his abdomen. "Jesus-goddamn-Christ!"

Lucas, who was also clutching his own injured hand, began to laugh in what seemed like genuine amusement. "Not quite, but I'll send you to go see him if you try that bollocks again, you little shithead."

Damien glared. "You're dead!"

"Wrong again, lad. Unless you mean dead bored, which if I'm honest, I'm starting to get a wee bit. You're keeping a man from his drink."

Damien was about to respond, no doubt to make more threats, but Steph cut him off first – not with her voice, but with the landlord's bell pulled out from under the bar. She rang it vigorously in the faces of the two arguing men.

"Pack this shit in!" she hollered. "I'm in no mood for child's play. Especially from you!" She scowled at Damien. "It's freezing cold, we're all stuck here, and we're in the bloody dark. Do you two not think things are bad enough without fisticuffs? Because you know something? If one of you gets hurt, I doubt there's an ambulance in the world that can get here tonight."

Or even this week, Harry thought.

Damien allowed his glare to turn into a grimace, before finally settling on a look of irritation. Lucas got back on his stool and quickly finished off his beer. He slid the empty toward Steph and said, "Two more, please. One for me and one for my new friend here with the broken hand."

Damien hissed. "It isn't broken, and I'm not your pissing friend."

"Well," said Lucas, offering a bottle of beer to Damien. "Perhaps you should be. It would make life easier."

"Come on, Damien," said Nigel from the far end of the bar. "If we're all stuck here, we may as well have a drink together. Could even be a laugh."

Damien turned his animalistic stare to the large, sweaty man at the end of the bar. "You think I want to waste a minute hanging around with a bunch of losers like you?"

Harry took offence. Being called a loser by a piece of scum like Damien did not sit well with him at all. "We don't want to be stuck with you either," he said, "but shit happens."

Damien turned his glare to Harry, his body coiled and trembling like a pissed off panther. *A panther ready to attack,* thought Harry, regretting his comment already.

Before further words were exchanged though, Lucas pushed the bottle of beer towards Damien. "How bouts I buy your beers all night if you sit down and join in? Be an amicable chappy!"

Damien smirked. "I don't need you to buy my drinks. I have enough money to buy your whole fucking family."

Lucas smiled his cheeky grin. "I very much doubt that, lad, but why don't we say I'm doing it to show my respect. I'm the new boy here and I obviously don't know how things work now, do I? So accept my offer as an apology."

Damien scrutinised the man's suggestion, but it seemed obvious that it had settled down his need for bravado. Harry admired Lucas's savvy. The man had swallowed his own sense of pride and manipulated Damien into behaving. The young thug thought he'd won, but it was apparent to everyone else at the bar that Lucas had just used a modicum of intelligence to control the situation.

"Okay," Damien finally said, snatching the bottle from Lucas. "Guess I can lower myself for one night and share a few beers with the peasants."

Everyone was happy to ignore the insult, ready to play along with Lucas's charade if it meant having peace. They raised their beers in the air and mumbled agreement.

Lucas put his hand on the bar; it was swollen and red in the candle light. "Don't suppose you could get me some ice, luv?"

Steph sighed and nodded. "Sure."

Damien suddenly slammed down his own fist on the bar and made the rest of them jump. Like Lucas, his hand was also swollen. "Yeah, I think I could do with some too."

There was a brief silence before Damien began laughing. It was the least hostile Harry had ever seen the lad and, before long, the entire bar was sipping their drinks and laughing right along with him. The tension seemed to float away.

But Harry had a feeling it wouldn't last.

7

"Dude, I'm starting to get totally frost-bitten. It's like *The Day After Tomorrow* in here."

Ben sighed. For some reason, Jerry had to speak almost entirely in film references. The fact that Ben's father owned a video store didn't help matters at all. Yet, despite his annoyance, Ben had to agree. It was getting uncomfortably cold.

"Can you hear me, B-dog?" Jerry shouted from the shop floor. "I said it's like *The Day aft-*"

"Yes, I heard you. Hopefully the power will come back on soon, but there's not a lot I can do about it in the meantime."

"What? You saw those fuses! The lights ain't coming on any time soon. You should just call your dad so we can get out of here."

Ben fumbled his way through the dark from the office back to the shop floor, bumping into various shelving units along the way. "I tried already! My phone's playing up. The display is all screwed."

"No shit? My phone is like that, too."

Ben paused. What were the odds that both their phones would be playing up? "Really? You think it's the weather?"

"I dunno," Jerry said. "Can the weather do stuff like that?"

"Something's responsible, not just for the phones but the power blowing out as well."

Ben crossed the shop floor over to the thick glass door at the front of the shop. It was still snowing outside; heavy round flakes that seemed to sizzle as they hit the ground. He and Jerry had been clearing the entranceway throughout the day, keeping the place as accessible as possible. Of course, in such bad weather, barely a soul came by all day anyway. To make best use of the time, Ben had decided to do a stock count, which had been spot-on bar two missing copies of *The Pianist* and a copy of *Brain Dead* that Jerry had swiped over six months ago.

Ben turned around to face the gloom of the shop floor and a thought crossed his mind. "Hey, Jerry, when did you go to the supermarket last?"

Jerry's response came from somewhere near the cash register. Ben hoped he wasn't messing around with anything. "Couple hours ago, why?"

"Did they say what time they were closing?"

"Nah, Cruella was serving me. I bought a Beano and left."

"You mean the manageress? Yeah, she's always so rude. I don't get her."

"I hope she gets eaten alive by zombies," said Jerry. "And not the slow kind – the shit-crazy running kind from *Dawn of the Dead 2004*."

Ben sighed at yet another film reference. "Maybe we should go across and see how the supermarket staff are getting home. Might be safer if we all go together."

"Dude!" Jerry cried out triumphantly. "That blonde girl over there is smoking hot. This could be the opening I've been waiting for."

"I'm sure she'll appreciate you getting her home safely. Just let me lock-up and we'll get going"

But before Ben could finish locking up, something hit the door.

8

The temperature had gradually swan-dived so low that Harry and the others shivered constantly. Steph's teeth also begun to chatter, leading everyone to giggle at her, which she didn't seem to appreciate at all. Eventually they'd all been forced to gather in front of the fire to try and keep warm.

"I'm starting to worry," said Steph. She was sitting on a thread-bare footstool and hugging herself tightly. "The snow doesn't look like stopping and we're going to freeze without the power on."

Harry looked over at the pub's front window. The large sheet of plate glass was starting to frost over, with icy spider webs creeping from the corners. The snow was falling heavier than ever.

Harry nestled into the sofa cushions to seek out their warmth, but found none.

"What's your drama?" said Damien from his standing spot at the left side of the fire's mantelpiece. In his thick puffer jacket he looked warmer than the rest of them. "A bit of a chill won't kill you, luv."

"Won't it?" she asked.

"Course not, you dopey cow. The power will come back on and the heating will kick on with it, so stop bloody menstruating."

Harry snapped, not quite sure why. "Didn't your father ever teach you to talk to women with respect?"

Damien was instantly enraged by the comment. "You don't talk about my father, you hear me? You're beneath him. What you gunna do about it, anyway? Teach me some manners? You ain't got the stones."

"You think so?" Harry challenged, still wondering what he was getting himself into and why.

Damien stepped forwards, but Steph halted him in place with a hand on his chest. "Behave!" she scolded. "Harry's right, you should treat women with respect – especially when they happen to be in charge of the only place with an open fire for miles. You're welcome to go freeze somewhere else, Damien, if you'd like. I'm not putting up with any of your games tonight. If it comes to having to separate you and Harry, Harry stays, you go."

Damien sniggered. "Why don't you two just shag each other and get it over with."

Harry blushed at the remark, but turned the emotion into anger and went to get up out of his seat. Lucas placed a hand on his arm and stopped him. The Irishman shook his head and eased Harry back down onto the sofa.

"Anyway," said Lucas, changing the subject. "Besides young Stephanie here – who I know is the world's finest barmaid – what do the rest of you call an excuse for a living?"

Stephanie laughed. "You cheeky git! I'm more than a mere barmaid. I plan on starting up a pet grooming business when I've saved enough money. Give me another year and I'll be there."

Harry had known Steph since she'd started at the pub a year ago, but he'd never learned about her aspirations. He wished he'd shown more interest in her life, instead of always relying upon her to show interest in his. A wave of guilt rose up in his gullet and stuck in his throat.

Beside the fireplace, Damien was rubbing at his sore hand and laughing to himself, apparently lacking any appreciation for Stephanie's ambitions. Lucas, however, seemed more interested. "Pet grooming?" he said, stroking at his chin thought-fully. "Giving haircuts to rats and baths to squirrels, huh?"

Steph giggled. "I was thinking more dogs and cats, but, hey, whatever. I love animals and they all smell better after a bath."

Damien's laughter erupted in a mean-spirited snicker that made Harry want to spit at him. "What you want to spend your time washing shit off Rot-tweilers for?" He winked at Stephanie. "I've got ways you can earn some *real* money, darlin'."

Stay calm, Harry told himself. Damien would knife you as much as look at you and violence just makes things worse. You made that mistake once before...

"So then," Lucas addressed Damien. "What is it that *you* do with yourself then, lad?"

"Don't ask," said Nigel from his space on the floor beside the fire.

"Because if he told you, he'd have to kill you," added Old Graham beside him.

"Is that true?" Lucas enquired, eyeing Damien up curiously. "Are you a man of mystery?"

Damien smirked. "Guess I am. I do a bit of this and a bit of that. Provide certain services and prod-ucts to my friends and customers."

Lucas stroked his chin again. "Interesting. So

how did you get into that type of thing, whatever it is exactly?"

"Family business, innit? Learned from the best – my old man."

Lucas nodded agreeably. "Sounds like a generous chap to pass on so much to his boy. Best thing a man can do is see his young ones right."

Damien beamed. "Old man taught me everything I know."

"So, where is this great man now?" asked Lucas, a knowing smile on his face that made it seem as though he already knew the answer. "I bet he's some great success, yeah? Sat back in luxury, watching his boy carry on the family trade? Am I right?"

Damien's face turned sour – not angry, but defensive and dangerous – like a cornered feline. "Not exactly," he said. "He's away at the moment."

"Vacation?"

Harry smiled as Damien squirmed against the wall and tried to merge with the peeling paintwork. He was rubbing his injured hand rapidly with rhythmic strokes. "Yeah," he finally said. "He's on a fucking cruise, innit. What's it to do with you?"

"Some cruise." Old Graham piped up from his space by the fire, but quickly turned his gaze to the floor when he was met by Damien's warning stare.

Harry wasn't sure if he wanted Lucas to shut up

or carry on, unsure if it was a conversation the group of them should be having. Lucas seemed to have a tendency to ask personal questions.

Lucas stood up unexpectedly. "A vacation, you say? Well, I hope he returns soon. Anyone for a beer?"

Talk about taking it to the brink, Harry thought, relieved that the conversation had altered course just as it neared an emotional minefield. It left Harry wondering what exactly had happened to make Damien so defensive about his father. Old Graham looked as if he knew, but when Harry glanced over at the old man, the pensioner looked away.

Steph's voice came over from behind the bar. She moved away from the fireplace and entered the flickering lights of the candles on the bar. "I think we have a problem, guys."

"What?" They all asked in unison.

Steph held an opened bottle of beer in her right hand and turned it upside down.

Nothing poured out.

"Jesus, no!" Old Graham cried, throwing his hands up at the sky as he realised what he was seeing. "The bloody beer's frozen."

Harry eye's widened.

Was it really that cold?

9

"Dude, what are you doing?"

The banging at the door got more frantic.

Ben glanced over his shoulder at Jerry. "What you *think* I'm doing? I'm opening the door."

"No way! It's like *The Thing* out there. If someone starts hammering on the door, trying to get in – you lock it, tight! Then you board it up with planks and nails."

Ben didn't have time for this. He let out a long sigh. "Do you have any planks and nails, because I don't. Movies aren't real, and this isn't a George Romero flick."

Jerry winced.

The banging continued. A silhouette flittered

against the pure white backdrop of the snow out-side the door. Ben was just about to open up when something occurred to him, making him pause. "Hey, who's there? Stop your banging, okay?"

Sure enough the banging stopped at his command.

"I said who's there?"

Jerry tapped his foot nervously. "Dude, I swear, if you let the Lost Boys in here, I'll never forgive you."

Ben shook his head again, certain that his friend had smoked one of his funny fags at some point during the last few hours.

"My name's Jess," said a girl. "I work at the su-permarket. Please let me in."

Jerry leapt up and punched the air. "Dude! That's the girl I was just talking about. The blonde fitty!"

Ben grinned. "Pity we can't let her in, just in case she's a zombie or a vampire?"

"Dude, stop fooling. Let her in!"

Ben couldn't help but laugh as he turned back to the door. The girl's silhouette continued to dance frantically against the snowy backdrop. Ben won-dered what on earth had gotten her so worked up.

"Jess," he said calmly.

"Yes, let me in."

"The door isn't locked," Ben cleared his throat and waited for a reply.

There was silence, followed by a "Huh?"

"The door isn't locked. It opens outwards. You keep bashing on it, but you need to pull it towards you."

After a further moment's silence, the door started to open slowly. The cold air rushed inside through the slowly widening gap. The girl that stepped inside looked very embarrassed.

IT TOOK ALMOST fifteen minutes for Ben to calm Jess down. Once he'd let her inside and locked the door – she insisted on it – the girl had started to catch her breath. The three of them stood now by the entrance, where they could just about make each other out under the moon's faltering glow and the green pulse of the fire exit sign.

"You're lucky," Ben said, patting her on the back. Her entire body was trembling. "We were just about to leave."

The girl glanced over her shoulder at the door behind her, as though she expected something to burst through at any moment. The wind was picking up outside and flakes of snow were whirling up and settling against the glass.

Ben raised an eyebrow. "What exactly happened to you out there?"

"Yeah," Jerry added. "Something give you the heebie jeebies, or what?"

Jess giggled, but it was a nervous sound. "I guess you could say something like that, but I'm probably just being silly. Least I hope so."

"You got us a bit freaked out," Ben said. "Banging on the door like that!"

"Sorry. I was just in a panic."

"Why though?" Ben wanted to get to the point quickly, disconcertingly aware of the fact that they would all have to get out of there soon. It was getting far too cold to hang around any longer.

"I left the supermarket to see if anybody knew why the power had gone out," Jess explained, "and to get away from my cow of a manageress. She drives me insane, but I just act really happy around her because I know it drives her insane."

Ben got Jess back on track. "Then what happened?"

"Oh right, well, it's the weirdest thing. I got lost!"

Ben and Jerry spoke in unison: "Lost?"

"Yeah, literally like ten steps out of the doorway. I couldn't find my way back at all. Every time I changed direction it felt like I was going round in circles. I couldn't see *anything* other than snow all around me. That's when I started to get, you know, a bit scared, so I got my phone out to call someone at the supermarket to come and get me, but my phone was all messed up. I totally freaked out and started calling out for help. That's when I saw it..."

Ben swallowed. He wasn't sure he wanted to hear what it was the girl saw – especially the bit about how her phone was all messed up the same as his and Jerry's. The last thing they needed was to be freaked out right now, but he asked the question anyway. It felt like he needed to. "What did you see?"

Jess shook her head and shrugged, her bleach-blonde hair glinting in the white light coming from outside. "I... I really don't know, but it had a face, you know? It was a man, I guess. A tall man."

"Like *Phantasm?* Dude!" Jerry left it at that. Sometimes *Dude* said enough.

Ben wasn't quite so impressed, though. "A face? You just bumped into someone, that's all."

Jess nodded. "Except the only thing I could make out on this person's face were his eyes – big, glowy white ones inside of a hood."

"A hood?" Another one of Jerry's fantasies took a hold of him. "What kind of hood?"

Jess shook her head, a blank expression on her face. "I don't know what any of that means, but it was like a priest's robe or something. I didn't see anything else – just the face – and I ran. Then I ended up at your door. Thank God!"

Jerry put an arm around the girl's waist and squeezed tightly. "Amen to that!"

Ben's common sense was telling him to dismiss the girl's story as paranoid nonsense, but part of him couldn't help but wonder...

Was something out there in the snow?

10

D amien had separated himself from the group and was now standing by the window in his bulbous puffer jacket, staring intently at the world outside. Harry and the other drinkers had remained around the sofa, a row of beers at their feet thawing in front of the fire. A couple were cracked due to the change in temperature, but most seemed to be returning to their more natural state of crisp, bubbling liquid.

Damien stared out into the night.

What is it with this weather? It just came out of freaking nowhere.

The cold was enough to freeze your eyelashes – not to mention the beer. If he was honest – which he rarely was if he could help it – he was worried. If the power didn't come back on soon, would it get even colder? Would he freeze to death? It seemed an absurd thought in this day and age, but he wasn't so certain. The ghost-white blanket swirling outside the window made him even less sure. It was like the whole world was freezing.

How did I get stuck in this dump on a night like tonight? The one Tuesday where I have serious business to attend to and this happens – and that fuckface Jimmy hasn't even turned up. I should be making plans for my future right now, but no, I'm stuck here with a bunch of deadbeats. Steph isn't so bad, but the others deserve a slap. Especially that fucking waste of space, Harry. Acts like he's better than me, but he's the biggest degenerate here.

Damien had noticed plenty of times how Harry turned his nose up whenever he and his mates were in the pub. Damien would have done something about it before now, but the guy wasn't worth the effort. Besides, despite his superior attitude, Harry pretty much kept to himself, and it was a bad move to pick fights with people who kept to themselves. People told tales when you started victimising innocent people.

Still, the geezer best wind his neck in, because Damien would put him down if he kept getting in his face. The thick Mick would get his, too, if he wasn't careful. Damien was sick of people treating him like a worthless thug, thinking they know all about him. They didn't know shit.

For some reason, when Damien thought about Lucas it stoked an anxious fire in his belly. It wasn't because he was scared of the man, but for some reason Lucas made Damien uneasy. Especially after the guy had damn-near busted his hand.

Damien shuddered as a cold breeze from under the pub's rear door made it all the way inside his collar. It was time to get back in front of that fire. He was freezing his nutsack off! He turned away from the window and saw Lucas staring at him from across the room.

Speak of the Devil!

Damien glowered at the man, who smiled back at him benignly like they were old buddies or something. The fire in Damien's belly grew hotter.

DAMIEN TOOK A LIGHTLY-FROSTED beer from Lucas and Harry wondered if he saw nervousness in the lad's eyes. Damien seemed to be getting less and less sure of himself as the night went by, as though some finely-oiled veneer of toughness was slowly starting to crack and peel. Harry took a swig of his own beer and cringed as the icy liquid passed over his teeth, making them ache a little. *Think I would actually prefer a steaming mug of coffee about now. When was the last time I felt like that?*

Lucas ended a conversation he was having with Steph and headed off towards the toilets. Suddenly alone, Steph took a seat beside Harry on the sofa. He could feel the warmth of her thigh against his as she settled into the cushions.

"You got anywhere you're supposed to be tonight, Harry?" she asked him.

He laughed. "You know me! When do I ever have any place to be other than here?"

"True," she said. "But I don't know why it is that you come here every night. It can't just be the drink? You could stay at home and pass out on your own floor if you wanted to."

Harry laughed again. "Yeah, but you wouldn't be there to pick me up afterwards."

Steph shook her head as though she didn't accept his answer. "I'm serious! Why do you come here?"

"I don't know. I guess it's because misery loves company. I think I come here to be among the living dead."

Steph raised one of her neatly-shaped eyebrow. "I don't follow."

"How can I explain it? On the weekends you get the kids in having fun, but during the weekdays you have guys like Nigel who sit at the end of the bar without saying a word to anybody all night, or guys like Old Graham who live in the past because they don't know where they fit in during the present." Harry took a swig of his beer and then looked Steph in the eyes. They looked to him like glistening pearls and, for a few seconds, he stopped speaking, just staring into them. Frightened that the pause might become awkward, Harry carried on with what he was saying. "I come here because it reminds me that there are other people who have nothing left in their lives except regret. If I stayed at home I'd lose sight of the fact that I'm not alone in misery – that I'm not the world's unluckiest man. It's strange, but sometimes that's the only thing that keeps me going. Doesn't matter how much I hate my life, I'm not unique and my pain isn't special. I'm never alone because I'm part of a club. The Living Dead Club. To be a member you have to stop living. You can walk around like a person, but really you're just a memory of who you used to be."

Steph rubbed a hand against her forehead. The various rings on her fingers glinted in the fire glow. "God, you're depressing. That's just about the most melodramatic thing I've ever heard. Have you always been like this?"

"No." Harry said, but did not elaborate. Once he'd been a positive, upbeat person, but now he wasn't – and that was that. The death of his wife, Julie, and his son, Toby, had left a charred, sucking wound where his heart had been. All he was left with was a star-shaped scar on the back of his hand.

Steph must have understood the feelings that her question provoked in him, as she changed the subject. "Hey, Graham?" she shouted.

The old man was sitting on the floor by the fire and flinched. "What?"

"Can you go upstairs to your flat and get some blankets and stuff? It's almost closing time but it doesn't look like the power is coming back anytime soon."

The old man nodded. "Good idea."

When Old Graham tottered over towards the bar on his way to the staircase in the corridor behind, Nigel shifted along the floor and filled his place closer to the fire. The man's greasy face turned in Steph and Harry's direction. "Is it okay for me to bed down here tonight, Steph? I'm parked round the back, but I don't fancy a night in the lorry."

Steph shrugged. "Can't exactly see you out on the street now can I?"

Nigel's face lit up. "Thanks, Steph."

Damien piped up from the opposite side of the fire. "So you live in a lorry then?"

Nigel nodded. "Sometimes I do. Travelling around the Continent most the time so what's the point in paying rent? I book a hotel when I fancy a soft bed and a warm bath, but most nights the driver's cab suits me fine. Never did much like being tied down in one place."

Harry wondered what that must be like. Such freedom to be able to lay your hat anyway and call it home for a night. Part of Harry yearned to disappear like that, to become a nomad with no emotional ties. But it just felt unnatural. A man without a home, without a family, wasn't really a man. It didn't seem right not to yearn for those things, or mourn for them once they were gone. He wondered what had led Nigel to live such an isolated life.

Damien sniggered. "So, you're basically one step up from a homeless person, huh, Nigel?"

Nigel shrugged. "Aside from the fact that I have a well-paid job and get to see a dozen countries in any given year."

"Where have you been recently?" Steph asked, smiling excitedly. "I bet you have some stories."

"I was in France last week, on my way back from

Amsterdam, and Copenhagen before that. There's some beautiful countryside along the way."

"Am-ster-dam." Damien said the word slowly as though he enjoyed the feel of it on his tongue. "I've been there. Next time you go, say hello to Cindy Suckalump. She'll give you a discount if you mention my name."

"Don't be so crude," said Steph. "I'm sure Nigel doesn't know what on earth you mean." The attention of the group suddenly turned to Nigel who was looking away sheepishly. "Oh my!" said Steph finally, realising that Nigel was just a man like any other.

Damien let out a raucous laugh. "Oh, he knows. Look at his face."

Nigel seemed embarrassed but was smiling nonetheless, like a ten-year old boy caught with his father's porno magazines. Harry leant forward and was about to speak, but was interrupted by a voice behind him.

Old Graham was holding something in the air triumphantly. "Got the blankets, folks. Brought me something else too."

"And what would that be?" asked Lucas, returning from the toilets and tucking his shirt back into his trousers.

"I think we need to know what the hell is going

on tonight," Old Graham explained, "so I brought down me old radio."

Steph slapped her hands together and congratulated the old man. "Excellent," she said. "If nothing else, we could get some music playing. It's getting a bit spooky in here."

"Now maybe we can find out just what the hell is going on with this weather and when the power will be back on," said Harry, but deep down, something told him he didn't want to know.

11

"What's the plan?" asked Ben. His body had gone from mild shivering to full-blown quaking now. It felt as if the very air were made of ice. "We need to get out of here s-soon. I'm freezing"

Jerry nodded agreement, his face lit by one of the dusty candles Ben had found in the bottom drawer of the office filing cabinet. His arm was still around Jess' waist, but she didn't seem to mind. Ben suspected that if she'd not had a fright earlier, her need for personal space might have been greater.

"Guess we should grab the beers from the office and try to make it back to yours," Jerry said.

Nice try, thought Ben. He was fully aware of his friend's lame attempts to create a social situation in which he could get Jess drunk, but he wasn't about to play along. "Leave the beers behind. They'll only slow us down. Let's get Jess home, then we'll go back and crash at mine. I've got to be back here tomorrow morning."

Jerry's face sagged. "Well, it would only be polite to invite Jess back as well. She may want company after the night she's had."

The two boys turned their attention to Jess and the girl began to fluster as all eyes were on her. "Well, I should, you know, really get back to my mum and dad. They'll worry otherwise. Another time though, yeah?"

Ben smiled as Jerry did the opposite.

Like I said, nice try.

"I think that's sensible," said Ben. "Where is it you live, Jess?"

"Costers Lane. You know it?"

Ben nodded. "Yeah, it's on our way. I live just past it."

Jess pulled away from Jerry's grasping arm and clapped her hands together. "Great. We should probably get going then."

Ben got the keys from the shelf below the counter and quickly locked the rear fire exit. It was not possible to set the burglar alarm, but seeing as it was half-ten at night and freezing, he was pretty sure his father would let him off this one time.

Pretty sure…

Ben inserted the key in the lock and turned it. "Ready?" he asked.

Jess and Jerry nodded.

They made their way out into the snowfield that had been a public footpath only hours before. It now seemed more like arctic tundra. Ben locked the door and they set off.

The wind continued picking up plumes of snow, which gathered in the air like wispy spirals. Ben's jacket had no hood. He had to cover his face with a hand to keep the newly falling snowflakes out of his nose and mouth. His feet immediately went numb inside his boots as he kicked and heaved through the thick snow. "I can't believe how bad it's got,' he said.

Jess replied. "I know. It's really scary! The snow was bad last year, but *this* is like the end of the world or something."

Jerry's expression lit up. "Like *The Day after Tomorrow*. I totally said that earlier."

"I wasn't being literal. I don't really think it's the end of the world."

Ben laughed.

Jerry blustered. "Yeah, well, I was just kidding.

Just saying that the snow is pretty bad, that's all. Most movies are totally based on science, so *The Day After Tomorrow* could happen."

Ben wiped his face clean of snow and let out a sigh. "The world isn't ending, Jerry. You thought *Jurassic Park* was based on science too, remember?"

Jerry jumped up and down in mock outrage. "Dude, don't even get me started on *Jurassic Park*. That shit could happen, too."

"No, it couldn't."

"Dude!"

Jess began laughing. "Is this what you two are like all the time? You crack me up!"

They both blushed. Ben hated when Jerry got him involved in one of his asinine nerd-fiction routines. It had been embarrassing him his whole life. It was his own fault; sometimes he just couldn't resist winding Jerry up. It was one of life's few pleasures.

"You know what?" said Jess, still giggling. "If we stop by my house, I can leave a note for my parents. I'll crash at yours like you said. It could be fun."

Jerry's face lit up and, if Ben was honest, he too was pleased at the thought of having Jess back to his place. She seemed cool, and it would be nice to have more than just one friend. All they had to do now was make it home, which at the moment seemed easier said than done.

TEN MINUTES LATER, Jerry had to stop. Jess wasn't thrilled about it because somewhere in the snow was the tall, hooded man that had frightened the life out of her earlier. She was certain of what she'd seen.

Well, pretty sure anyway.

"Dude, I can't see two inches in front of me!" Jerry bumped into the back of Ben, sending them both into a stagger, the deep snow making it hard to keep balance.

Jess laughed at them. "Come on, Ant and Dec. I'm freezing my tits off here."

Jerry regained his balance, pushing against Ben's shoulders to steady himself. Ben huffed, most likely irritated that he was being used as a steadying post.

"Hey, if you want me to warm them up for you," said Jerry with a smirk, "just let me know."

"Nice try," she said. "But I'm not as easy as that."

Ben chuckled and pointed at his friend. "Wounded!"

"Hey, she said she wasn't easy – not impossible."

"Well, I must admit that's closer than you get

with most girls."

"You ain't so hot yourself, Gandalf."

"I told you to stop calling me tha-"

"Children, children," Jess interjected. "Put away the testosterone and try to remember I'm not a Star Wars figurine. I don't like being fought over, and my packaging stays on."

"Worth more like that anyway," Jerry muttered. "Besides, I thought most girls liked being fought over."

Jess stopped walking and put her hands on her hips. "Well, I'm not most girls."

The three of them shared a laugh and they continued struggling onwards, crunching their footprints into the twinkling snow. The increasing blizzard made it difficult to see – and to hear – but they all saw clearly the shadowy silhouette standing in front of them.

Jess raised her hand and pointing a trembling finger. "It's him. The man I saw earlier."

Jerry put his arm around her. "It's cool. Nothing to worry about."

Ben stepped towards the stranger. "Sir? Are you trying to get home? We are too. Perhaps we could help one another?"

The shadowy figure stayed still, obscured by the veil of blustering snow and darkness.

"Let's get the hell out of here, Ben," Jerry urged. "I have a bad feeling about this."

"Me too," said Jess. Although she could not make out any of the stranger's features, she knew it was the hooded figure from earlier. She felt it.

The stranger remained silent, not speaking or moving, but undeniably there.

"Come on, dude. This is the type of situation where somebody ends up on the end of the meat hook."

Ben shot Jerry an angry look. "Jerry, do you always have to be so annoying? There's no such thing as monsters. This isn't one of your stupid horror movies. I'm sick and tired of-."

Ben's speech was derailed by an explosion, not of sound but of light. Behind the shadowy figure, a palisade of flames ignited, rising from the very snow itself, blotting out the darkness and drenching their freezing bodies in intense heat. The sudden change in temperature made Jess's skin pop and tingle, but her legs were still numb, buried by the snow.

The flames behind the stranger were mesmerizingly bright, illuminating his features in all their glory. He wore magnificent silver robes that almost seemed to sparkle against the blazing backdrop of vertical fire. The hood over his head showed nothing but the red hot swirls of his eyes.

Jess laughed as the inappropriate image of a Vegas magician presented itself in her head. Maybe she was losing her mind.

Jerry shouted at Jess from behind her, but she couldn't move, her legs paralysed by fear. Her eyes remained fixed on the hooded figure and the flames behind him. Whatever she was seeing, it couldn't be real.

The lurching figure finally started to move. From beneath the silver robes came a crooked hand, all bony fingers and bulbous knuckles. It began to draw something long and grey, a slither of sharp metal.

Jess flinched. Is that a sword?

"He's about to get stabby," said Jerry. "Who is this guy?"

Ben made mumbling sounds, like he was trying to say something, but couldn't find any words.

Jess regained the use of her legs and started backing away. "Ben," she said, "I think you should back away and come over here with us."

Ben turned and stared at Jess with wide, fearful eyes. "No shit!"

The three of them ran for it.

"Who the hell *is* it?" Jess managed to ask mid-run, the words coming out in huffs and puffs.

Jerry answered in the same out-of-breath way. "You mean *what* is that, don't you? It ain't no man."

The conversation went no further as the three hurried away from the hooded figure. The snow slowed their escape down to a stumbling crawl and Jess couldn't help but worry that if the creature pursued them they had slim hopes of getting away. "Is it thing following us?" she asked, trying to move faster, despite her clumsy snow-bound strides.

"I don't know," said Ben. He looked back over his shoulder. "I think-"

While Jess tried to catch up with Jerry a few yards in front, she waited anxiously for Ben to finish his reply. After several seconds, her heart surged with so much panic that she had to turn around herself.

When she looked back, she saw that Ben had stopped several yards behind her. He was still following after her and Jerry, but he was making slow, almost laborious progress. Beyond him, Jess could see nothing except snow and darkness. The burning palisade and the robed stranger were gone.

"Ben," she called out. "What are you doing? Get a move on!"

It was a few moments before he replied to her. "I...I don't feel right. I..." He fell down in the snow, his face disappearing.

Jess panicked. She had to go back and help Ben, but that meant heading back towards the stranger with the sword. .

Up ahead, Jerry stopped in his tracks, swaying and tottering like he couldn't gain control of his knees. He looked confused as to why everyone had stopped.

Jess trudged her way over towards Ben, who was still down on his hands and knees, face buried in the snow. Within a few minutes, she managed to make it back to him.

"Hey, what's wrong," she asked, getting frantic.

Ben managed to roll onto his side and looked up at her. The sight made her stomach churn. His face had turned white as the snow, except for his lips, which were bright red with blood.

Jess swallowed a lump in her throat. "Jesus, Ben, are you ok? What's happened?"

"I...I don't know."

Jerry came rushing up beside her, and immediately dove down into the snow. "Ben! Ben, what's wrong, buddy? Shit, dude, you're bleeding."

Ben managed to laugh meekly at his friend's arrival. Scattered specks of blood flew from his mouth and covered the snow in pinpricks of red.

"Oh my god," said Jess, covering her mouth. "One of your fingers is missing!"

Ben stared down at his hand like he didn't recognise it. The strangest thing of all, Jess noticed, was that the finger stump wasn't bleeding. It was capped by a glistening patch of red, but it wasn't moist at all. The wound seemed more like the surface of sandpaper than raw flesh.

Jerry reached out a hand to his friend. "Come on, B-Dog. Let's get you out of here."

Ben reached out to take Jerry's hand, but when their hands made contact his arm crumbled away at the shoulder as though it were made of sand. The stump bled for a few seconds then appeared to glaze over. It left Ben staring at them with the same look Jess imagined soldiers wore when they realised they were holding their own intestines. Ben's glistening eyes dried up until they looked like two lumps of clay set into his face. His lips cracked.

It took a moment for Jess to realise that Ben was dead.

It took several more moments for Jerry to understand it too, but when Ben's entire body crumbled away to ashes and melted into the snow, he was finally forced to accept that his friend was gone. How and why made no sense at all.

Jess allowed herself the luxury of screaming, and she didn't stop until she was completely out of breath.

12

Harry's world felt better from beneath the snug security of the thick quilt. Despite the fact the cold was a little more tolerable, Harry still eagerly awaited the power to click on. It'd been almost three hours now and closing in on midnight.

"Come on, old man," Damien shouted. The lad had declined one of Old Graham's blankets, as it would probably ruin his hard man image, so he was instead closer to the fire than everyone else. He also had on his thick padded coat.

"Yeah," Nigel joined in. "Haven't you picked anything up on that piece of junk yet?"

Old Graham sat on a footstool by the fire and

fiddled with his radio. It hissed and crackled. "I'm trying," he grumbled. "Nowt's happening."

"When was the last time you even used that thing?" Damien asked.

"It's been a while, but I knows how to work a bloody radio, lad. My generation grew up with the things."

Lucas reached out a hand from his perch on the armrest of the two-seat sofa. "Give it here, old timer. I know my way around a puzzle."

Old Graham obliged and handed over the crackling radio. Lucas immediately set about twiddling its knobs and pressing buttons. A frown filled his face gradually like liquid filling a beaker. "I think the thing's a dud, fella."

"Nonsense! I've used it a hundred times."

Lucas gave it a whack. "Well, it's gone on strike tonight."

Harry was curious. "I've never known a radio to switch on and not pick up anything at all. They usually get something, even if it's only faint."

"Not if the antenna's faulty," Lucas said. "You'd get nothing but static. Let's say you're right though. Let's assume the radio is working and still we're getting nothing. What does that mean?"

Harry started to think about it, but couldn't come up with an answer. "I guess it would mean that nobody's broadcasting, or that the radio waves aren't getting through."

"Exactly," Lucas said, as if he was revealing the most obvious fact in the universe. "So those are two options. The third and final one is that the radio has popped its little electrical clogs. What's the most likely, Harry Boy?"

Harry felt silly, but worried at the same time. "I suppose it *is* just the radio, or the weather affecting things."

Lucas smiled as if he'd successfully explained algebra to a monkey. "There you go! No need to as-sume the wor-"

Old Graham cried out. "Got something!"

Harry and Lucas broke off their discussion and turned to the old man; so did Steph, Nigel, and Damien. Old Graham waved his hand at them all and ushered them closer. His left ear was half-an-inch from the radio's speaker. At first, all Harry could make out was more hissing and crackling, but as he got closer...

"What is that?"

"I don't know," Old Graham said without turning his attention away from the radio. "I can't make it out, but something's definitely there."

Everyone gathered around and listened to the radio pop, hiss, and crackle, but behind those noises was something else. At first it sounded like horns blowing – trumpets even – but then there was...

Voices.

Garbled, disembodied speech that made sense to Harry for only mere seconds: ...*Pillars...Salt...Sin...*

Nigel straightened his back and stepped away from the radio, which quickly returned to giving out nothing but empty static again. "Did anyone else hear that? Could anyone understand it?"

Old Graham shook his head. "Not really. Something about salt?"

Nigel shook his head. "Pillars. It was pillars."

"Pillars of salt," Steph added helpfully.

Damien turned his back on the group, walked back over to the other side of the fire, and then turned back to face them. "Pillars, Salt, Sin, that's what it said." He pulled at his earlobe. "Guess my hearing's better than you old farts."

Harry felt like screaming '*shut up*' at the top of his lungs, but refrained. "Damien's right. It said: Pillars. Salt. Sin."

Lucas sat back down on the perch of the armrest. "What in heaven does that mean then? Sounds downright biblical."

Harry didn't disagree and thought about it for a moment, wondering who was broadcasting it. "Does anybody know what Pillars of Salt and Sin actually means?" He asked the question earnestly because he had no idea.

Steph was the first to offer an opinion. "Isn't it from a Coldplay song?"

Harry raised his eyebrows. "You think we just caught part of a song playing?"

Steph shook her head and seemed to doubt her own answer. "It didn't sound like singing, and the line in the song goes quite quickly. The words on the radio were drawn out and slow."

"Plus, that song doesn't contain the word, sin," Damien added.

"No, it doesn't." Steph agreed.

"Okay," Harry said. "Anybody else got ideas?" He looked around and raised his eyebrows. "What about you, Lucas?"

"Can't help you there, fella. It's probably nothing but Prayer Time with Father Bob for all I know. You can find all kinds of religious mumbo jumbo if you fiddle about enough. Either way, I need to go and visit the latrine again, so I'll leave you folks to ponder." Lucas got up from the sofa's armrest and headed towards the toilets again, while the rest of them continued their conversation.

"I'm sure it's nothing," said Old Graham wrapping a wool blanket around himself and pulling it tight around his shoulders. His words still fluttered slightly as the cold strangled his central nervous system. "No point worrying about it now. I'll put the radio on the bar if anyone wants to have another go. I need to get warm."

Nigel nodded and pulled up his own blanket. "Yeah, it's getting a little too nippy for my liking. Do we have any more wood for the fire?"

Steph nodded and headed off towards the bar, but before she got there the sound of screaming made her turn back around.

"What the hell was that?" said Nigel

Harry leapt up from the sofa and placed his beer bottle down on one of the nearby tables. "Someone's outside."

Steph stepped away from the bar. "Harry, where are you going?"

"To help them."

"I'd advise against that, Harry Boy." Lucas was returning from the toilets. "You go out in that weather and you might not come back."

"We can't just do nothing," said Harry. "Someone is screaming."

Lucas walked over to him by the pub's exit and pointed to the frost-covered window. "Look out there, fella. You'll be blind the second you step outside, and trying to make it in a straight line for ten steps will leave you a disorientated sot. You'd probably struggle to walk ten steps in a straight line on a normal night."

Harry scowled. "The fuck's that supposed to mean?"

Damien stood laughing by the fire. "He means you're a worthless drunk, Harry, and everybody knows it."

The hackles of Harry's neck rose. "What did you just say to me?"

Damien stepped towards Harry, but was still a good nine feet away. "I said that you're a no-good, stinking drunk, and that if someone is hurt out there, screaming for help, the worst person that could turn up to help them would be you."

Harry wanted to use words to retaliate, as that was the man he was – but none came to mind. The only thing that filled his head was a blind, boiling rage. He leapt across the room, landing a punch square on Damien's nose, spreading his cheeks and scrunching up his face. Both nostrils gushed blood immediately.

Damien didn't go down. He staggered backwards, clutching his nose in stunned bewilderment.

Everyone else in the room stood frozen and silent, their mouths open, their eyes wide.

Damien regained control of himself, dropping his hands so the blood and mucous ran down the light-blue shirt inside his puffer jacket. "You just made a big fucking mistake," he snarled. "Cus I'm going to kill you."

Harry's soul deflated as he realised the seriousness of his actions. What had made him act so violently? That wasn't him at all. Was it? Either way, he'd chosen a course of action and would have to stick to it.

Harry clenched his fists and spat defiantly. "Try it, you little fuckweed!"

Damien started towards him, taking each step casually as if he had all the time in the world. Harry tried to swallow but found a lump blocking his throat. He raised his fists and prepared for his first ever bar fight.

Lucas jumped between the two of them and placed a hand across Damien's chest. "Calm down there, fellas. Thought we had an agreement? We're all going to play nice tonight."

Damien sneered. "Try telling that to your man here; wrecked a perfectly good designer shirt. He'll pay for it, though."

Lucas sighed. "You gentlemen can settle up another night. There's no time for it now. There's some lass screaming out there and our Harry Boy was about to do the noble thing and go offer assistance. You should do the right thing and let him."

Damien shook his head in disbelief. "*You* were the one telling him *not* to go out there."

"Well," said Lucas, "that was before he was in as much danger inside as he is out. Besides, there's a chance he might freeze to death, so you should be all for it."

Damien backed off slightly, but pointed a finger at Harry. "We'll finish this later."

Harry was unsure what to do, not wanting to lower his fighting stance until he knew the situation was truly defused. He looked at Lucas who nodded at him reassuringly. He slowly lowered his arms and moved back towards the pub's exit.

"Wait!" It was Steph. She sounded worried. "Let me find you a torch or something."

"Yeah," Old Graham agreed from under his blanket by the fire. "At least take a blanket with you."

Harry waved a hand dismissively. "I'm sure someone's just slipped over. I'll be straight back. It's just a bit of bloody snow."

"I'll be waiting when you get back," said Damien.

Harry sighed. He stepped towards the pub's exit...

Clonk!

...before falling to the ground clutching his head

as the door swung inwards and clubbed him in the forehead.

The world cast into darkness as a gale rushed in from outside and extinguished all the candles on the bars.

Harry moaned in pain.

"Shit! Harry, are you okay?" Steph asked from somewhere in the darkness.

Harry ceased his moaning and tried to get up. Pressure mounted in his skull, a swelling above his left eye. Reaching forward onto his hands, he planted his knees on the floor and prepared to get back to his feet. It was then that he realised someone was standing in front of him in the darkness.

"Who's there?" he said.

Everyone stood still in the darkness and waited for an answer.

"My name is Kath. I'm the manageress of the supermarket across the road."

A collective sigh of relief filled the room. Steph quickly relit the candles on the bar.

"Try coming in a little slower next time," Harry said, rubbing his forehead. "You almost broke my skull."

Kath laughed nervously. "I'm so sorry. I guess the weather has put me in a bit of a panic." The woman moved away from the doorway and towards the light. "Oh, that's better. I was starting to forget what it was like to be able to see properly."

Kath offered her hand to Steph and Steph shook it.

"Pleased to meet you, I'm Steph. Why were you screaming out there?"

"No, that wasn't me. It would no doubt be that silly girl."

Harry moved over to the bar. "Silly girl?"

"Yes, Jessica. She's just some ditsy teenager who works for me. She went wandering off into the snow when the power went off."

"We should go look for her then," Harry insisted.

Kath sighed. "Don't bother wasting your time. Peter went after her; she'll be fine. I'm sure they bumped into each other out there and that's what startled her."

"You sure she'll be okay?" Steph asked. "We should check to make sure."

Kath's response was abrupt. "If she needed help there would have been more than one scream, wouldn't there?"

"Guess that makes sense," said Lucas, taking the top off a newly defrosted beer with his molars. "I say we top up that fire and get ourselves snug beneath those blankets."

"Good idea," said Old Graham, already making his way back to the fire. The rest of them followed, spreading the blankets into a line, before tucking themselves in side by side like sardines.

Steph brought over a crate of bottled beer and placed it by the fire to hopefully thaw out. Harry passed an already recently thawed bottle to their new arrival, Kath. "My saviour," she said, supping the beer greedily. "After the day I've had I could see myself becoming quite the alcoholic just to cope." The comment brought a stiff silence. "Did I say something wrong?" Kath asked. "It was just a joke."

Despite Harry expecting Damien to use the opportunity to revisit their earlier animosity, he declined to speak. Instead he stayed quiet and drank his beer.

"So," Steph asked, "what exactly have you been through tonight, Kath?"

"God, if only you knew. The whole world has gone crazy. The electricity went out, my phone stopped working, and at one point I thought I was going to freeze to death. Thank heavens you're still open, because I don't know how on earth I would have made it home in this snow."

"Your phone isn't working?" said Damien.

Kath shook her head. "No, it doesn't work at all. The landline didn't either."

"Guess the power affects the towers, or whatever you call 'em," said Old Graham.

"Maybe," Kath agreed, "but don't the landlines work even when the power's out?"

Harry nodded in the dark and rubbed at the throbbing lump on his forehead. "I think you're right. Don't they work off static signals?"

Lucas laughed. "Any telephone technicians in the house? Anybody?"

"What's your point?" Harry asked.

"My point is that none of us really know how the phone lines work."

"That's right," Nigel said. "Didn't they go digital or something a time back?"

From the middle of the group, Steph cracked open another beer. Her words were beginning to slur slightly as she spoke. "Don't suppose it matters. We're stuck here not knowing all the same. This is the worst weather I've ever seen, it doesn't surprise me that everything's gone down the pan. Not like we have a government that actually knows its arse from its earlobe, is it?"

Kath chuckled. "Tell me about it!"

"Now, now, Ladies," Lucas put both hands up. "A pub is no place for politics. You can go to a stuffy wine bar for the likes of that. A good old-fashioned boozer like this is meant for people to forget their troubles, inept governments included."

Steph laughed. "Aha! So you think the government is inept as well?"

Lucas grinned. "Sweetheart, I think they're *all* inept – and trust me, I've seen a few. I always say that religion and politics are just clever ways to make discontent people content with their discontentedness."

Old Graham snorted. "Good one."

Kath turned to Lucas, disapproval on her face. "I take it you're a nonbeliever then, erm..."

"*Lucas*, my dear woman. You can call me Lucas. To answer your question: *yes*, absolutely I believe in the Almighty Father. I never condemned Him now, did I? I condemned the eejits that try to run things in his name."

After a moment's thought, Kath seemed to accept this. "Well, perhaps I can agree with you there."

Harry joined in. "What's your Almighty Father's plan for tonight? Besides freezing us all to death that is."

"Do I detect a heathen?" Lucas asked.

Harry swigged his beer. "I'm just a realist."

"That's just slang for being a moody sod," Lucas quipped.

"Why don't you believe, Harry?" Kath asked.

"Because if I believed that there was someone responsible for all the things that have happened in my life then I would be so consumed with rage that I don't think I'd be able to go on living."

"Is that because you're such a loser?" Damien asked.

Harry wanted to get angry, but he was too tired. Maybe it was the beer, or something deeper inside of him that was just giving up. His heart felt weary.

"You've lost someone, haven't you?" asked Lucas.

Harry turned in the Irishman's direction. "What?"

"The only time a man gives up hope like you have is when they've lost a loved one...a child perhaps. Was it a boy or a girl?"

"*It*," Harry spat, "was a boy. Toby."

There was silence, thick enough that a snow plough would have blunted against it. Harry had never let anyone in The Trumpet know about Toby. It was his place to escape from all the pity and well-wishing that his onetime friends and family had become consumed with since the accident. This pub was his place to come and be alone with his pain, to remember his son the way he wanted to.

"I'm sorry," said Damien. No one else spoke.

Harry didn't say anything either. He was consumed by a deep sadness. Not just for Toby or Julie – he always felt sadness for them – but sadness because he knew he could never come back here again. The Trumpet's sanctuary of anonymity was gone.

"Okay," said Lucas, raising a beer in the dim light of the fire. "We'll change the subject, but first: Here's to Toby, may his soul be somewhere safe and pleasant."

The group raised their bottles and said Toby's name. Harry stared into the fire.

13

Peter hadn't seen Jess, or anybody else, for almost an hour, not since he'd parted ways with Kath. Earlier, the two of them had heard screaming and he was certain it was Jess. Kath had chosen to head for the nearby pub, caring only about herself, but Peter had decided to do the right thing and go to find his friend. It had not gone as well as he'd hoped.

Peter wasn't one to lose his cool easily; no one in Poland was, not after what their grandparents had lived through. It gave them a unique perspective on what really mattered in life. Yet, Peter had to admit to himself that he was starting to get anxious.

Peter had been used to the freezing cold of his hometown, near Warsaw, but he'd never known conditions like this. It reminded him more of the Arctic Circle than Great Britain – the place he'd come to follow his dreams and earn money he could only dream of back in Poland. England had become as much a home to him as his own homeland, even if he wasn't always made to feel welcome.

But tonight, Peter would have given anything to be back home with Momma and Poppa. He'd never felt as alone as he did right now.

"Jess," he called out into the emptiness. "Jess, are you ok? It is Peter."

There was no response. He'd almost given up hope of finding Jess, but that didn't stop him worrying about why he had heard a scream. Jess was a nice girl, attractive and funny. Most of the Polish people in the town stuck to their own and socialised with each other – especially when it came to dating. It was easier that way and provoked less xenophobia than if the Polish men went around sleeping with the English women. But Peter often yearned to spend time with Jess, and thought about kissing her.

Peter hoped she was okay.

"Peter, is that you?"

Peter stopped in his tracks. The snow crunched beneath his polished work shoes. "Jess, is that you?"

"Peter, I'm over here. I need help."

Peter turned a full circle, unable to pinpoint where Jess's voice was coming from. "Jess, I hear you, but I not see you. Jess?"

The voice came closer. "Peter, I'm here. Help!"

Peter turned another circle. He spotted something in the distance and trudged towards it. "Jess, I...I see you."

In the near distance, Peter could just about make out a grey shape in the howling blizzard. A sigh of relief whistled from his cold, blue lips and he began to head toward it.

JESS AND JERRY fled in terror after witnessing Ben turn to dust. They were too much in shock to comprehend what they'd witnessed. They just knew they had to get out of there.

"I don't have...a goddamn clue...what just happened," said Jerry, fighting his way breathlessly through the snow.

Jess was beginning to slow down. They hadn't gone far, but in the deep, sucking snow, moving any distance was an endurance test. "I need to stop," she said. "I've got a stitch."

Jerry halted and looked at her. Then he grabbed her arm and pulled hard. "Are you nuts? That thing will get us. You never stop when there's a demon on your arse. Have you never seen *Friday the 13th*?"

Jess pulled back, her chest rising and falling in great heaves. "There's...no such thing as...demons."

"There is too. *Exorcist* was based on true events and so was *The Entity*."

Jess shook her head. "They just say that so idiots like you go to watch it. That thing wasn't chasing us when we started running. I think we can stop for a second."

"You saw what it did to Ben!" Jerry seemed to struggle with something internally, before going on, like he was fighting back a wave of tears. "It killed him, and if we don't get moving it'll get us too."

Jess nodded. "Okay, but where the hell are we going? I can't see anything and I've already got lost in this snow once tonight."

Jerry pulled on her arm again and the two of them started moving. "We need to find the pub. There is always someone there till late."

"The pub it is then," said Jess, getting her wind back and making a move.

~

TWENTY MINUTES LATER, the two of them came to a stop at the bottom of the hill leading up to The

Trumpet. It had taken the last of their energy, wandering around in the white darkness of the growing blizzard, to find it, and if it hadn't been for the fear and adrenaline dominating her system, Jess was sure she would've keeled over by now.

"Thank God we found it," she said. "I don't think I can get much colder. My nipples could cut cake."

Jerry stared at her chest.

"That wasn't an invitation to ogle my chest. Just take my word for it, I'm cold."

Jerry shook himself as if escaping a hypnotic trance. "Sorry! Well, it's one thing finding the pub, but let's hope somebody's still in there. Else, I don't know what we're going to do. With the Siberian weather and Flame Boy on our tail, I don't know what'll kill us first."

Jess shuddered.

"Sorry," he said. "I know you're scared."

Jess didn't admit it, but it was true. They were both fighting back the pangs of panic. Jerry's cheeks had gone clammy and looked like they were burning up despite the chill. Jess worried that if they didn't get under cover soon, they'd be in danger of getting frostbite or hypothermia.

She started to take the first steps up the hill, sticking to where she imagined the path lay beneath the snow. She peered up at the pub, which loomed over them ominously. "I think I see a light in there," she said.

Jerry squinted. "Yeah, I think I do too. There must be people inside."

The two of them hurried, taking steps as quickly as possible in the knee-high snow sloping upwards. As Jess neared the top, she became more and more certain that there was light inside the pub. Not electrical light, but a flickering, glowing light from a torch or-

"I think they have a fire in there," said Jess, giddy at the thought of warmth.

"*Jurassic Park!*" Jerry fist-pumped triumphantly. "Let's get our black asses in there."

Jess's brow wrinkled. "We're not black."

"Come on!" Jerry grabbed Jess by the arm and started helping her up the hill...

...but a noise from behind made them stop.

"Is that...growling?" Jess turned slowly as the low grumbling grew louder. It did indeed sound like growling but, when she looked back, there was nothing other than the drifting, windswept snow. She turned back to Jerry. "Let's just get to the pub, okay?"

They picked up as much speed as they could, still hampered by the chilling embrace around their ankles and shins. When the growling started again

it seemed to be coming from all directions, vibrating through the air all around them.

Jerry put his hand on Jess's back and pushed. "I don't like the sound of whatever's making that."

Jess was about to agree when she found herself off balance, her toe stubbing up against some hidden brickwork or stone beneath the snow. As she crumpled, her leg twisted and folded beneath her, leaving her facing back the way she had come. She shrieked at what she saw.

So did Jerry.

14

"Harry snapped out of his wallowing, leapt up in front of the fire. "The hell was that? More screaming?" He started for the pub's exit again. "What's going on tonight?"

The others emerged from underneath their blankets and duvets by the fire. Steph hurried up beside Harry and put a hand on his back, clutching his jacket. "That scream sounded really close," she said. "You think it was the same person as earlier?"

"I hope so, otherwise that means there's something even more screwed up going on out there. A single person screaming is a lot better than two people screaming."

The cries continued, closer and more urgent.

"Go on, Harry," Steph urged. "It sounds like they're right outside."

Harry nodded and made for the door, but, before he managed to get there, it sprung open. Luckily, his forehead was nowhere near this time and he avoided a second blow from the thick wood. "What is it with people flying through this bloody door?"

Two flailing bodies – a boy and a girl – tumbled through the entrance and ended up in a crumpled heap on the floorboards. Harry saw that they were just a couple of teenagers.

He offered them his hand. "Come on in why don't you."

The girl ignored his hand and sprang to her feet unassisted. She rushed over to the still-open door and slammed it shut, heaving her weight against it and sliding her arm up to the bolt, pulling it across with a forceful *Clack!*

Damien stepped up beside Harry, peered down at the teenage boy on the floor and then across at the panting girl slumped against the door. "What the fuck you two tripping about?"

The girl looked back at Damien, her chest heaving in and out beneath her fleece. Her eyes were wide and she said nothing.

Damien turned his glance to the boy instead. "What about you, knobhead? You got anything to say, or shall I kick your arse back outside? You've interrupted a private party and it's bad manners to crash."

"No," the girl said urgently. "Please, let us stay!"

Damien went to speak but Harry cut him off, confident that he would take a more appropriate line of questioning than the young thug. "You can both stay. Of course you can, but what on Earth has gotten you so frightened?"

"There's something out there," said the boy on the floor, still trembling on his back, but now propped up on his spindly elbows. "There's something out there, like a big freaking dog or something. It was like...like...*Jaws* with fur."

There was silence in the room as Harry and the others studied the newcomers and considered their wild suggestions. The girl was nodding in agreement and they both seemed scared half to death by something, but what they were claiming seemed like pure...

"Bullshit," said Damien.

Harry nodded, actually agreeing with Damien for once and finding the sensation strange. "It was probably just a stray dog," he said, "stressed out by the weather. I'm sure it's unpleasant out there for anyone, dogs included."

The teenagers seemed to calm a little, although

both of them kept glancing back at the door nervously. Eventually the boy got himself up off the floor and put an arm around the girl. They spoke between themselves for a moment, too quietly for Harry to make out the words. Boyfriend and girlfriend, he supposed, before asking them, "Beer?"

This seemed to be just the ticket as the two youngsters started smiling. Yet, despite them relaxing, Harry couldn't ignore the bile rising from his stomach.

It tasted like dread.

～

JESS WATCHED the elderly man come from behind the bar with more blankets, while beside him, a large greasy-skinned man had a shopping bag filled with food – sausage rolls, chicken, ham, and stale-looking bread. Jess's mouth watered as the snacks were handed out amongst the group. She was surprised by how hungry she was.

"You say it was halfway between a Great Dane and a bull?" Kath asked Jess, her sneering lips spattered with porkpie crust.

Jess couldn't believe it when she'd found Kath at the pub. A spiteful part of her had hoped the old bag had got lost in the snow. Jess made a mental note to find out where Peter had gone to. It wouldn't have surprised her if Kath left him in the supermarket to guard it overnight in the freezing cold. Kath had it in for Peter ever more than she did Jess.

Kath cackled. "Well, *bull* is exactly what it is, young lady."

"Yeah, as in *bull-shite!*" said a voice from somewhere else.

Jess sneered at the person who had spoken. "You're Damien Banks, aren't you?"

Damien's face lit up. "You've heard of me? Well, you'd be a fool not to have."

Jess folded her arms. "Yeah, I've heard of you. You're the dickhead that deals smack. Your mates are always causing trouble at the supermarket – knocking stuff over and threatening us all. Basically acting like immature little boys. Same as you are right now."

Damien's smug expression dissolved into anger. The flesh in his cheeks changed from primrose to burgundy. "You better watch that mouth sweetheart. This is my pub and–"

"Actually," said the barmaid – Jess thought she'd heard her name was Steph. "It's my pub tonight, Damien, and we've all agreed to get along. That includes you, too, sweetheart. Don't poke the natives!"

Jess nodded. "You're right, I'm sorry."

Damien smiled and held up his beer. "I forgive you, but only cus you've got nice tits."

"She's, like, sixteen, dude!" Jerry shouted, eye-balling Damien with suspicion.

Damien sneered. "You want to call your dog off, sweetheart? He's likely to get himself neutered."

Jess turned to Jerry. "I don't need you to fight my battles."

Jerry stepped closer and spoke in a hushed voice. "Sorry, it's just that this guy is bad news, a right wannabe gangster."

"I know," she whispered back. "Everyone is aware of Damien Banks, which is why you should just stay out of his way. He's dangerous enough on a normal night, let alone one where everything's gone to hell. Let's just finish our beers and try to stay out of his way until we can get help."

Jerry nodded and re-joined the group. They were all resuming their positions in front of the fire

"So, lass," said a good looking man with an Irish accent, "with a somewhat calmer mind, do you want to spin us your yarn about the furry beast you say you saw outside?"

Jess didn't answer and instead looked quizzically at the man who'd offered to help her up off the floor when she'd first arrived. He was good looking too, but more tired and weary looking.

"Don't worry," he said to her and smiled. "Lucas always speaks like that. You'll get used to it."

Jess laughed. "Oh, well, I guess it was like you all said: just a dog or something."

Lucas frowned. "Come now. If that was what you thought at the time then you wouldn't have burst in here screaming like a banshee. At the time, you thought you saw something. What?"

Jess was hesitant, nervous at the thought of bringing it all up again after she'd managed to convince herself it hadn't happened. "I er...I really don't know. It was all so confusing."

"It wasn't a dog," Jerry spoke up. "I've seen a hundred different breeds of dog and there's nothing even close to what we saw tonight."

The others switched their focus from Jess and listened to Jerry as he continued. Don't tell them, Jess was thinking. They'll think we're both insane.

"We'd just started to climb the hill," Jerry said, "when we heard growling. It started off just like a dog's, but a dog's growling can't make your bones rattle like this. We started to get our asses out of there, but Jess slipped over."

"I tripped on something under the snow," Jess explained. "That's when we saw it."

"Saw what?" asked the elderly man of the group. "What did you see?"

There was silence for a few moments and it became unclear who would be the one to answer. Jess decided it would have to be her. "It was big, bigger than anything wandering around a housing estate should be. It had thick, oily fur that was totally free from snow, as though any flakes that tried to settle on it just melted. In a way, it really *did* look like a dog, but it was just way too big... and besides, its face was all wrong."

Jerry supported her as her voice began to weaken. She appreciated it and had already started to consider him a friend. Relationships were forged easily at times like this, she realised. "Yeah," Jerry said. "Its face was much flatter and rounded – more like an ape than a dog, except its mouth took up half its face. It was full of teeth; rows and rows of them like those chomp-monsters in *The Langoliers*. You ever see that movie"

Damien scoffed. "How could you make out all that detail in a blizzard?"

Jerry shook his head. "I don't know. It was as though there was a glow around it, like a ball of light."

Damien shook his head, obviously not buying any of it, but didn't say anything. Jess saw a similarly incredulous expression on Kath's face as well. Screw you both, she thought.

The others stayed quiet too, until Jerry finally said in a croaky voice, "We haven't even told you about the sick bastard that murdered my best friend – turned him right into dust."

Everyone stared at Jerry like he was insane. Only Jess knew he wasn't.

WHEN THE TEENAGERS finished their wild story about a hooded figure turning their friend into dust, Harry was rendered speechless. Of course, he didn't believe such a ridiculous tale, but the story still managed to unsettle him. Whether it was true or not, *something* had obviously sent the kids running.

Harry swigged his beer and stared into the fire, listening to the conversation of the group rather than taking part in it. He tuned in to what Kath was saying.

"You silly, attention-seeking, twit," the woman said. "You're just trying to frighten everybody. I've never heard such codswallop in all my life."

Jess slapped her palms against her forehead in dismay. "I watched Jerry's best friend die tonight. If you hadn't been too busy abandoning me then you might have been there to see it too."

"How dare you! I did nothing of the sort. I

shouted and looked everywhere for you, but you'd wandered off carelessly."

Jess sneered. "Like hell you did. You're full of shit."

"That is *it,* young lady!" Kath's voice quivered with rage. "Don't you bother coming into work tomorrow because you are fired."

Jess laughed. "We're in a pub, *Kathleen*, not at work. I can say what the hell I like to you. Don't worry though because I quit anyway."

"Music to my ears. Now I can employ someone with half a brain."

"Actually, you need to hire someone without a brain, then they won't mind working for a pathetic bully like you. I understand though, Kathleen, it must be difficult being a spinster."

"You spiteful cow! You know nothing about me."

Kath threw off her duvet and leapt to her feet. For a second, it looked as though the older woman was going to go for Jess, but instead she turned away from the group and departed towards the toilet.

"You two don't get on then?" Lucas quipped from the edge of the group.

"No shit," Jess replied. "Got to tell you though, it felt really good saying that to her."

"Yeah, I'll bet," said Harry. "Maybe you should

just let things lie for now, though. Who knows how long we'll be stuck in this situation together."

"Don't worry. I'll leave her alone, so long as she doesn't get in my face. I need to ask her where the warehouse guy went first though. She treats Peter like dirt and I need to make sure he's alright."

Jess shoved herself up onto her feet and headed after Kath. Once she'd taken half-a-dozen steps, a body crashed through the window.

15

"Peter!" Jess screamed.

Harry watched the girl drop to her knees, scrambling over to the body that was now splayed across the pub's wooden floor. The injured boy was barely conscious, covered in blood and murmuring deliriously in what sounded like an Eastern European accent. Freezing cold wind and swirling snow flew in through the broken window and extinguished what little warmth had managed to remain inside the pub.

Harry clambered across the room and skidded to his knees beside Jess and the injured boy she had referred to as Peter.

Jess blinked at Harry; a hollow stare consuming

her delicate features. Tears leaked from her grief-stricken blue eyes. "Help him, please."

Harry choked on his words. "I...I...what's... what's happened to him?"

"I don't know," cried Jess. "Just please make him alright."

"*I'll* tell you what happened," said Jerry, rushing over to join them. The others in the pub stood on the periphery, watching curiously. "It's whatever was outside. It's the demon in the robes and the fiery sword."

Harry blinked. "You're speaking gibberish!"

"You reckon?" Jerry contested. "Then why don't you tell me what can chuck a guy through a pub window like a ragdoll, huh?"

Harry had no answer for that. Jess shoved him hard on the arm. "You're not helping. You need to help him."

"Okay," said Harry, shaking himself into action and raising his voice. "Let's get him someplace comfortable. I need someone to bring me blankets, bandages, anything like that. Is there a first aid kit here?"

Steph stepped forward and nodded. "There's one in the back. I'll go get it."

Harry smiled, glad to have help. Once Steph rushed off, he turned to the others. "Nigel, help me carry Peter over to the couch by the fire. I need the rest of you to get that window covered up before we all freeze to death."

There was a mumbling of agreement and everyone got to work. Harry slid his right arm underneath Peter's shoulders and instructed Nigel to get his legs. He did so without argument.

The two of them shuffled their way across the bar, careful to avoid twisting or jerking the patient in their care. In the corner of his eye Harry was aware that the others in the pub were upending a table and pushing it up against the open window. Damien was also amongst the group and in fact seemed to be the one taking charge.

"Okay, Nigel," said Harry, coming to a stop besides the sofa, "you lower Peter's legs and I'll lower his body. Carefully does it."

The two of them eased Peter down, one inch at a time, until finally he was resting securely on the sofa. Amidst the glow of the fireplace, the severity of the boy's wounds became evident. Shards of glass protruded from deep gashes all over his body and poked through his torn clothing like alligator teeth. One of the boy's eyes had also been mangled beyond repair. It dripped blackish-red gunge. Harry felt his stomach tighten.

Who the hell did this? Who could make such a

mess of another human being?

"Peter, everything is going to be fine now." Jess had arrived and was speaking soothingly to her friend, stroking a hand across his forehead. "You're safe."

Peter muttered something in reply but it made no sense, more of a gurgle than discernible speech. Harry continued to examine the boy's body and was shocked to discover yet more wounds, more cuts, and more blood. Not to mention an ankle that looked like it was attached to the boy's shinbone back to front, sticking out at a gruesome angle.

Harry placed a hand against Peter's icy cheek. "Who did this to you?"

Peter opened his remaining good eye and seemed to concentrate for a moment. His eyeball kept flicking left and right as if it had a mind of its own. His mouth formed the words: "*Skrzdlaty Diabel.*"

Harry frowned. "Peter, can you tell me in English?"

The boy took a wheezing breath. It seemed to take every ounce of strength from him, but he managed to utter another word: "Winged..."

"Winged what?" asked Jess, tears streaking her cheeks.

Peter gazed at her and almost managed a smile,

like he had only just realised she was there. "Winged...demon."

Peter lost consciousness.

Jess went to put her hands on him, perhaps to shake him back awake, but Harry prevented her. "Let him rest."

Jess leaned up against Harry. He could feel her shaking as she looked up at him. "What do you think he meant?"

"I don't know," said Harry honestly. "Probably shock."

Jess shook her head. "If it wasn't for all the other things that have happened tonight I may have believed you. There's something out there, Harry. Something in all that snow that's evil."

Harry hated to admit it, but he was inclined to agree with the girl. Something most definitely was wrong tonight, but *what?*

"Harry?"

Harry spun around to find Steph holding a green plastic box. A first aid kit. He took it and thanked her, but she didn't hear it, too busy looking down at the bleeding casualty on the sofa. Eventually, her attention turned back to Harry. "He's a mess."

"I honestly don't know what could do this to a man....or why."

Jess sobbed in the background.

Steph's expression grew dim, her skin becoming ashen even in the orange glow of the fire. "Are we in trouble here, Harry?"

"I don't know; but I can tell you one thing: I've never wanted to get out of this pub so bad. There's something out there, Steph, and we're trapped in here."

Steph swallowed. "I'll go check on the others. Just do what you can for him, yeah?"

Harry nodded and turned back to Peter. Jess was perched on the armrest of the sofa, looking sick to her stomach. He wondered how close she was to the boy. Wasn't Jerry her boyfriend?

Harry knelt down beside Peter. The heat of the fire pinched at the flesh of his back, making it itch, but he put up with it for now. He placed the first aid kit down on the floor and popped open the lid. Inside were the things one would expect to find: gauze, bandages, tape, alcohol wipes, and plasters. He also found an eye dressing which he plucked out of the contents first.

After applying the dressing to Peter's damaged, oozing eye and securing it around the back of the boy's head, Harry moved on to the other wounds. He unbuttoned Peter's work shirt to get a clearer look.

Jess slapped a hand across her mouth.

At first, Harry wasn't sure what he was seeing. He unclasped the final button on Peter's shirt and pulled the fabric away. A film of glistening blood covered the boy's chest and stomach, flowing from deep channels scored into his flesh. As Harry took it all in, he realised that the gashes weren't just random injuries.

"Somebody has carved words into his chest."

Jess looked like she was going to throw up. "It's sick. W-what does it say?"

"Hold on." Harry pulled a couple of alcohol wipes from the first aid kit and ripped them from their packets. He gently rubbed at Peter's wounds, clearing away as much of the blood as he could, fighting away fresh tides that sought to replace it. Slowly, the words became clearer.

SEnD...

Out...

ThE...

S...i...N...N...e...R.

"Send out the sinner?" Harry said the words out loud, hoping his brain would come up with some interpretation that made sense.

"What does it mean?" Jess asked.

"I have no idea," Harry replied. In fact, Harry had no understanding whatsoever about the kind of monster it would take to carve words into someone's chest. He took a deep breath and let it out. "Maybe we should go get the others."

Jess agreed.

They dressed as many of Peter's wounds as they could and left him sleeping on the sofa. The rest of the group were still stacking furniture up against the broken window and pulling the pub's long curtains around the whole thing, trying to keep out the freezing gusts from outside.

"Good job," said Harry.

Those at the window turned around. Each of them looked shaken and out of breath, even Damien. Kath was the only one who didn't appear to be bothered. Harry watched the woman as she sat down on a nearby chair and began to pick at her nails as though she had not a care in the world.

"Harry Boy. How's the nipper?" asked Lucas.

Harry rubbed at his eyes and let out a sigh. "Not good. Someone's made a real mess of him, blinded him, and cut words into his chest."

Damien overheard this and stepped away from the window. "Someone carved words into him? That's harsh, man. What's it say?"

Harry shrugged. "Something about sin."

Steph slid another chair up against the barricade, reinforcing it further. She turned to face

Harry. "Sin? I don't understand. What exactly did it say?"

"God knows," Harry said. "Just the words of a psychopath."

Jess spoke up. "It said: send out the sinner."

"The fuck does that mean?" Damien demanded. "Does someone in here know what's going on out there?"

Harry pointed his finger at Damien. "Calm down. It probably doesn't mean anything. We just need to stick together and everything will be fine. No one needs to panic."

Damien snarled. "I ain't panicking, I'm pissed off. It's obvious that this is personal. Whoever's running around out there like Freddie-Krueger-on-acid has a grudge against someone in here."

"Nonsense," said Harry.

"Maybe not," Lucas chimed in. "You don't use a human being as a memo-pad and hurl them through a window unless you're trying to send a wee message. Maybe what's happening tonight is all down to one person. Wouldn't that be an interesting twist?"

A silence fell over the group as they scanned one another suspiciously, trying to work out who was the sinner.

Harry wondered if it was him.

16

Nigel Sutcliffe had sat and watched the unfolding situation with quiet interest. Things started out strangely enough that evening, if only for the dire weather conditions, but once the lights had blinked out, things became truly bizarre. What concerned Nigel most was all this talk about a 'sinner'.

He sat, shivering, on a stool by the bar, listening and watching as the others all argued incessantly about the injured boy with the chest carvings. Who was the sinner, they demanded, and who was outside in the snow? Nigel decided it was a conversation he was better off avoiding. Because he was very much a sinner. Sometimes, he felt as though he'd been born to sin.

But was he *the* sinner? The one the person outside was looking for?

Maybe he was worrying over nothing. Nigel didn't care what happened to his immortal soul. All that mattered to him was how much pleasure he could find in life. The skinny bitch he'd fucked and killed in Amsterdam last week had been a particular highlight. God how she'd screamed. He smiled at the thought. But his reminiscing was interrupted by the arrival of Steph at the bar.

She handed him a beer. "It just about defrosted in front of the fire," she said.

Nigel thanked her. "Just what I needed. Things are a little crazy around here tonight, huh?"

"Tell me about it! I feel like I'm in a horror film. Still haven't decided on an emotion yet, but I'm stuck somewhere between dazed and terrified."

Nigel put his hand on her shoulder and squeezed. His pinkie ring slid over the fabric of her delicate blouse and stirred something within him. The solid gold ring had a dolphin insignia and was his most prized possession – a memento of his first victim, a twelve-year-old blonde with chubby cheeks like a prepubescent Drew Barrymore. He'd bitten it off her finger as she wailed and squirmed in the back of his lorry. He'd worn the dolphin ring ever since, enjoying the way it rubbed against his penis as he masturbated over his dying victims.

"I'm sure there's nothing to worry about," Nigel reassured Steph. "I think whatever's going on tonight is personal."

"Personal? You mean 'the sinner'?"

"Whoever's out there causing trouble obviously has it in for one of us; but you know what I think?"

Steph shook her head.

Nigel pulled his hand away from her shoulder, already missing the warm throb of her flesh. He picked up his ice cold beer and took a deep gulp before placing the near empty bottle down on the bar. "I think this is a tiff over drugs. The only people I know sick enough to smash a kid to pieces and lob him through a window are smack-heads and dealers, and we just so happen to have our very own aspiring drug lord right here with us."

Steph looked across the room at the others then looked back at Nigel. "You think this is all about Damien?"

Nigel shrugged. "He's the biggest sinner *I* know. Beat some kid into a coma last year, didn't he?"

"I don't know," Steph admitted. "I heard that too, but whether it's true or not..."

"Well, it's certainly within his nature from what

I've seen tonight. He's been glaring at Harry all night, and he threw a punch at the Irish fella."

Steph glanced over at Lucas, who was standing by the fireplace. "What do you make of him?"

"Lucas? It's strange how he turns up for the first time on a night like this. Maybe he's the eyes and ears for whoever's outside. Could be some drug lord looking to come into the area and put Damien out of business. Maybe they're making their move tonight because they're hoping the snow will keep the police away."

"You're really sure it's about drugs aren't you?"

Nigel shrugged. "I don't know anything for sure. One thing I *do* know is that if whoever's out there is looking for a sinner, it's not me. I'm a decent, God-fearing man."

Steph laughed. "Good for you, but I don't believe anyone's one hundred per cent innocent. No one's perfect. It's where people's hearts are that matters."

"That's a lovely way of seeing the world and it's no doubt why you're such a lovely woman."

"Nigel, you'll make me blush, you charmer." She gave him a quick hug around the waist. "I'd best go check on the others. There are more beers to hand out."

Nigel nodded slowly, taking in the scent of her. "Vital work. You'd best get started."

Steph sauntered away, leaving him to enjoy the sight of her lithe figure fading into the darkness as she left the candle-light of the bar. Nigel felt himself get hard.

Was tonight the night?

Steph was the main reason he kept coming to The Trumpet to drink. From the first time he'd seen her behind the bar, squeezing her tits together as she innocently leant over tables to wipe them clean. Nigel knew he was going to have her right then, and the more he watched her sexy little backside wiggling around the pub, the more he knew he needed to have her soon. He'd been waiting for the right opportunity.

It had finally come.

Tonight was the night. The lights were off, the roads were closed, and a group of psychopaths roamed the snowbanks outside. If Nigel did Steph tonight, he could make it look like somebody else's doing without any trouble at all. And if the others inside the pub were, for some reason, to find out, he would just have to deal with them too. He could be in his lorry come morning, a hundred miles away. Even snow this heavy couldn't keep his rig from moving.

Nigel put his hand in his trouser pocket and rubbed at the flick knife pushing against his throbbing erection.

Yes, my little prize, tonight is most definitely the night.

17

"What the hell do we do?"

Harry heard Jess's voice, but had no answers for her. Peter had remained unconscious since they'd patched him up and his condition only seemed to be getting worse. He needed immediate medical attention, but there was no way to get any. They were stranded inside the pub, with someone outside meaning to do them harm.

"We just need to do the best we can for him, right now." Harry said. He could see the anguish on Jess's face, but he was powerless to do anything about it. He wasn't a doctor and could do nothing about the snow keeping them inside. Still, he felt like he was letting the poor girl down.

"He'll be okay," said Jerry, coming over and placing an arm around Jess's shoulders. "We just need to keep him warm."

The only place in the pub left with any warmth at all was by the fireplace, and Peter was now taking up most of the space. Harry decided to move over to the bar to join the others.

Steph was busy handing out fresh beers.

"Got one for me?" he asked her.

Steph smiled. "Sure, Harry, here you go."

"Is anybody else wondering what we're going to do for warmth now that Peter is taking up the fire?" said Kath. She had shown very little concern for her injured employee.

"Already on it," said Steph. "Damien and Old Graham are down in the cellar looking for anything we could start a fire with. I'm pretty sure there's an old steel dustbin we could stab some holes in and use as a furnace."

Lucas laughed. "This gal is something else, don't you reckon?"

Harry looked at Steph for a moment and their eyes met. "Yes, Lucas, she most definitely is."

"You think the kid's going to snuff it?"

Harry was taken aback by Nigel's harsh wording. "What?"

"I overheard you talking to the girl. I could tell by your voice that you don't hold out much hope."

The negativity irritated Harry, but it was probably only natural considering the situation. "I can't say – I'm not a doctor – but I know enough to see that the poor lad's suffered more than anyone should."

"You ever seen anyone in such a state before?" Lucas asked.

Harry conjured up images from his memory but quickly stopped himself. "No, I haven't," he lied. "I've never seen injuries like it before, which is why I'm not sure if he'll last the night."

"Well, then," Lucas replied, "perhaps we should be worrying more about who – or what – did this to the lad. There's someone out there looking to do us all harm, and we've got enough on our plates with the weather alone."

"I agree," said Steph from the other side of the bar. "I don't like any of this. I feel like we're cut off from civilisation. The phones are dead, the electric's off, and we can't go outside because some madman is knifing people up. I don't even want to think about what the rest of the country is like. I'm starting to get really freaked out. This isn't normal."

"We don't know there's a madman outside," said

Harry. "Perhaps Peter made an enemy and they've got what they wanted just by hurting him."

Nigel posed a question that made Harry's logic falter. "Why throw him through the window?"

"Yeah," said Steph. "If they wanted to kill Peter they would have been better off leaving him outside in the snow. Throwing him through the window makes it pretty obvious they were trying to frighten everyone inside the pub."

Lucas put his beer down on the bar with a *clink*! "Maybe it was a message for the sinner," he said.

"More talk about this bloody sinner," said Nigel, banging down his own beer on the bar. "Why are we buying into this bullshit? If someone is crazy enough to carve words into someone's chest then I think it's fair to say they've lost a certain amount of marbles – probably all of them."

"You're probably right," Harry admitted. "How would we even know who's a sinner and who isn't, anyway?"

"Exactly," said Nigel, seemingly satisfied.

Steph pushed another recently-thawed beer over to Lucas, who was about to finish his current one. . "Nigel seems to think that it's all about drugs, and that Damien is the one they want."

"Well, well, well. Is that right, now?" Damien emerged from the bar's staff area and moved through the hatchway. Old Graham was with him and seemed to be cringing. Damien did not look happy. "So you think I caused all this, do you?"

Nigel shifted on his stool. "I didn't say that. I...I was just talking to Steph about who could be out there and...and..."

"...and you thought you'd blame everything on me? Why's that then? Is it because you think you're better than me? That I'm just some fucking mug?"

"No, I just thought..."

"You thought shit!" Damien tensed up like a wild animal.

Lucas leapt up from his seat and stood in Damien's way. "Do I have to tell you again? Calm down for a spell, fella; it's no good for the blood pressure."

Damien turned his anger towards Lucas. "What are you talking about, you thick Mick?"

"I had your word that you'd behave," said Lucas. "The only reason our Nigel is looking to blame people is because he's afraid."

"Hey," Nigel protested. "No, I'm not."

"We're all afraid," Lucas continued. "And when people are afraid they flap their gums. Tisn't personal; just what people do to try and make sense o' things. Stops their minds floating away."

"Yeah," said Nigel. "I was just talking shit. Figured that, because you're a tough guy, you'd have some tough enemies."

"You'd better keep your accusations to yourself from now on," said Damien, "because kicking your arse would be a nice way to warm up!"

Nigel nodded. "So, we're good?"

Damien nodded. "Yeah, we're good for now."

Harry was glad Damien had been reined in yet again. In fact, he started to wonder whether the thug was really the bloodthirsty psychopath people made him out to be.

"Can we get a beer for Damien?" Harry asked, trying to encourage peace.

Damien shook his head. "Not now. I found that old dustbin in the basement, but I need help dragging it up. It's an old-fashioned wheelie bin but the wheels have rusted off. We should be able to start a decent fire in it and get some goddamn heat in here."

Harry raised an eyebrow. "That's great. I'll come and help you."

Damien shrugged and walked back through the hatch, disappearing through the narrow door behind the bar. Harry followed him into the rear corridor and then down the stairs into the cellar. At the bottom, Old Graham waited next to a rusty old double-wide dustbin. The rest of the cellar was a mess, with mounds of wood and cardboard rotting away in the corners.

"You going to help or not?" Damien asked, tipping the dustbin onto its edge.

Harry hurried over and grabbed the other side, while Old Graham kicked away the debris that covered the route to the stairs. The pensioner turned out to be quite spry for his age.

"After three," said Harry. "One...two...three..." He and Damien heaved, heading for the bottom of the stairs with the steel dustbin. The container was empty, yet still substantial in weight and thick with rust. Harry felt his hands chafing under the pressure. "How are we going lift it up the stairs?" he asked as they neared the bottom step.

Damien laughed. "Back giving out on you? We'll just lift it, step by step. Piece of piss."

The two of them stopped at the stairway and righted the drum back onto its base, dropping it down with a *Wong!* "Okay," said Harry. "You ready?"

"Ready for what? A bit of lifting?"

Harry shook his head, unwilling to get into a pissing contest. He turned to look at Old Graham. "Maybe you could gather up some of this cardboard so we can use it for the fire?"

Old Graham nodded and got to work.

Harry signalled to Damien and the two began to

lift. They hoisted the bin onto the first step with little effort, and then again onto the second and third. By the fourth, Harry was starting to lose his breath. "Can we stop a sec," he said.

Damien grunted. "Maybe if you didn't drink so much, you'd have more stamina."

Harry felt his pulse quicken as he fought the urge to lash out, but decided to let his actions argue for him. "Right, come on then! Let's get this bloody thing up there." He tried to sound full of vigour, despite the tightness in his chest. "Last thing I want is for your delicate little body to get cold."

Damien snickered but didn't rebuke. The two of them continued hoisting the steel dustbin upwards. They scaled the fifth step and then the sixth. The seventh and eight were hard work but they managed to shift the deadweight up using their feet to give it an added shove. With only two more steps left, Harry yearned to release the weight he carried. His shoulders burned with fire and his lungs started to cramp. Damien was right, a year of constant drinking had left Harry in the physical state of a man twice his age. He felt ashamed.

Just two more steps though and it would be done. He could make it.

They hoisted the bin once more. Damien began to slide it up onto the next step, but as he did so, the bottom edge of the dustbin struck against the outer lip of the step. Harry pushed his side up, trying to clear the centimetre needed to get the dustbin up onto the step, but he couldn't manage it. He strained harder and willed his biceps to contract, but instead his arms lowered against his control. Harry's grip failed, then gave out completely.

Damien cursed as the weight in his hands suddenly doubled. Harry watched helplessly as the lad tried to keep the dustbin under control by attempting to trap it with his leg. But it was futile. The hunk of steel twisted sideways and fell away from them both.

Harry stumbled forwards onto the step above as the dustbin struck his shin before beginning a spiralling journey down the old stone staircase. All of the hard work getting the dustbin to the top had been wasted, and it was Harry's fault. But as he watched the rusty steel careen towards the bottom of the stairs, he felt a hundred times worse. Old Graham was bending over, gathering up all the cardboard just like he'd been asked. The old man was oblivious to the danger hurtling towards him.

The dustbin flew through the air.

A moment later, so did Old Graham.

18

Jess couldn't stop worrying about Peter. She worried too about her mum and dad. They would be fretting. Usually they would stay awake until she return home from a late shift, finishing off a bottle of wine and arguing before finally retiring to bed. Jess hoped they were too drunk tonight to notice that she wasn't home yet. With a bit of luck they would have had one of their rare nights of fondness and gone to bed early for a bit of nooky. What better way was there to stay warm on a night like this? Jess knew that probably wasn't the way of things though. Her parents were more likely to throw things at one another than show affection. They hadn't always been like that.

Jess convinced herself that her parents would

be fine. Peter was a much bigger concern than her parent's marriage problems. She looked down at her sleeping friend, surprised to find that his injuries still had the ability to shock her. Beneath the bandages, Peter's left eye was caked with foul-smelling custardy puss, but that wasn't what disturbed her most. It was the deep carvings sliced into the pale flesh of his chest. SEnD Out ThE SiNNeR.

Whatever it meant, it was the work of a sicko. Peter never did anything to anyone. He was a quiet boy, sweet and gentle. Not like the usual, football-obsessed, dickheads that lived in the area, or a thug like Damien. Despite the blood on Peter's face, Jess could still make out his gentle features, his soft lips. She suddenly wondered what it would be like to kiss him. She wondered if he'd ever thought about kissing her.

Bloody hell, Jess, she thought. Peter's lying here, dying, and you're thinking about making out with him. Jeez!

At that moment, Peter opened his good eye. Jess didn't notice at first, but when he started to moan it startled her. He continued moaning until the strangled noises eventually began to form words. "Jess...ica."

Jess nodded and smiled, tears gushing down her

cheeks. "Yes, yes, it's me. I was so worried about you, Peter. What on Earth happened to you?"

Peter focused intensely on her for a moment, lips puckering as if preparing for some great speech. She hoped it wasn't going to be a final one. "Jessica..." he grimaced, "listen...to me."

She put a hand against his cheek. It throbbed heat like a radiator. "I am, Peter. I'm here."

"Get away," he said, "out of here."

Jess blinked. "What do you mean?"

A hiss of air whistled in Peter's nostrils as though forcing its way past a blockage. He repeated himself, but more weakly, like he was going to lose consciousness again at any moment. "Get away. They are...coming."

Peter's good eye rolled back in his head, disappearing behind his drooping eyelid. Before Jess had time to consider what he'd been trying to tell her, she was alerted by a crash. Followed by cries of pain and screams of agony.

What the hell's happening now? I don't think I can take any more.

Making her way over to the bar area, Jess saw commotion taking place. Lucas, Steph, and Nigel were standing around, looking concerned.

"What's going on?" she asked Lucas.

"Dunno, lass. The menfolk went downstairs to

get us something to build a fire. Next thing I know there's a load of caterwauling." He moved into the doorway behind the bar and faded into the shadows. Before disappearing completely, he turned back. "Well, you coming or not, lass?"

Jess stood for a moment, then nodded. She followed after Lucas and they headed into an unlit corridor at the back of the bar. The sound of someone in pain became clearer, and so did the noise of people bickering.

Lucas sparked his lighter and gave them light. "I think they're down there," he said, referring to an open doorway on their left. It led to a narrow staircase, leading down. A breeze floated upwards from the cellar beneath. It tickled Jess's cheeks and the inside of her nostrils.

Lucas placed his hands either side of his mouth and shouted down the staircase. "You fellas okay down there? We heard yelling."

"We need help." The voice was Harry's. "Graham is hurt. I screwed up. I screwed up rea-"

"Just bring some blankets and whatever is left of the first aid kit." The new voice was Damien's and it cut Harry off mid-sentence. "Graham's hurt, but he's gunna be alright. No need for anybody to get their knickers in a twist."

Jess couldn't help but feel faint. Peter was at death's door and now Old Graham was injured too.

Two down... How many more to go?

KATH ALMOST FELT BAD.

Almost.

It'd been Peter's decision to run off and look for Jess. Nobody made him do it. Ironically, it was Kath who eventually ended up finding Jess, and that had proven even more how idiotic Peter had been for not listening to her. Still, she couldn't help but ruminate over what had happened to the boy. Someone had messed him up real nice.

Probably crossed the wrong people, Kath assumed. Polish Mafia or something. At least she hoped so. The alternative was that there really was a psychopath out there in the snow?

Not that being trapped inside The Trumpet with her current companions was any better. There was Lucas, prancing around like a drunken parody; Nigel, an ugly man who lacked any discernible personality; Steph, a low-class tramp; and that insufferable girl, Jess. Of all the people Kath could be trapped with, Jess would have been last on her list. Her little buddy from the video shop was no less irritating, backing up her absurd stories just so he could get into her filthy knickers. And that thug, Damien, was a walking billboard for dysfunctional youth if ever she saw one. To complete the agony, was Old Graham, a pensioner stinking of piss and beer, and Harry, a hopeless case from what she could ascertain. It was obvious Harry was a drunk because of the weathered look on his face. It was the same look her father used to have. Alcoholism was a slow, draining sickness which killed a man one drink at a time while making him neglect everything that was important. But no matter what anybody said, it was not a disease, it was a choice. A selfish, weak, and pitiful choice. Nobody ever forced a bottle to an alcoholic's lips.

Maybe if Kath's father hadn't been such a dead-beat she would have finished her History degree and actually done something with her life. Instead she'd ended up supporting him all the time until she hit twenty-eight. The day she found the old drunk lying on the living room floor, rapidly fading from a severe heart attack, had been a godsend. The vision of him pleading with her to call for help, while she stood there shaking her head at him and watching him die, was a significant turning point in her life. It was the day she decided she would no longer let anyone take advantage of her. She would look out only for herself. Everybody else could go right to Hell.

All around Kath, the degenerates inside the pub with her scuttled like ants, clutching blankets and bottles of water to their chests while taking them from one place to the next.

Something was going on, but Kath didn't really care. She was only with these people for safety, and the last thing she wanted to do was get involved. She would remain by the bar, warming her hands over the candle flames and waiting for the power to return.

Slowly, everyone filtered behind the bar and left the pub empty. Kath suddenly found herself alone in the flickering shadows. She cleared her throat. "Well," she said out loud. "I'd best go see what those idiots have gotten themselves into."

Kath stood up and headed for the darkness of the corridor behind the bar.

19

"I'm so sorry, Graham." Harry looked down at the old man's twisted leg and felt the urge to punch himself in the face. How could he be so stupid, getting caught in a testosterone contest with a kid fifteen years his junior? He was pathetic and for the first time was finally realising it. He put his hand on Old Graham's shallow chest and could feel the man's ribs through tissue-paper skin. The scar below Harry's knuckles reminded him that he had a habit of hurting people.

"Harry," Old Graham whispered, not to be quiet but because he was obviously winded by his ordeal. "Harry, don't worry. I'm okay, it's just me leg. Get it fixed up in the morning, good as new."

Harry didn't want to lie to the man. "I don't

think tomorrow's going to be any better. I'm not sure if we can get you help soon enough."

Old Graham snorted. "Then just put me in a bathtub full of whiskey. By the time I drink meself dry, the snow will have gone and the ambulances will be back on the road."

Harry smiled. "I'm really so-"

"If you say you're sorry one more time, son, I'll break my other leg just to shut you up."

For reasons he couldn't quite understand Harry felt like crying. All the times he had labelled Old Graham a nuisance, and he'd never taken the time to see what a kind forgiving old soul he was. Harry had stopped taking the time to know anyone after the crash that had taken his family. He realised how selfish that had been.

"Can I do anything for you?" Harry asked Old Graham.

"No, just get me a beer, and a snog off Steph, and we'll call it quits.

Harry laughed. "I'll do my best, but I'm thinking I'll only be able to manage one of those."

Old Graham opened his eyes wide like a startled rabbit. "What? You mean we're out of beer!"

Harry stood up, wanting to laugh his ass off, but somehow finding it impossible. Laughter was a luxury he was all out of.

In the hallway above, a sphere of light began an ethereal descent down the shadowy staircase. By the time it got down to the last few steps, the source of the glow revealed itself. Steph was carrying a tray full of candles. She set them down on the floor.

"Hey," said Harry, quietly taking her to one side. "I think he's going to be okay for now. Tough as old boots, that one."

Steph smiled. "Old Graham? Yeah, I could have told you that. Took a bullet in the Falklands. Didn't even realise till he was back at base half a day later."

Harry frowned. "He tell you that?"

"Yeah," said Steph, keeping her voice down. "It's one of his stories I like to believe; makes me think of him as a hero."

Harry thought for a moment then nodded. "Yeah, I think it's one I'd like to believe too."

Steph stroked a hand against Harry's shoulder and rubbed all the way from his elbow to his neck. The feeling made his stomach flutter and filled him with a mixture of excitement and remorse.

"How you holding up?" she asked him.

He didn't know what to say. After a while, he said, "I really don't know. With all that's happened tonight, I'm starting to wonder if I'm losing my mind."

"Me too. I feel like we're the only people left in the

world and we can't go outside because we'll either freeze to death or get eaten by monsters. Something isn't right, but I keep telling myself that everything will be okay. I hope I'm not just being naïve."

Harry reached out and gave her hand a squeeze. "We have to keep reminding ourselves that this is reality, not one of Jerry's horror movies. Whatever is going on is really strange, maybe even dangerous, but as long as we stick together, we'll come out the other end of this and find out what the hell has been going on all night."

"I hope so, because this is starting to feel too much like a nightmare."

"My whole life is a nightmare," said Harry. "I'm getting pretty sick of it."

"When this is all over, I'm gunna take a holiday."

"Yeah," said Harry. "Me too. Maybe I'll go skiing."

Steph stared at him for a moment looking confused, but then broke out in hysterical laughter. After a moment, Harry was surprised to find that he was joining her. Maybe laughter wasn't a luxury he was completely out of just yet.

Or maybe Steph is just a master of getting blood out of a stone.

Or feelings from a torn heart.

"Oh Harry," Steph patted him on the shoulder. "You do make me laugh! I'm really going to have to get to know you better when this is all over, but trust me it won't be while we're skiing. Give me sand and sun, so that I never have to see another flake of snow again."

"Okay, deal. Anyway, do we have a plan on what to do next?"

Steph nodded. "Damien said the dustbin was just too heavy to get up the stairs, so we'll have to come down here and start a fire. He said a small windowless room like this would be easier to heat anyway. We just need to leave the door at the top of the stairs open so we can breathe. He's not as stupid as he looks, you know?"

"Yeah, I've noticed that," agreed Harry, wondering why Damien hadn't condemned him for dropping the dustbin from the top of the stairs. The lad knew it had been Harry's fault, yet for some reason, he was making out as if it had been an impossible task to begin with. Tonight had muddled Harry's entire opinion of the Damien. He wasn't ready to trust the lad, but he was at least starting to consider it.

"Everyone's upstairs," said Steph, "gathering stuff to burn. We're going to leave Peter in front of the fire. Jess said she'd stay with him, but there's not enough room for anybody else."

Harry nodded. "We'll have to keep an eye on them both. It may not be safe for her to be alone. I'll go see if she needs anything and then go help the others."

"Okay, Harry. I'll get Old Graham nice and comfy, then get this place lit up. See you in a bit. Mind yourself in the dark."

Harry moved aside to let Steph past with her candles and then he started to climb the stairs. He was taken back to earlier when he'd tried to climb up with the dustbin. He had a lot of making up to do to Old Graham, that was for sure, but at least Damien had turned the disaster into a sustainable plan B. It would be warmer in the cellar once they got the fire going and Harry started to feel far more hopeful about their situation.

The corridor at the top of the stairs was pitch-black, but Harry could make out a dim, flickering light coming from the bar's candles at the far end of the hallway. He felt his way towards them and found Lucas standing at the bar. The Irishman was busy gathering beers and a large bottle of Famous Grouse whisky into an empty crisp carton.

"Getting essentials, I see?" said Harry as he re-entered the bar.

Lucas held up an uncapped beer and swigged from it, letting out a lip-smacking sigh at the end. "Don't ya know it! I asked the old fella what he needed and all he said was beer and plenty of it. Can't deny an injured war hero now, can I? What kind of man would that make me?"

"Never thought of it like that." Harry fired off a mock salute. "Keep up the good work, private."

Lucas returned the salute. "Will do, Major Jobson, sir!"

Harry continued on from the bar and over to Jess at the fireplace. She flinched, as though he'd startled her. It wasn't surprising, really; sounded as if the poor girl had been through it worse than anyone else tonight. Other than Peter of course.

"You okay?" Harry asked her.

"Fine." She stroked Peter's forehead with a damp cloth she'd no doubt warmed in front of the fire. "I can't leave him here alone, and I don't think it would be right to move him either. Jerry has gone to find us some snacks. He'll be back soon to keep me company. Anyway, I have *this* if I get into any real trouble." Jess reached down beside the sofa and came up with a great shiny piece of metal.

Harry nodded. "The last call bell. Good idea. Not a single man whose ears won't prick up at that sound. Just ring if you need help, okay?"

Jess seemed proud for a moment, but her sombre expression soon returned when she went back to nursing Peter. When she spoke again, she did so without looking Harry in the eye. "How's Graham doing? I heard his leg's pretty painful."

Painful wasn't a good enough word to describe the result of Harry's stupidity. "Luckily, there's no bleeding," he said. "I think it's broken, but he's okay for now. Chipper as ever, long as he has us bringing him beer all night."

"He seems like a nice old man. I hope he's okay."

Harry nodded. "Me too."

He thought Jess was going to speak again, but instead of replying he caught her looking over his shoulder. Her eyes grew wide as if something concerned her.

Why is she staring like that? Harry wondered. *Is something behind me?*

Harry spun to find Damien standing close behind him. As usual the lad's face was a syrupy mixture of frowns and scowls, but there seemed to be something else in his expression too.

"Come with me," Damien said simply, before walking off in the opposite direction and leaving Harry wondering what to do.

Should Harry follow? Or should he grab a weapon and prepare to fight? It was hard to tell when it came to Damien. After the last few hours, Harry decided the lad had earned the benefit of the doubt, so he followed.

Damien had headed over to the pub's rear corridor, which led to the male and female toilets, the rear fire door, and the seldom-used dance floor at the back of the pub.

"Take a look," Damien said to Harry as he caught up. He was pointing at the exit door. "Look through the window at the top."

For a second Harry had visions of doing as he was told and having his head rammed through the glass. Wasn't that the kind of thing gangsters do? Made you dig your own grave? Harry sighed. If something was going to happen, it was going to happen. He stepped toward the door.

"Look through," Damien ordered again.

Harry moved up against the door and put his face against the glass. There was no prompting necessary on where to look or what to focus on. It was clear for him to see.

"We have big problems," Damien said.

Damn right they did!

Outside, towers of flame seemed to rise from the snow in all directions – ten, maybe even twenty feet high. The fire formed a wall around the pub like a fiery prison.

But was it intended to keep them all in? Or to drive them out?

What terrified Harry most, however, was the three giant crucifixes standing in the centre of the inferno. Each of them possessed a struggling victim being roasted alive by the flames. Their screams held no sound, but Harry could feel their agony as their flesh blackened and peeled from their bones, leaving behind charred husks of flesh.

"This nightmare just got worse," said Harry. "I think I'd like to wake up now."

20

Damien had gone while Harry had been staring out the window.

Was the horror show outside not interesting enough for him?

Harry took another glance outside, blinking so that he knew what he was seeing was real. The fires still burned high, whipping back and forth in the growing blizzard while sizzling snowflakes filled the air like locusts. It was bizarre and unsettling to see both flames and snow mingle together in the same space; like two separate nightmares merging into one.

Harry started to feel like he was in a Salvador Dali painting, with the world melting away around him. He needed to make sense of the situation, but should he tell the others? He wasn't sure, but was astounded by the fact that he wanted Damien's advice about the matter. He couldn't deny that the lad was calm under pressure.

But where had he gone? And why?

Harry glanced out the window one last time before moving away. It seemed like a bad idea to take his eyes off the flames outside, but he couldn't stay there all night. It was freezing next to the fire exit, and an aggressive draught snuck under the door and rattled the wood on its hinges.

Back in the main pub area, the others members of the group were travelling back and forth, seeking out fuel for the furnace. Nigel was busy tearing cushions from the chairs and snapping the legs into kindling. Kath was gathering up beer mats halfheartedly.

"Hey, Kath," he said to her. "Maybe we can find something bigger to burn? I don't think those will last very long."

The woman shot Harry a look that made him feel like she wanted him to die. Harry shivered, but a second later it was as if the look hadn't happened, as Kath was now smiling at him politely.

"I guess you're right," she admitted. "I'll go search for something else." She threw down the pile of beer mats and they hit the table with a *slap!* Then she walked off towards the bar like a stroppy teenager.

Kath was an odd lady.

There was still no sign of Damien. Harry tried to figure out where he'd gone, and why so suddenly? And why had he chosen only Harry to lead into the exit corridor? It didn't seem that anybody else knew about the flames outside yet. With the windows barricaded and the pub up on a hill, it was impossible to see anything outside other than darkness. So the question remained: did Harry tell the others what Damien had shown him.

Harry made the decision. He clapped his hands together. "Everybody listen!"

Lucas and Nigel turned their attention to Harry. Kath reappeared from behind the bar. At the far end of the room, Jess stood up from the sofa, leaving Peter asleep under the watchful eye of Jerry. Harry moved into a spot where they all could see and hear him. He clasped his hands together and tried to find the right words. "I think there's something that we all need to be aware of."

"And what would that be, Harry Boy?" asked Lucas, lifting himself up onto a bar stool. "Please tell."

"It's not easy to explain, but I think we can all agree that tonight is a strange night."

"No argument there," Nigel said. "I'm starting to get a bad feeling."

Harry pushed himself to continue, his were palms sweating. "I think we can agree that there are dangers tonight, more than just the cold."

"You mean what happened to that stupid boy, Peter?" said Kath. "I'm sure whatever trouble he has gotten himself into was something he deserved. That doesn't mean that *we're* in any danger."

"You bitch!"

Harry turned to see Jess storming toward Kath from the other end of the pub. Jerry seemed unsure whether or not he should be following after her or remaining where he was.

Lucas moved away from the bar to intercept Jess in the middle of the room. "Calm down there, lass."

"I swear to God, Kath!" Jess bunched her hands into fists. "If you say one more thing about Peter – and I mean, *one more thing* – I'm going to scratch your goddamn eyes out. This happened because of you, because you allowed him to wonder off alone."

Kath snorted. "I'm not his babysitter. He's a grown man, and if he can't look after himself then he should have stayed in Poland. God knows we don't need his kind here."

"You...you racist!"

"Call me whatever you like, dear. I'm only saying

what most of the country thinks. Peter was probably a petty criminal like the rest of them. Tonight he got his comeuppance."

To everyone's surprise, Jess's small frame managed to escape Lucas's grasp. She leapt towards a nearby table, snatching at the nearest thing she could find, which happened to be an empty pint glass. Harry watched in horror as Jess flung the glass through the air, pitching it with all the aggression of a baseball player.

It hit Kath's forehead with an almighty *thonk!*

Immediately, the woman hit the floor, clutching at her face and screaming. A second later she was back on her feet and furious, like a champion boxer rising after a fluky haymaker. She was not happy. Her bloodstained forehead was testament to it.

"I'll kill you!" Kath growled, as a line of blood trickled down the side of her nose.

"Nobody is going to kill anybody!" Everybody turned to see Steph storming out from behind the bar. Damien was with her. "What the hell is going on? Why is Kath covered in blood?"

"The little bitch threw a glass at me. She's insane."

Steph turned to Jess with such ferocity that the young girl flinched and took a step back. "Is that true? Are you causing trouble in my pub?"

Jess nodded and took another step back.

Steph pointed a finger. "Go look after Peter – NOW! – and if I see you move for the rest of the night, I'll throw you out in the snow myself."

Jess moved so quickly it was almost a sprint.

Then Steph turned to Kath. "There's a little kitchenette with a sink in the back. Take a candle from the bar and clean yourself up."

Kath still bristled with fury, but she was beginning to simmer down. Slowly. "That girl should be locked in a padded cell."

Steph sighed. "Well, for now we don't have that luxury, so the best I can do is keep you two separated. Jess will be staying up here with Peter, so you come downstairs with the rest of us. Now, go get that blood cleaned up before it freezes on your face."

Kath nodded unhappily and left the room, while Lucas and Nigel went back to their tasks. Steph and Damien approached Harry.

"What happened?" Steph demanded. Her breath fogged in front of her.

Harry ran a hand through his hair. "I don't know. I was trying to get everyone together so I could tell them something and it all kicked off. Those two really don't like each other!"

Steph shook her head wearily. "Tell me about it.

I'd call the police if I could. There's no excuse for that kind of violence."

"It wasn't just Jess's fault," Harry told her. "Kath doesn't seem to have much respect for anyone else."

"I don't doubt it. But violence is violence, and on a night like this things are tense enough."

"Speaking of tension," said Harry. "There was something I was trying to tell everyone before it all went Pete Tong. Come with me."

Steph followed. Damien too.

The three of them made it over to the exit door in the rear corridor. Harry pointed to the fire exit. "Look through the window, but try to stay calm."

"What do you mean?" Steph said. "You're worrying me."

"Just look, and then we'll talk."

Anxiety etched itself across Steph's face, but she obliged nonetheless, moving up against the door and peering through the glass for several seconds. "Jesus Christ," she said finally.

"You see! You see what we're up against?"

Steph turned back around to face Harry. "Of course I do. The snow out there is getting insane. We need to get that fire going right now or we're all going to freeze. I don't like this at all. This is bad."

Harry didn't understand. He pushed Steph to

one side and peered through the glass again for himself.

The fire was gone. In fact it was as though it'd never even been there. The snow was deeper than before and there were no shallow areas where the heat of the flames would have caused it to melt. Everywhere Harry looked was cold, bleak, empty, and white.

But there was no fire. No fire at all. Nor were there three crucifixes or burning bodies.

"There were flames!" Harry mumbled. "Flames everywhere."

Steph looked confused.

Harry looked at Damien, who was stood silently with his arms folded. "Tell her. Tell her what we saw."

Damien shrugged. "I don't know what you're talking about?"

Harry blinked, then shook his head in disbelief. "What am I talking about? You saw it! In fact it was *you* that showed me!"

"Think there's a stripe missing off your Adidas, mate. I dunno what shit you're chatting."

"No, no, no. You saw the flames too! Why are you doing this, Damien?"

Damien didn't answer. He just walked away, leaving Harry alone with a confused-looking Steph

"I swear it!" Harry told Steph adamantly. "Damien's playing games. I don't know why, but he is."

Out of the blue, Steph hugged Harry and whispered in his ear. "If you say there was a fire outside then I believe you, okay? Just don't get yourself worked up, because I need you tonight. I would have gone insane if you weren't here helping me."

Harry eased her back and looked at her. "Y-You really believe me?"

Steph nodded. "Yes! Now go make yourself useful. Old Graham was asking for you, so go see him. I'll get all the toilet paper and hand towels. We're going to have to get that fire going soon."

Harry nodded and Steph left him in the cold corridor, wondering why Damien had not backed him up. *Just when I thought we were finally getting along, he makes me look like a lunatic, right in front of Steph. Stupid, Harry. Real stupid! You should never trust a snake.*

But Damien wasn't worth the time right now, not when Steph had made it clear she needed Harry's support. She was playing nursemaid, host, and leader, all at the same time. She was putting everyone else first, while all they did was bicker. Harry wanted to take some of the strain off of her, and he would, but first he was being summoned to attend to other business. Old Graham wanted to speak to him and Harry wasn't about to keep the old guy waiting. He owed him too much already.

Before Harry left the corridor, something caught his eye. At the far end of the rear corridor was a light, coming from the pub's unused dance floor.

Was somebody in the back room?

Harry stepped forward cautiously. It was probably just one of the others, looking for something to burn, the light coming from their candles.

"Hey, who's there?" Harry asked.

No reply. The light seemed to get brighter, pulsing rapidly.

Harry continued down the corridor, creeping anxiously as he awaited a response. When none came, he called out again. "I said who's there?"

Still no response. Harry was left with the decision whether or not to investigate. Tonight was a night where strange things were happening and wandering off alone was a bad idea. Nevertheless, his feet carried him forward.

Harry had to shield his eyes with his forearm as he took the final few steps towards the backroom. The pulsing light was blinding.

Inside it felt like a sauna, humid and hot. After hours of freezing, the aura of warmth was heavenly, but it was unnatural as well. There was no rational explanation for the backroom of The Trumpet to feel like the Brazilian rainforest, especially when it was snowing outside.

Rather than retreat, Harry stepped out onto the stiff wood of the dance floor. It creaked beneath his weight. From the end of the room, the bright light continued pulsing. It was coming from behind the elevated DJ booth erected against the far wall, but as Harry got closer the light began to weaken. He hopped up the three steps at the edge of the dance floor and hurried towards the booth. The light continued to fade. Harry had the feeling that if he didn't get a look inside the DJ booth quickly, he would miss something important. Harry unlatched the door and rushed inside.

His heart skipped a beat.

It was the most wonderful and the most painful thing Harry could ever have hoped to see. He choked back a sob. "Toby?"

Cowering before him, engulfed by a rapidly fading glow, was Harry's son. Toby hadn't aged at all since the crash. He peered up at Harry with the same deep, soulful eyes he had always had.

"Daddy." Toby's voice was an echo, seeming to come from the walls themselves. "Daddy, I'm scared."

It was impossible, an evil trick. Yet, somehow,

Harry found himself speaking only affectionately. "It's okay, Toby. Daddy's here."

The light around Toby died, returning the room to near darkness. He looked just like a normal six year old boy now. "You promise you'll keep me safe, daddy?"

"Yes, son. I'll keep you safe." Harry reached down to Toby, but the boy shuffled backwards out of his grasp.

"No, you won't," Toby said spitefully. "You can't keep *anyone* safe. My daddy was strong. He taught me to ride a bike and would buy me chicken nuggets whenever I wanted. You're not him! You're weak. Weak and pathetic!" The words hissed and crackled from Toby's mouth, not at all like the voice of a child.

Tears fell from Harry's eyes. I am weak, he thought to himself. I failed you, Toby. I let you get hurt, and all I've done since is feel sorry for myself. But you're not my son.

The apparition of Toby was so accurate that it sent a chill through Harry's bones. But it wasn't perfect. Harry could see the lack of humanity in its malignant eyes.

"I have to go now, Toby," Harry said, backing away slowly. "I think you should go back to wherever you came from."

The malice in the creature's eyes gave away its age. There was something ancient and inhuman bubbling away beneath the surface as it cackled at Harry. The piercing sound filled the room.

"Running away is all you're good for, maggot. You watched your family die and have been running away ever since. You are pathetic, wasting the life that He gave you. Death will embrace you soon. Leave this place Harry Jobson and be done with it. Your time is over. Reckoning is here."

Harry didn't understand, but he knew he had to get away. By taking Toby's form, the creature had specifically targeted Harry, plucking at his grief like strings on a guitar.

Harry didn't take his eyes away from the DJ's booth as he sidled backwards along the dance floor, but it didn't stop him noticing the light source growing behind him.

Harry spun around.

His heart stopped all over again.

Thomas Morris stood by the exit to the pub's backroom. The man who had taken everything from Harry was here, and smiling at him like an old friend.

"Long time no see, Harry," the apparition hissed. "You're looking...older."

Harry said nothing.

"You really gunna ignore me? With the history you and me have? Thought you'd have more to say."

Harry's fists clenched. "I have nothing to say to you!"

The apparition of Thomas Morris laughed again. "You never were much of a talker. You prefer to let actions speak for you, right?"

Whatever this thing was, it was not Thomas, and it could do Harry no harm. If it could, then why hadn't it done so already? Harry stepped around the image of his old enemy and headed for the door.

Harry was thrown backwards and hit the floor hard.

Thomas immediately loomed over Harry. His inhuman eyes were filled with the same malignance that Toby's had been. "You will pay for your action-sss," it hissed at Harry. "Everyone will pay. It is time for...retribution."

Harry cowered on the dance floor. The apparition had hit him; but how? Harry decided not to hang around to find out. He leapt to his feet and rushed for the door.

The apparition shouted after him, words both wicked and baleful. "You will die tonight, Harry Jobson. Death's cold embrace awaits you. Go outside and face your end. Do not delay what is already certain."

"Fuck you!" Harry shouted back. He reached the door to the pub's corridor and glanced back one last brief second. It slowed him down, but he couldn't help it.

Thomas Morris was nowhere to be seen.

Harry realised he was shaking. He took a series of deep breaths but still couldn't relax. He needed to get out of that room right now, return to the others and tell them what he'd seen. Not that they would believe him.

He would just have to try to make them believe him. After what he had seen in the last hour, Harry knew that they were in great danger – from a source he could not make sense of.

Harry was about to leave, when the back room presented him with another gift. This time his heart kept its rhythm. Perhaps he was becoming used to seeing the impossible. Lying on the floor was his wife, Julie. Her body and face were battered and bruised, bones splintered and askew. Just like what she had looked like after the car crash that had killed her.

Harry gazed down at the twisted forgery of his wife and allowed his heart to scream for a moment. The final image of his wife's dying form had always stayed with him, but never had he confronted it face-to-face. Not since the night it happened.

Julie tilted her head towards him, broken bones scraping and grating against each other as she moved. "Harry..." She spoke in a condemning whisper. "Why did this happen to me? Why are you not with me?"

Harry ground his teeth. This wasn't his wife. This wasn't Julie. Whatever it was, it was defiling the memories of dead people. He owed it no explanations.

"You're dead, Julie," Harry said, stepping over the twisted body and heading into the corridor. "And I'm not afraid of joining you."

21

Damien wasn't sure why he had lied. Harry had made himself look a right muppet in front of Steph, but the fact was he was telling the truth. There had been flames outside, but they'd suddenly disappeared. Damien could have backed Harry up, but had instead decided to leave him hanging.

Did the thought of Steph and Harry possible copping off together irritate Damien so much? He didn't think he was so petty. Steph wasn't like the usual girls Damien fucked. She was strong, with a mind of her own, and took control in the same way he did. He respected that.

But it was more than simple jealousy. Damien

had gained a degree of pleasure from Harry's frustration. Over the last few hours, Harry had shown himself to be an alright bloke. He may have been a deadbeat, but the geezer's heart was in the right place. Maybe what pissed Damien off was the way Harry constantly played the part of the wounded soldier, always making people want to come up to him and ask if everything was okay. *Oh, poor Harry, so full of pain and anguish, yet he still keeps going. What a guy!*

Damien scowled. Harry had no right to make out like his problems were worse than anyone else's.

He did lose his son though...

Damien shook his head and stood up from the cushion-less bench. He was beginning to lose sight of things. Tomorrow would be a new day and he would go back to not knowing any of these people.

Jess and Jerry were sitting nearby, with the dying polish kid who'd come through the window. Damien had chosen to stay near to the three of them just in case they needed help. He'd been impressed by the way Jess had glassed the old bird. Took balls.

As he stretched his legs, Damien continued to brood about Harry. Damien had things tough, too, but no one cared about his problems. No one ever gave a damn that his old man used to beat him black and blue growing up for no other reason that he felt like it. *Trying to toughen you up, boy! Teach you to be a man.* No one cared when the locally-feared, notorious gangster, 'Big Jan', had made Damien deal drugs at ten years old. *No one will suspect a kid,* his old man used to say, *so get yourself on that corner and don't come home till you've sold it all.* And no one cared when Damien's old man, 'Big Jan', had tried to pin an assault charge on him just to boost his street cred. *People need to fear you like they fear me, Damien. Time to get a name for yourself.*

The rage that ever flowed through Damien's veins began to heat up. When his old man had gone down last year, he'd felt free for the first time ever. But it hadn't lasted. Damien had been ordered to take over operations and report to his father in the nick via regular phone calls. *Keep the money safe for me, Dame, for when I get out. Make me proud, son.*

Yeah, I'll make you real proud, dad! I'll live up to the name of 'Big Jan'.

Except Damien had never felt so small than when he was trying to be big like his father. For him, violence was an act, a well-rehearsed skill. There was no joy in punching a rival's face, only emptiness. To his father it came easily. Like when he kicked the shit out of a local street dealer until he was a whimpering, bleeding mess on the ground. A kid no older than Damien.

Gazz Brown had been tough. He'd managed to knock Damien spark-out at a party and taken his stash of e. Damien's father had not been happy – the supply had been his. Not happy at all. In a drunken rage, Big Jan – along with a group of 'the boys' – had taken Damien to go find Gazz. They'd found him round the back of the local supermarket, selling the e to the warehouse workers. Big Jan saw red – had gone red in fact. Like a wild bull, he had torn into the youth, cracking bones and shattering teeth, stamping and kicking long after the boy's beaten body lay unconscious on the ground. It took almost ten minutes before the boys dragged him away, but by that time someone had called the Police. Somebody had to go down for it.

But not Big Jan.

Gazz ended up in a coma and Damien fessed to the crime. He'd gone to juvi for a stint, while ironically the fuzz got his old man twelve months later for Class A dealing. Big Jan went to Hewell Prison for 15 years just as Damien was getting out of kid's knick. Upon his return, Damien had become feared on the local estate, viewed as a vicious, animalistic thug who had gone down for beating someone into a coma. His old man would have been proud.

But tonight was supposed to be the night when Damien did something to make *himself* proud. He was going to disobey Big Jan for the first time and do the right thing. Instead, he'd found himself trapped inside a rotten pub with a bunch of losers.

Losers like Harry, who only care about their next drink.

Finally it clicked. The reason Damien hated Harry so much was because the man cared more about getting wasted than anything else. Damien's father had been no different, except it had been drugs instead of booze. Every time Damien looked at Harry, downing pint after pint, night in night out, he thought about how much he hated his father.

But Damien realised he had got Harry all wrong. Harry had been a good man and a good father, a bloke who cared so much about his family that, when they'd died, he'd just given up on life. Harry's family had been his entire world – the exact opposite to Big Jan – and when they had died, part of him went with them. Damien finally understood Harry's endless drinking.

And he could forgive it.

"I should apologise," Damien told himself, "but first I gotta go take a piss."

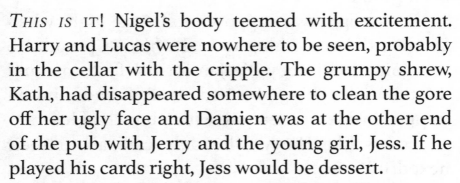

THIS IS IT! Nigel's body teemed with excitement. Harry and Lucas were nowhere to be seen, probably in the cellar with the cripple. The grumpy shrew, Kath, had disappeared somewhere to clean the gore off her ugly face and Damien was at the other end of the pub with Jerry and the young girl, Jess. If he played his cards right, Jess would be dessert.

But first he had Steph to gorge himself on.

I'm finally going to fuck her.

Nigel had watched with delight as everyone departed, except Steph who had gone toward the toilets alone. This was his chance. He would follow her in, knock her out cold, have his way with her, and then slit her throat with his trusty pen knife – *sharpened to perfection*. By the time he dumped her body outside in the snow, no one would be any the wiser. Nigel would plead ignorance of Steph's whereabouts and, while everyone would fret and worry, that would be the sum of it. What else could they do but impotently panic? Only Nigel would know the truth.

First thing in the morning, he'd hop in his lorry and get the hell out of there as fast as the snow would flatten before his tyres. He would spend a few months in France maybe, enjoy some of the pussy on the South Coast. It was the easiest thing in the world. Raping and killing unsuspecting women had become as second nature to Nigel as taking a leak. Just another need to be taken care of. An itch to scratch.

Nigel eased open the door to the men's toilets, where he'd seen Steph enter. The door creaked ever so slightly, but the sounds coming from inside, of Steph gathering up supplies, drowned out any noise he made.

The toilets smelt of stale piss and the room was lit by a single candle Steph had placed on the middle of three sinks. She was at the far end of the small space with her back to the door, gathering up bundles of handtowels from a storage cupboard.

Perfect! She won't even see it coming.

With well-practiced grace, that belied his lumbering appearance, Nigel struck his blow. He clocked Steph from behind, hooking his fist into the side of her jaw and knocking her cold. The clunky Dolphin ring on his pinkie finger gave the blow a little extra impact. Steph's body flopped sideways, collapsing into one of the toilet cubicles. Her head hit the ceramic bowl inside with a resounding *thump!*

"Good, girl," Nigel grinned, "helping Daddy like

that. You've found us a room and got yourself ready."

He knelt over Steph and fumbled at her clothing, squeezing her breasts through the material. He could barely see in the dark, but that only made it more exciting. He'd fantasied about this moment for so long that every touch of her flesh was enough to send small beads of ejaculate spurting from his swollen cock.

He rolled Steph onto her back and slid his eager, trembling fingers beneath the waistband of her jeans. Despite the perishing cold, the flesh of Steph's belly and groin was surprisingly hot.

Steph murmured incoherently.

"That's it, you little slut, cry out for your Daddy. He won't help you."

Nigel fumbled excitedly at the buttons on Steph's jeans. He ground his teeth in frustration when they refused to pop easily. Taking a deep breath, he steadied his excited hands and concentrated. The buttons came loose one at a time.

Pop.

Pop.

Pop.

"That's it, darling, let's get you out of these clothes."

Just as Nigel was about to start tugging down

Steph's jeans, he was alerted by a presence close be-hind him. He spun around.

Then bit his tongue as something struck his jaw.

"What the fuck is going on here?" a voice demanded.

What the fuck indeed, thought Nigel as he unwill-ingly went to sleep on the piss-soaked floor.

22

Harry had been on his way to the toilet when he heard the ruckus.

After seeing the apparitions in the dance hall, Harry had hurried downstairs to the cellar to regroup. The vision of Thomas Morris had reached out and struck Harry, but he was almost certain that was the extent of the physical threat. If it could have done any real harm then surely it would have done so. Harry had no clue what was going on, but there was no need to panic the others with what had happened just yet, at least until he could figure out what to tell them.

It turned out that Old Graham wanted to speak to him about a rather embarrassing matter. The old man had needed to piss badly, but couldn't get up with his leg the way it was. Harry understood the predicament, and accepting responsibility, but at first didn't know what to suggest. Then he spotted the half empty bottle of Famous Grouse that Lucas had brought down. He gave the bottle to Old Graham who immediately necked the rest of the contents. "For the pain," he said. Then Harry had given him the old man a few moments alone to refill the bottle.

Now Harry was on his way to the urinals upstairs, with a candle in one hand and a whisky bottle full of geriatric piss in the other. He hadn't expected to run into trouble again so soon after his last encounter, but something was definitely happening inside the toilets as he approached.

The men's toilet was dimly lit by candlelight, and it was too dark to see clearly what was happening inside. There was some sort of scuffle going on. A soft wet thudding that was immediately recognisable.

Someone's getting a beating.

Candle in hand, along with the whiskey bottle full of urine, Harry ran forwards, lighting the room in a narrow sphere as he moved. At the back, he found...Damien. And then he found Nigel. Damien was beating the bigger man to a pulp, like he was tenderising a piece of beef. His knuckles made soft *whapping* sounds as they bounced off Nigel's swollen face. What upset Harry most, was the sight of Steph lying unconscious in one of the cubicles. As Harry swooped the candle towards her, he saw that her jeans were unbuttoned.

Damien looked up and noticed Harry, but it was too late to give an explanation. Harry smashed the whiskey bottle full of piss over Damien's head so hard that it might have killed him.

Part of Harry hoped it did.

BESIDE THE FIREPLACE, Jess watched over Peter, with Jerry beside her. She watched her sleeping friend turn paler and paler, and could not tell whether it was down to the cold or blood loss. Most of Peter's wounds were bandaged, but they wept constantly.

"You think he's going to wake up?" Jerry asked, tugging Jess out of her thoughts. His usual exuberance was absent for the time being and he had remained quiet for a while. Jess wondered if he was thinking about Ben; trying to make sense of what had happened to his best friend.

Jess shrugged. "He woke up once before, so who knows. How are *you* doing?"

"Me? I'm cushty? It's *this* one we need to look after." He pointed at Peter. "He looks bad."

Jess shrugged again. "I think he might have it easiest of all, being asleep. Right now, I want to know how *you* are. You know...after what happened to Ben."

Jerry's face crumbled like a moist sandcastle and, for a short moment, Jess thought he was going to cry. He didn't, though. "It's stupid," he said, "but I miss him already."

"That's not stupid at all."

"Feels like it. I just keep wishing it was me. I wish I was the one that was dead and Ben was still alive."

"Now *that* is stupid." Jess shook her head despairingly. "He wouldn't have wanted you to be dead, would he?"

Jerry shrugged. "Wouldn't surprise me. All I ever did was annoy him."

"Then why did he always keep you around?"

Jerry looked away from her and stared into the fire. "Fate, I guess."

Jess wasn't sure she understood. "What do you mean, fate?"

Jerry rubbed at his eyes and somehow succeeded in making them look even more tired. "Ever seen the play, Blood Brothers?"

"No.".

"It's a film about these two brothers who get separated at birth. A mother has twins and can't afford to keep them both, so she gives one away to the rich family that she works for."

"Okay," said Jess, still not really following, but willing to listen.

"Somehow, the baby boy she gave away ends up making friends with the son she kept – his twin brother. They have completely different upbringings, one rich, one poor, but somehow they become best friends. Despite everything, they're really very much alike." Jerry stared at Jess and this time she was certain he would cry, but still he did not. He smiled instead. "That's like me and Ben. You get what I'm saying?"

Jess didn't. But then she thought about it a little harder and ventured a guess: "You and Ben were... brothers?" Jerry didn't answer her but Jess knew it was a hit and not a miss. It still didn't quite make sense, though. "Did Ben know?"

Jerry finally allowed a tear to escape his eye. He blinked it away and it crept down his cheek. "We... we had the same dad, but I never told him that. My mom only told *me* when I was ten. By then I'd already been friends with Ben for three years."

Jess was shocked. "Why did you never tell him?"

Jerry wiped the tear from his face, but did nothing about the new ones that ran down to replace it. "Ashamed, I guess. My mom told me it was just a one-night stand and that it was while Ben's dad was still with his mum."

"You kept it to yourself because you didn't want to hurt Ben or break up his family. I understand."

Jerry avoided looking directly at Jess as he spoke. "Ben idolised his father; thought he was this great businessman. Truth is that the guy was a small-time jerk with more skeletons in his closet than Norman Bates, but if I told Ben what his father – what *our* father – was really like, it would only have hurt him. I didn't want that. He was my brother."

Jess felt emotionally winded by the story and had to remind herself to breath. What a beautiful sacrifice for someone to make, she thought, before hugging Jerry very tightly.

"What's that for?" he asked her.

Jess pulled out of the hug and kissed Jerry's cheek. "For being such a kind human being. I don't think you realise quite how rare that is. Ben was lucky to have you as a friend, Jerry, and even more so as a brother." Jerry whimpered. Jess patted him on the back. "Sorry, didn't mean to upset you."

Jerry wiped his eyes with the back of his arm.

"It's okay. Think I needed it. Clears my head for what really matters."

Jess frowned. "And what's that?"

"What do you think? You saw what happened to Ben. There's something evil out there and it's not going to stop till it gets us all. If Peter could wake up and speak, he'd tell us to get the hell out of this messed up situation."

"Peter already did warn me," Jess blurted out. "He said I needed to get away."

Jerry was silent for a moment, then took a deep breath. "No one believed us about what we saw, and I guess we kind of just let it go because we were embarrassed, but we both know that we're not crazy. There's something out there that isn't human, Jess. It killed Ben."

"I know," she said. "We have to get away."

23

"Make sure it's tight"

"I am!" Harry tugged the curtain ties around Damien's wrists and felt them dig into the boy's flesh. "Any tighter and I'll cut his arms off."

"Good," said Nigel. "Exactly what the dirty little rapist deserves."

When Harry swung the whiskey bottle at Damien's head it'd instantly shattered, sending streams of Old Graham's salty piss all over the both of them. Harry could still smell the vinegary pong on his clothes.

Once Nigel regained consciousness, he and Harry had dragged Damien's limp body into the bar and heaved him up onto a chair. They were now in the process of restraining him to it as tightly as possible. The last thing they needed was Damien waking up and endangering anybody else. They had enough on their plate as it was. Harry still hadn't forgotten about the incident in the dance hall. Chaos, it seemed, had started coming at him from all directions.

Steph was lying downstairs on a pile of blankets, covered by an old duvet. She'd stirred briefly when they lifted her from the toilet floor, but remained unconsciousness ever since. Lucas was currently looking after her.

Harry felt sick for nearly trusting Damien.

"Nigel, I don't know what would have happened if you hadn't walked in when you did. Steph is so lucky you were there."

Nigel's chest puffed up proudly. With the beating his face had taken, Harry thought he looked like a dishevelled bear. "I'm just sorry the little perv got the drop on me before I could take him down. My head's banging."

Harry gave the curtain ties one final, haughty tug. He was satisfied that Damien was now adequately restrained. "Vicious sod really did a number on you, didn't he? Soon as the phones are working, we'll call the police and get him squared away."

Nigel seemed to flinch. "Police...yeah"

Harry looked at him. "You okay?"

"Yeah, yeah, of course. Just a bit dizzy. Need to sit down, I think."

Harry stood up, his frigid kneecaps popping. "I can keep an eye on things here. You go and rest, Nigel."

"You sure? Can I get you anything?"

Harry thought about another beer, but for some reason he said, "No, I'm good, thanks."

Nigel walked away gingerly, clutching at his ribs and holding his head. Harry tried to imagine the pain the guy was in. He was lucky to be alive after the walloping he took.

Harry stepped back and examined Damien. What could make a person so wicked as to want to rape and beat a person? It made his heart ache to think of the amount of hatred that infected the world. Damien was just one tiny ant in a whole colony of remorseless monsters. Harry started to wish that he'd asked for that beer after all. His mind couldn't cope without it.

A strangled snort came from Damien's direction and for a moment Harry thought the lad was going to wake up. His eyelids fluttered and his nose crinkled as though a fly had landed on it. But then he fell still again.

"What do we do with you now?" Harry asked.

"Can't exactly leave you in the middle of the room to freeze now, can I?"

Or maybe that's exactly what you deserve.

Harry's fists clenched themselves automatically as he thought about how frightened Steph must have been on that grimy toilet floor. He had to take deep breaths until the anger passed. It would drive him insane if he wasn't careful.

Harry needed to get away from Damien – just being near the dirtbag made him sick – but it wasn't an option. Damien could wake up and try to escape. The only place warm enough to keep the lad prisoner was by the fire, but that was already taken up by their casualty, Peter.

Prisoners. Casualties. What the hell is happening tonight!

The only other place was the cellar – once they got the new fire started at least – but there was no way Harry was going to put Damien anywhere near Steph. He was never going to let the kid anywhere near her ever again.

Harry walked over to Jess and Jerry. Both of them were on their knees tending to Peter's wounds. Jess looked up at him as he approached and managed a weary smile.

"Hey," Harry smiled back. "How you two holding up?"

"It's starting to feel a bit like that film, *Alive*," said Jerry.

Harry raised both eyebrows.

Jerry sighed. "You know...that movie where the plane crashes? The one where they're all freezing to death, one by one? They all start to eat the dead bodies to stay alive? In other words, it's freezing."

Harry shrugged his shoulders. "Sorry, never saw that film."

Jess spoke. "We want out of here, Harry."

Harry hadn't expected that. Sure, it was an obvious thing to say, given the circumstances, but Jess was an upbeat person and didn't seem the kind to complain. "We all do," he said, "but that's not possible right now. You know what it's like out there. It's not safe."

Jess nodded. "That's what I mean. It's not safe here either. The snow is getting deeper and deeper outside, and it's getting colder and colder in here. There's something out there that killed our friend and we don't want to hang around here until it gets us. We weren't lying about what happened to us. There's something out there."

Harry pictured the flames outside, growing from the snow like shimmering beanstalks, with burning corpses hanging from them. Then he thought about the thing pretending to be his son, and how he need to tell someone. "I believe you. I saw things out there in the snow, too, which is why I don't understand why you would want to go out there."

"Because we're sitting ducks here," said Jerry. "I'd rather take my chances running to safety than waiting here to freeze to death. Do you really think we can all just sit around drinking beer and waiting for things to go back to normal? I hate to say it, but I think normal took a bus out of town. We're all going to die if we stay here."

"No one is going to die," Harry stated firmly, "but I agree that we may not be safe here."

Jerry narrowed his eyes. The cold air, fighting against the licking heat of the fire, made his cheeks blush like cherries. "So, you'll help us then?"

"No," Harry said quickly. "If we go outside we'll be frozen stiff in a matter of minutes, or the victims of something even worse. It would be insane to leave here before morning. Even then, I'm not so sure. I agree we're in danger here, but I think we would be even worse off out there. We need to dig in and prepare."

Jess's lower lip trembled and she blinked several times. She looked at Harry pleadingly. "So what do you suggest? That we wait here until someone else comes flying through the window? Or until Damien tries to rape someone else?"

Harry felt his lips pull back in a snarl. "Damien won't be hurting anyone else, don't you worry about that."

Jess shrugged as if his assertion meant nothing to her. "Fine," she said, "but there's something out there that's less than friendly. You really just expect us to wait here till it tries to get in?"

"No," said Harry. "We prepare ourselves. If whatever is outside tries to get in..."

Jess and Jerry both looked at him. "Yeah?"

"We make it wish it hadn't."

24

J ess decided Harry was crazy. He had to be. Why else would he suggest bunkering down in the pub and waiting for whatever was outside to get in? He didn't understand the situation, and perhaps that made sense. Harry hadn't seen what she and Jerry had seen; hadn't seen Ben's body disintegrate into a billion bloody granules of sand. No one else understood that there was a seven-foot psychopath out there with a film prop from *Braveheart*.

Braveheart? Jesus, I sound like Jerry.

Once Harry was far enough away, Jess turned to Jerry and whispered. "Are we really going to stay here?"

"You mean batten down the hatches like the kid

from *Home* Alone?" Jerry ran both hands through his messy hair and sighed. "What choice do we have?"

"Maybe Harry's right," she admitted. "Maybe we'll freeze to death out there as soon as we step through the door. I just don't like feeling trapped, you know?"

Jerry nodded.

"So what do we do?" Jess asked.

"Arnie-up, I guess. Get some weapons and take it to the first thing that comes through the door."

"Whatever happens, I don't think they'll be using the door." Jess looked down at Peter who was still sleeping on the sofa. He seemed more peaceful now and she wasn't sure if that was a good or bad thing. "I think windows are more their style."

Jerry chuckled humourlessly. "No shit."

Jess placed her hands on her hips. "Should we get started?"

"I think before we do anything we need to stoke the fire. I'm freezing my nuts off, and I think Peter's turning blue."

Jess looked down at Peter and saw the azure tint at the edge of his lips, like a thin line of biro. "I'll go and check with Harry," she said. "They're building a fire downstairs. Maybe we can get some stuff to burn."

Harry was stood with Lucas. The two of them were examining Damien in the chair and muttering. Jess couldn't believe what Damien had tried to do. She had known he was a jerk, but...

Something felt off about the situation. Damien Banks was a lot of things, but Jess never pegged him as a rapist. Still, how much could you know about a guy, really?

"Harry," Jess said, approaching him and Lucas. "The fire is struggling and we need something to burn."

Harry nodded and rubbed at his chin. The stubble there made his face seem dirty. "Yeah, I know," he said. "We'll get it going again soon with some of the chairs Nigel broke up. I forgot to say earlier that I think I'll have to leave Damien up here with you and Jerry. The only other option is to put him in the cellar, but with Steph..."

Jess waved a hand. "That's fine, I understand. We'll keep an eye on him."

Harry stared into her eyes. "If he so much as twitches you need to shout down and get me."

"Yeah, course. If he tries anything I'll ring the bell or whack him with the fire poker. You tied him pretty tight by the looks of things, anyway."

Harry looked down at Damien's swollen wrists

and seemed proud of himself. "I knew Boy Scouts would come in handy one day."

Jess laughed. "I knew there was something out-doorsy about you."

"No," said Harry. "That's just how I smell."

Jess laughed again, this time louder. "You're suddenly in a cheery mood."

Harry stared into space for a moment before making eye contact with her again. "Guess I decided it was time to start taking part."

Jess didn't know what he meant. There were a lot of things she didn't understand tonight. "Taking part in what?"

Harry smiled. "Life, I guess. Now, let's go find you something for that fire."

"Sounds like a plan." She took Harry's free arm as he grabbed a candle from the bar. Lucas nodded to them both as they passed, letting them know he was happy to stay behind and supervise Damien. As the two of them sauntered towards the bar, Jess felt a surreal feeling of safety that made her wonder if she was in some sort of denial about the fear she'd felt only minutes before. Strangely, Harry's light-ened mood made her feel that things might just work out okay.

Jess blinked twice and refocused her mind. Her skin felt tight under the prolonged attack of the cold. The chill felt like razor wire pulled tight around her flesh. She couldn't wait to get in front of a renewed fire. Maybe she could even grab a short nap. She was exhausted. According to her watch it was almost 3am.

Jess descended the stairs while Harry lit the way with a candle. At the bottom they entered the cellar and were immediately met by Steph, who seemed to be recovering well from her ordeal. Old Graham lay on the floor beyond, snug beneath a blanket and seemingly quite drunk if the sound of his slurred singing was anything to go by. At the edge of the room, in shadow, sat Nigel, Kath was also in the room, but Jess didn't care to pay attention to that old cow.

Steph took a step towards Jess and Harry and it became obvious that she was still a little shaky. "We have a problem," she said only to Harry, as if Jess were not even there.

Harry's happy demeanour soured slightly. "Steph, you should be resting. What's so important that it can't wait?"

Steph raised an arm behind her and pointed to a makeshift fire in the centre of the room. The steel dustbin was half-stuffed with wood and cardboard. Several chair legs pointed upwards like giant fingers.

Jess knew straight away what Steph was going to tell them and she didn't want to hear it. She shook her head in despair. "That's all we could find to burn, isn't it?"

Steph changed her focus to Jess and nodded solemnly. "The cardboard recycling was done yesterday morning and we're all out of coal. I was going to buy some from the supermarket to stock up. If we burn all the tables we still might not have enough."

"We just need to last till morning," said Harry. "We have plenty of wood until then."

"I'm not so sure. Two separate fires is going to take a lot of fuel, but even if we can last till morning, what then? I don't think this is just a bit of bad weather. Something's happened. I'm sure some group of scientists someplace know exactly what is happening, but I think it's starting to become pretty obvious that things are bad. We can rely on this all being okay come morning. Nobody is coming to help us and it's only getting colder."

"We're going to freeze to death," said Jess coolly, as if stating a fact.

Steph nodded. "Unless we do something about it."

"Then let's do something about it," said Harry.

25

"What the Hell do we do?" asked Nigel, still shrouded in shadow.

Harry thought for a moment. "Steph, you're absolutely sure that there's nothing else we can burn? What about in Graham's place upstairs?"

Steph shook her head. "Nigel already checked. It's like a closing-down-sale up there. Barely enough furniture to fill one room. We'll burn what's there, but it's not much."

"Hey," said Old Graham from the floor. "That's all my worldly possessions you're talking about... actually on second thoughts, you may as well burn it."

Harry thought again, shivering as he did so. He

wondered whether he was as cold as he felt or if it was just his mind exaggerating. Before he had time to decide which, his musings were interrupted by Jess.

The girl asked a question. "What about the supermarket?"

Harry looked at her. "What do you mean?"

"Yes," Kath chimed in from the other side of the room. "What do you mean?"

"I mean," Jess said, impatiently, "that the place is full of, like, a thousand cardboard boxes, plus all the bags of coal in the warehouse. If we grab one of the trolleys we can cart it all over here. There're painkillers and other stuff, too, that we could give to Peter."

Old Graham piped up from his resting place in the middle of the room. "Don't bloody forget about me!" he slurred. "I could use some pain relief too."

"Then we have a plan," said Steph.

"Not yet we don't," Kath objected. "That is supermarket property you're talking about. I can't just let you in to ransack the place. It's theft."

Jess cursed out loud. "God sake, Kath, you still don't get what's going on, do you? Screw the supermarket! Our lives are more important."

Kath snickered. "That's debatable."

Harry was starting to see why Jess hated the

woman so much – she was wretched indeed – but before things got out of hand again, he decided to butt in. "Come on, the both of you. Fighting isn't helping. Enough people have already gotten hurt tonight."

"Yeah," said Kath, rubbing the swollen cut on her forehead. "I'm well aware of that, thank you very much."

"Look," said Harry in his calmest tone. "We're lost without you here, Kath, and if you were kind enough to let us into the supermarket then we'd all be in debt to you. Our survival would most likely be down to you and we won't forget that."

Kath seemed smug, as if her previously sour expression was just painted on and was now melting in the heat of the candle she held in front of her. "Well," she said. "I guess I can't just let you all freeze, but I hope you realise the sacrifice I'm making. I have responsibilities that can't be taken lightly."

"Thank you," said Harry. Resisting the urge to slap the woman. "So, you'll give us the keys?"

Kath laughed, as if someone had tried to convince her that the world was made of mashed potato. "Don't be ridiculous," she said. "The store keys are to remain with an authorised key holder at all times."

"What are you suggesting?" asked Steph.

"That should be obvious. I'm going to have to be present at all times. I'm coming along."

Harry bit his lip, seeing no other way to proceed. If the woman wouldn't hand over the keys, he would have to take her along. The alternative was to man-handle her, and he wasn't sure he could do that.

"I also must insist," Kath continued, "that Jess is to remain here. Her employment was terminated earlier tonight and ex-employees are prohibited from entering the premises. Petty vindictiveness is all too common these days, I'm afraid."

Harry caught the sight of Jess about to explode and quickly moved the conversation on. "Okay, that's fine. It's too important that Jess stays here, anyway, to keep watch over Peter and Damien. We can't risk her going outside." Jess seemed to settle down, but Harry couldn't help but wonder how long he could keep the two women from each oth-er's throats. "Okay. Let's just get to work. Sooner we do this the better. I'll go ask Lucas if he's up for the trip. Nigel, would you be okay to watch over things here?"

Steph grunted. "What would we ladies do without a man to protect us, eh?"

Harry leaned in close to her and spoke so that only she could hear. "After what you've been through tonight, there's no way I'm going to leave you on your own. Nigel's a big guy and I'd feel safer with him around. It's more for *my* peace of mind than it is yours." Steph seemed affected by Harry's words but he didn't have time to wonder about how she felt about it.

"I'll keep em safe," said Nigel. "You can count on me."

Harry reached forward and shook Nigel firmly by the hand. "I know I can. Thank you. And if that piece of shit upstairs tries to get free, you have my permissions to throw him on the fire."

Nigel nodded and Harry made towards the stairs, starting to climb them one by one. As he ascended, he thought about whether or not this really was a good idea, to leave the modest safety of the pub and venture out into the snow. After what Jess and Jerry had said about their friend, Ben, and with Peter being thrown through the window, Harry half-expected to meet a fire breathing dragon outside. *Not to mention giant plumes of impossible fire climbing into the sky while people burn to death on crosses.* But without a well-fuelled fire, they were all doomed. There was no choice involved in what he had to do. The risk of death was better than the certainty of it. Whatever was outside, he would just have to face it.

It was time to start facing problems and doing something about them.

"Harry Boy, I take it you've been informed of our grave situation?"

Harry entered the bar area to find Lucas. The man was watching over Damien. "Yeah, they told me," Harry said. "Nothing's going right tonight, is it?"

"You can say that again. Still, I'm guessing you're a fella with a plan."

Harry nodded. "And you'd be right. Kath and I are going to go raid the supermarket for supplies. I wanted to ask you to come along."

Lucas' reaction was unexpected. The man seemed suddenly afraid. "Well, are you sure that's the best course of action, Harry Boy? Should I not stay here and keep an eye on the womenfolk?"

"Nigel will do that. Plus, Jerry is by the fire with Peter." Harry moved forward and placed a hand on Lucas' shoulder. "I really need your help. We need the bags of coal they sell at the supermarket and I won't be able to carry them all on my own. We're going to use a trolley, but we will still have to lift it over the snow."

Lucas shuffled uncomfortably, but seemed to come round to the idea. "Well, okay, I guess. I have little choice in the matter, do I? Can't let an honest fella like yourself down. Bring on the snow, I say."

Harry patted Lucas on the shoulder again. "I really appreciate it. We'll be fine. Quick in and out, military style. Like you said earlier, I'm Major Jobson and you can be Captain Fergus." Harry snapped off a mock salute and stood straight.

Lucas chuckled and returned the salute. "Sounds like a plan. I just can't help but worry about bumping into something unpleasant out there. I'm not the bravest of men, you know?"

Harry understood the man's fear; in fact he felt it himself. "I've been trying not to think about it too much," he admitted, "but it's either a quick trip to the supermarket or a slow wait until we freeze to death. I'd rather die trying than trying to die."

Lucas clicked his fingers and did a little jig. "I like your spirit, Harry Boy. When do we depart?"

"No time like the present."

26

A baseball bat and a handful of kitchen knives was the best they could do. Harry hadn't expected guns or a flamethrower, but he'd hoped for something a little more intimidating than kid's toys and cutlery. Still, what they had was better than nothing.

"Right," he said, handing the baseball bat to Kath and arming himself and Lucas with a chef's knife each. "The plan is to get across to the supermarket quickly and quietly, sticking together at all times. Once we get there it's over to you, Kath, because you know where everything is."

Kath nodded and took over. "Our main priority is, of course, the coal, so we will gather that first.

However, nobody touches anything else without my say so."

"Would you mind if we breathe the air?" asked Lucas.

Kath planted her hands on her hips. "If you're not going to obey my rules then we can forget this whole thing, right now."

"Fine," said Lucas. "Although, we could just tie you up like our young friend, Damien, then take the keys for ourselves."

Kath's face dropped in horror.

Lucas chuckled. "Just pulling your leg, lass."

Harry slid off his stool and straightened himself up. "Okay, Nigel, you keep an eye on everything here and we'll be back as soon as we can. Jerry, you make sure that Damien stays tied up nice and tight."

"No," said Jerry. He was holding the fire poker down by his thigh and shaking his head. "I'm coming with you."

Before Harry had time to object, he found that Jess had beaten him to it. "Are you insane?" she said.

"No, I'm not," Jerry replied. "Just tired of being useless. That's all I ever was when Ben was around and I'll be damned if I'm going to carry on being like that now he's gone."

"That's very...noble," said Harry, "and we all un-derstand you wanting to honour your friend, Jerry, but there's no need to take the risk. We've got it covered."

"Dude, I don't know you and you sure as hell don't know me, but one thing you'll learn real soon is that all of the shit me and Jess told you about is real. None of you have seen what's out there. But I have."

"What's your point?" said Harry.

"My *point* is that I'm more qualified than you to go out there and face down the crazy, so what right do you have to tell me anything?"

Harry shrugged. He didn't have the energy for this. "We don't have time to argue, so I guess you'll be coming along, too, then."

Jess placed a hand on Jerry's shoulder and nudged him to face her. Harry couldn't hear their conversation, so he decided to take the remaining time to check up on Steph. She was standing behind the bar, relighting candles that had gone out.

"You okay?" Harry asked her. "You've been through a lot tonight."

She smiled at him, her features so tired and faded that she looked like a shivering ghost in the candlelight. "N-no more than normal," she said, chattering. "This place was never exactly The Ritz to start with. I'm used to trouble."

Harry took her hand and felt a jolt run through

his skin when he felt her squeeze back. The room was freezing, but her palm throbbed out heat. He smiled at her. "You don't have to pretend, you know?"

Steph's eyes welled up as though a tap had been turned loose somewhere inside of her. "You mean I should just be honest and say that I think we're all going to die tonight?"

Her words hit Harry like a punch to the kidneys. Just when he'd started to find some strength and positivity inside of himself, Steph had lost hers. It was tragic because he knew that his strength had, in part, come from being around her. He'd taken advantage of Steph's emotional strength and now the poor girl was drained. He squeezed her hand tightly. "No one is going to hurt you, Steph. I promise. I agree, some weird business has been going down tonight, but things will work out. Don't be scared."

Steph laughed and wiped at her nose and face. The skin of her wrist glistened as she pulled it away. "There's nothing to fear but fear itself, huh?"

Harry smiled. "Something like that."

"You just get back here in one piece, okay! Then I'll stop crying."

"Okay, deal."

Steph let go of Harry's hand and pushed him away. "Well, get going then."

Harry turned around and saw that Jerry, Kath, and Lucas were all waiting for him. They formed an orderly queue by the door. Lucas still seemed reluctant to go outside and Harry couldn't say he blamed the guy.

It was time to get going. A sheen of ice had started to form on the wooden surfaces of the tables and snow drift was gathering around the front door wherever it could find the thinnest of cracks. Whether or not they went outside, the weather was coming in to get them sooner than later.

Harry marched to the front door and placed a hand against the bolt, ready to slide it across and yank open the door. For one quick moment, he lost the nerve he needed to continue, but he took a breath and forced the fear deep down into his gut. "Let's go," he said finally, pulling open the door and stepping out into the snow.

～

OUTSIDE, the landscape was blank as an unused canvas. Harry could see nothing but white. A white so pure that its gleaming intensity made his eyes ache. But, despite the blankness, there was movement everywhere. Shifting, dancing specks of snow swirled in the air, each individual flake part of a greater never-ending whole. A blizzard. Harry thought about rushing back inside, regretting the plan already, but when he looked over his shoulder he could no longer see the pub.

Lucas, Jerry, and Kath were following closely behind, linking arms to form a human chain. Each of them seemed worried. They were looking for Harry to lead them.

But lead them where exactly? These people's safety is in my hands and I don't even know what to expect.

"You alright there, Harry Boy?"

Harry turned to Lucas. "I'm just...thinking."

"Well, perhaps you'd like to do your wonderings some place a bit warmer. I don't know if you've noticed, but it's a tad cold out here this evening."

Harry nodded and started moving. The snow enveloped them past their knees. They had to swim through it more than they did walk. It wouldn't be long before the snow was deep enough to swallow a man whole. The effort of each step left them panting.

Several minutes passed.

The snow went on forever.

"Do you have any idea of where we're going?" Kath shouted from the back of their human chain, struggling to be heard over the howling wind. "We should have been there by now."

Harry had been thinking the same thing.

"We're lost, aren't we?" said Kath, accurately reading in on the meaning of Harry's silence. It had been more an accusation than a question.

Instead of Harry answering, Jerry did. "Yeah, we're lost," he said, "but Harry's not to blame."

Harry raised an eyebrow. "What do you mean, I'm not to blame?"

"I mean that the snow *made* us lost."

"Don't be ridiculous," said Kath.

"Come now," said Lucas, stopping and halting everybody in the line. "Let's hear the boy out."

Jerry prepared to give his explanation. The others gathered around close, each of them shivering, except for Lucas who seemed to be coping slightly better. "It's not normal snow," Jerry explained to them. "It's magic snow."

Nobody spoke, although the incredulity was clear on their faces.

"Yeah, yeah," said Jerry, deadly serious. "You don't believe me, I know, but I'm telling you that this snow is unnatural. It's a force being wielded by something evil."

Harry decided to humour the boy. "Wielded by who?"

"Who you think? The guy in the robes and hood. The guy with the flaming sword. The snow is just his tool to trap us or get us lost and confused. Then he comes to kill us, just like he did Ben. I know you think I'm full of shit, but something killed my friend."

"Okay," said Harry, trying his best to remain open-minded. "But, if you believe that, what the hell are you doing out here?"

Jerry smashed a fist against his open palm. "Because me and the monster out here have unfinished business. If he turns up, I'll be the one to face him while the rest of you make a run for it."

"Why would you want to do that?" asked Harry asked. "You're just a kid, not Rambo."

But Jerry seemed perfectly sane as he spoke. "I need to take responsibility instead of letting other people do things for me. If this is the end of the world then the least I can do is make it hard for the bastard who started it. I'm going to give him the arse-kicking of his life."

"Erm....fellas?" The group turned to face Lucas, who was looking at them queerly. "That *bastard* in question," he pointed over Harry's left shoulder, "is right over there."

Harry spun around to see a shape in the distance. The dark silhouette of a man, taller than a man should be, was gliding towards them, slowly and methodically, as if it had all of eternity to reach them. In the last year there had been many nights that he had jerked from a nightmare, but this was the first time he'd ever felt like he was drifting *into* a nightmare.

And that nightmare was coming right at them.

27

"I'd better go check on Old Graham," said Steph, leaving Jess and Nigel to look after Damien and Peter. Harry and the others had been gone for almost half an hour. With the exception of Kath, Jess missed having their numbers around.

She turned to Nigel. "Best settle in. It's already been a long night."

"Yeah, I guess so," Nigel replied.

The two of them slid down on either side of the fire, leaving the middle clear so that its warmth could reach Peter on the sofa. Damien was still tied to a chair, though not as close to the fire as the rest of them. They'd dumped an assortment of blankets on him to keep him. Jess pulled a duvet over herself and let out a shiver.

"Not getting any warmer is it?" Nigel commented. "Don't they say you should all huddle together to share warmth?"

"Yeah," Jess agreed. "They do say that."

Nigel patted the floor beside him. "Well? You want to come over?"

"No...it's okay," she said. "I'm warm enough for now, but thanks for offering."

For a half-second, Jess thought she saw anger flush through Nigel's face, but when he spoke he sounded harmless.

"Don't mention it," he told her. "I just don't like to see a young girl suffer."

Jess giggled. "What a gentleman."

"Unlike some." Nigel nodded towards Damien.

"I still can't believe Damien tried to hurt Steph."

"Well, believe it! The lad's an animal. He's lucky I didn't fucking kill him."

Jess was taken aback by the sudden outburst of anger. "Wow! Calm down. I was just saying it was a shock, that's all."

Nigel rubbed at his eyes and shook his head. His gold pinkie ring glinted in the fire light, the image of a dolphin flashing into her vision for a split-second. "I'm sorry. I just wish I was there to stop him sooner."

"You stopped him soon enough," Jess said. "He

never got to hurt Steph. Well, not in *that* way, you know?"

Nigel nodded and smiled, but something about his expression made Jess feel uncomfortable. It felt like she was being looked at through a mask and that Nigel's smile was hiding something.

But what?

"Do you mind holding the fort for a couple minutes?" Jess said. "I want to check if Steph needs anything."

"No problem," Nigel said, looking her hard in the eyes.

Jess shivered again, and she was certain it wasn't because of the cold. She stood up and hurried away. She didn't know why, but she suddenly didn't want to be near Nigel. It was as if a veil had lifted, revealing him to be someone else. It was spooky.

Nigel remained by the fire. Jess suddenly felt stupid and paranoid. Nigel didn't look like he would hurt a fly. But neither did frogs, until they shot out their slimy tongues and pulled you in to swallow you whole.

Jess stepped behind the bar and immediately felt the warmth coming up from the fire in the cellar. She shuddered at the pleasant feeling and started to take the steps downwards.

At the bottom, she found Steph sitting near the

makeshift brazier with Old Graham. The two of them were chatting away as if they didn't have a care in the world. Steph looked up at Jess as she approached. "Everything good up there?"

Jess shrugged. "I wouldn't describe anything as good at the moment, but things are...stable."

"How's Peter?"

"Bad. I don't know what to do for him. I'm hoping that the others come back soon. They've been gone a while now."

Steph bit her lip. Her face was swollen on one side where she'd been struck and her right eye was half-closed. Jess wondered quite how much Steph had been affected by what happened to her. It was obvious she was trying not to show any emotion, but the feisty barmaid didn't seem quite as tough as usual. "Are you okay?" Jess asked her.

Steph seemed to snap out of a trance. "I'm fine. Just a bit worried, I guess, but that's to be expected, right?"

"Hell yeah. You'd have to be made of stone not to be worried tonight. Speaking of which, how well do you know Nigel?"

Steph looked confused. "Nigel? Pretty well, I guess. Why?"

"He just makes me feel a bit...uncomfortable."

Steph shook her head. "He's never caused any

problems in the eight or nine months I've known him. Keeps to himself, more or less."

"A nice guy...f-from...what I seen...tonight." Old Graham had fallen into a drunken haze, but still managed to fade in and out of the conversation. "A nice...guy. Can I have another drink?"

"No," said Steph. "We need to lay off the beers. We're all getting a bit too heavy headed."

"Maybe, I'm just being silly," said Jess.

Steph smiled. "I'd say so. Nigel saved me from being raped tonight! He's a good guy."

Jess nodded. Maybe she really was paranoid, just as she'd suspected earlier. Having Steph confirm it made her feel much better. She would go back upstairs and look after Peter, thinking no more about it. But first she wanted to check on Steph's injuries. They looked pretty bad and Jess felt bad that Steph always seemed to be the one looking after everyone else. Jess wanted to try and look after her for a change. "Let me have a quick look at your face, before I go back upstairs," she said. "You look pretty beat up."

Steph waved a hand. "Don't worry about it. Just a bruise."

"I'd feel better all the same. I did first aid a couple months ago." Jess slid down onto the floor besides Steph.

Half-asleep, Old Graham murmured something from the floor. "Let the girl...take a quick...gander."

Steph sighed and leaned forward. "Okay, then, but keep your hands away. It hurts bad enough as it is, without being prodded."

Jess leaned forward slowly and cringed at the sight of Steph's bulging cheek. Her misty blue eye was bloodshot and teary. A second injury on her forehead seemed just as painful. The throbbing bump that was already turning purple around the split in its centre. "Jesus, you really took a whacking, didn't you?"

Steph sighed. "Think I fell against the toilet bowl. Don't really remember much more than that. Someone came out of the dark and hit me."

"Someone? You don't remember anything at all?"

"No. I just remember being hit."

Steph went to pull her head away, but Jess stopped her. "Hold on a sec. Let me look." Jess examined the swollen gash on Steph's cheek, and noticed something. Something at the centre of the bruising, a patch of skin lighter in colour than the surrounding tissue. It formed a shape, perhaps matching the surface of whatever had struck her. The outline seemed to resemble a...

Jess' eyes went wide.

Her mouth gaped open.

The mark resembled a dolphin.

Jess scratched at her head while she tried to understand why she recognised the shape. It didn't take her long. "Holy shit! Nigel!"

"Did I hear someone say my name?" Nigel had reached the bottom of the stairs and was heading into the cellar.

Jess's stomach cramped up as she tried to think of something to say. "Oh...hi, Nigel. Yeah, we were just talking about you. Steph just told me what a nice guy you are."

Nigel grinned like a hungry fox. Jess finally saw through the man's disguise. His mask had slipped.

And beneath lay a monster.

～

WHEN JESS HAD SUDDENLY EXCUSED herself, Nigel had been concerned. Maybe his fumbled attempt at getting the girl to sit beside him had eroded the harmless veneer he worked so hard to maintain. It was possible that Jess had seen his true intentions.

Now, as Nigel walked down into the cellar, he wasn't entirely sure. Jess certainly seemed jumpy at his presence but, considering the events of the last few hours, that was perhaps understandable. Steph seemed glad to see him, though. She smiled and waved a hand at him when he'd entered the cellar. It wasn't surprising she trusted him. After all, he'd been working on gaining her confidence for the last eight months. As far as Steph was concerned, he was as harmless as a three-legged kitten with pneumonia.

Dumb fucking whore.

It didn't matter if Jess suspected anything. They were both just his prey now; new victims to add to his mental highlight-reel of rape and torture. He figured he had at least an hour to have fun with them before he'd have to slit their throats, stash the bodies, and take a finger for his collection – and that was only if Harry and the others managed to make it back from the supermarket without freezing to death first. If they did make it back, Nigel would have a story all ready for them, and his trusty flick knife ready in his pocket just in case they didn't believe it.

"Everything okay?" Jess asked him, still not giving away whether or not she suspected anything. "Shouldn't someone be watching Damien and Peter?"

Nigel nodded, trying his best to look solemn. An emotion he couldn't actually *feel* at all, but one he felt he was adept at emulating. "That's what I wanted to talk to you about, sweetheart. I think Peter's waking up. I heard him say your name."

Jess didn't react for a moment and Nigel wondered how well his lie had gone down. Finally, she said, "That's wonderful. G-great news."

"Well," said Nigel, offering out his hand, "you going to come see the poor lad or not? I'm sure you're the thing he'd like to wake up to."

Jess shifted uncomfortably, as if determined not to get up, but eventually she had no choice but to concede.

"Be right there," she said. "I just need to talk to Steph about something first. Girl problems, you know? Shall I see you up there in five minutes?"

The girl knew.

And she's trying to warn Steph, the little bitch!

Nigel closed his eyes and fought the urge to rip the girl apart right there and then, tasting her wet insides as she gulped her dying breaths. He had to work *real* hard to control himself and keep his cool. He would be nowhere without his *control.* Far better to have fun once everyone was tied up and under his power. That way there could be no surprises and the party could really get started. Killing Jess now would just cause chaos.

"I think you should probably come right now," Nigel suggested, keeping his voice soft so as not to alarm an unsuspecting Steph. "What if he doesn't make it and this was his last chance to speak to you, Jess?"

Steph placed an arm around Jess and gave Nigel a scolding look. She'd pay for it later. "That's a little bit harsh, Nigel," she said. "Let's not condemn the poor boy just yet."

"Thanks," Jess replied.

"I do agree with him though, honey," Steph added. "You should go right away. Peter hasn't been conscious much at all tonight and you wouldn't want to miss out on anything he could tell us about what's happening outside."

Nigel grinned. *That's a good girl. Always so eager to help daddy, aren't you? Just like when you knocked yourself out for me in the toilets.*

Nigel reached his hand out towards Jess again. "That's what I was trying to say. I didn't mean to upset you. I'm sure Peter's going to be just fine, but right now he needs you."

Jess looked like one of the cats Nigel used to strangle as a child, before he moved onto women and children. Trapped and terrifyingly aware that death was rapidly approaching, yet powerless to do anything about it. The girl was afraid, and the sight of it made Nigel's cock hard. He liked it so much better when they knew it was coming. Loved the look in their eyes.

Jess started to get up, ignoring Nigel's outstretched hand and rising tentatively on her own. Nigel moved away to give her space, waiting patiently at the bottom of the stairs. To his irritation, Jess instead turned to Steph and held out a hand. "Will you come with me? I'm not sure I'll cope if Peter takes a turn for the worse."

Nigel clenched his jaw. *Don't even try it! Just take what's coming to you and stop making things hard.*

Steph shook her head and Jess seemed to deflate like a leaking balloon. "I can't. I need to stay here and look after Old Graham. You'll be fine, don't worry. I'm sure Peter will be fine."

"But Old Graham's asleep," said Jess, sounding desperate.

To Nigel's dismay, Steph seemed to pick up on the girl's subtle pleas. She stared at Jess, as if trying to work her out. Nigel held his breath, waiting for the outcome.

"Okay," said Steph. "I'll come with you, but we'll have to be quick."

Nigel tapped his foot irritably as the two women huddled together and headed for the stairs. It was clear now that Steph had picked up on something in Jess's tone, but Nigel doubted she had any idea of what was really going on. She wouldn't figure out the truth until it was far, far too late.

Nigel crept up the stairs, making sure the women were following close behind. He kept his steps slow, so that Jess couldn't fall behind and whisper something to Steph without him hearing.

When they reached the top, Nigel stepped aside and ushered the two women in front of him. He manoeuvred them into the candlelight of the bar and they re-entered the freezing lounge. It wasn't even biting cold any longer, but a far deeper sensation, like his very blood was turning to ice in his veins. Ice seemed to cling to everything, and breathing felt like sucking in cold steel. "Come on," he said to them, "let's get over by that fire."

The women walked ahead and Nigel kept close behind, rubbing his palms against his arms to try to generate some friction and heat – but the only thing getting him *hot* right now was watching Steph move. He thought about all the things that he could do to that sexy, slender body that would warm him up for the rest of the night. The only thing left to figure out was the best way to take Jess out of the picture. For now, he'd let things play out and wait for an opportunity to present itself. The flick knife in his pocket made Nigel consider just stabbing the girl in the eye and being done with it, but that would be a waste.

He had to have his fun with her first. If Steph was going to be the main course, then Jess would be dessert. *I'll eat her nipples as cherries,* Nigel thought as he let slip an excited laugh. He quickly stifled it when the women looked at him.

"Something funny, Nigel?" Steph asked.

He quickly shook his head. "Just the craziness of tonight making me a little loopy. I get the giggles when I'm nervous."

"And why would you be nervous?" Jess asked in a tone that he didn't like at all. It was almost goading.

"Well," he said, "there's a lot to worry about tonight, isn't there, sweetheart?"

Jess took a step backwards and was nodding as though she knew a punch-line to a joke that no one had told yet. Nigel felt his blood pressure rising as he fought the urge to rip into the girl and punish her insolence. She kept her eyes fixed on him as she continued stepping backwards. Steph was watching from a few feet away, visibly unsure of what was about to unfold. Nigel took steps of his own, keeping pace with Jess.

"Or are you nervous," Jess said, "because you lied about Peter being awake? Look at him, he's still unconscious."

Nigel grinned. *Of course* Peter was still unconscious. The kid was as good as dead. *Pity he isn't awake. He could have watched while I fuck his girlfriend.*

Jess took another step backwards, placing herself up against the wall beside the fire. No more space to retreat. Nigel continued approaching.

You're trapped now, bitch.

"Or," Jess continued, "are you nervous because I know that you're the one who tried to rape Steph?"

Nigel looked at Steph and watched the sudden shock wash over her. She took a sharp intake of breath. Jess's revelation had sucked the wind out of him as well. He'd expected her to try and blow his cover, but the fact that she'd done it right in front of Steph hurt him. Nigel hadn't wanted Steph to know the truth about him until the very last moment.

Nothing to be done now, though. Time to start ripping flesh.

Nigel lunged at Jess like a cobra striking. Overcommitted to attacking, he was powerless to change direction as the teenager swung at him with the fire poker she'd somehow managed to grab without him seeing.

The last thing Nigel thought as the steel rod arced towards his skull was...

28

"You want another piece of me, huh? Well, if it's Mortal Kombat you want then that's exactly what you're going to get, you cross-dressing freak."

Harry managed to reach out and grab Jerry before the lad ran off to his peril. "Hold it," he said, clutching the boy by the collar.

Jerry struggled to get free. "Dude, not cool. Let go of me. Him and me have got unfinished biz'ness."

Harry shook the lad. "This isn't Star Wars and that's not Obi Wan Kenobi."

Jerry looked outraged. "Obi Wan is one of the good guys, you dork!"

"Yeah," said Harry. "*I'm* the dork."

"Fellas, while I'd love to have a discussion on the

many wee sides of the force, I think we should get going, pronto."

Harry nodded to Lucas and then looked into the distance at the approaching figure. "Okay, let's get back to the pub."

Everyone agreed. They turned, ran...

...and stopped in their tracks.

"Holy shit!" Jerry cried out as ten foot flames exploded from the snow before them, cutting off any chance of escape. Harry felt the heat spread in a wide semi-circle around them, leaving no place to go but directly towards the robed figure.

"Time to enter the Thunderdome, bitch," Jerry snarled.

"You reckon we should fight?" Harry asked everyone.

"You got a better idea?" Jerry said, limbering up.

"This is insane," said Kath. "We need to run."

"Where?" asked Harry.

"Don't suppose anybody has a fire extinguisher?" Lucas asked, fanning his hands against the rising flames behind them.

Harry took several steps forwards. It was probably a stupid idea. "What do you want from us?" he demanded of the stranger in the snow. The robed figure stopped moving, still buried too far inside the blizzard for Harry to make him out clearly. Despite that, he could feel the stranger's stare boring into him, digging at the corners of his soul. "I said, what do you want?"

Silence.

Then: "WE HAVE COME FOR...THE SINNER."

Harry shook his head. *What the fuck is with this guy? Did he overdose on bible studies as a kid?*

"Who exactly is the sinner?" he asked.

More silence.

Then: "YOU ARE, HARRY JOBSON."

Harry stumbled as his knees ceased functioning for a moment. Was he really the sinner? The cause of all of the havoc tonight? It seemed insane, but...

He's right...I am a sinner. But how did anybody ever find out?

"Come on, Harry Boy, time to go." Lucas grabbed him from behind. At first Harry thought it was to turn him over to the hooded stranger, but it wasn't. Lucas and Jerry both dragged Harry backwards through the snow, heading through a small gap in the wall of fire.

"What are we doing?" Harry asked wearily as they dragged him along by the armpits. His legs trailed in front of him uselessly.

"Running for our lives," said Lucas. "What the blazes do you think?"

"The supermarket must be nearby," said Jerry, struggling with Harry's weight. "At least I hope so."

"It is," said Kath. "We're here."

Harry looked up to see the dim shape of a building present itself through the blizzard, only twenty yards ahead.

They were going to make it.

Lucas and Jerry continued to drag and pull him across the snow. Kath overtook them, searching her pockets frantically, no doubt for the building's keys.

Harry had a question, and he shouted it out. "Where's the stranger? Where did he go?"

They reached the supermarket's locked fire door and dumped Harry down. Lucas stared down at him and offered his hand. "I don't bloody know where it is, but get up and be ready in case it comes back."

Kath pulled her keys from her pocket and started sifting through them. "I can't see a thing out here."

Harry managed to stand, his legs turning from jelly to gradually-setting cement, not yet firm, but getting there. He looked back in the direction they'd come from and found his heart stopping in his chest. "You'd best hurry up and get us inside, Kath. I mean right NOW!"

Coming through the snow, with a steady and

methodical purpose, was the hooded figure; but this time he was not alone. There were other robed strangers getting nearer. Dozens of them. Their ghostly visages melted into the background of the whirling blizzard and there could have been an endless legion of them out there for all Harry knew.

Kath frantically tried her keys on the lock. Lucas fell to his knees, muttering. Harry thought he heard the Irishman say something about 'an army of Christ', but there was no time to ask about it. The robed strangers were approaching quickly, almost seeming to glide across the deep deep snow.

"How's it going?" Harry urgently asked Kath.

"I'm trying," she said, sounding close to tears. "I'm sodding trying."

As if things could get any worse, Harry heard something awful.

Growling.

The sound was so guttural that it might have emanated from a pack of rabid wolves. Alongside the army of strangers were a dozen beasts. They fit Jerry's description of the creature that had attacked them. Giant dogs with innumerable teeth in their salivating jaws

"Hell hounds," said Jerry. "Just like the one that attacked me and Jess. Believe me now?"

Harry clutched the chef's knife tightly in his

hand, but had a feeling it would prove useless. "Jerry," he shouted. "If we live through this, I will be the first in line to apologise for not believing you, but now's not the time for humble pie."

Jerry seemed buoyed by the vindication and actually began to smile. He moved to Kath and picked up the baseball bat she had propped against the supermarket's door and hefted it over his shoulder.

Lucas was still on his knees, but had stopped his incoherent rambling. He fixed his gaze on Jerry. "What the b'jaysus are you doing, lad?"

Jerry narrowed his eyes. "I'm getting even."

With that, Jerry trudged through the snow at a speed as close to running as possible in the thick snow. He held the baseball bat high above his head as if it were a holy sword of Justice. The strange army of unearthly figures continued approaching with their hell hounds. Jerry didn't seem concerned by any of it as he picked up speed.

"Jerry, get back here!" Harry shouted, but his words faded into the blizzard.

What is that boy doing?

Harry watched as Jerry came to a halt six feet in front of one of the giant dog-like beasts. He stuck out an arm and made a 'bring it' motion. "Let's go, Cujo!"

Jerry swung the baseball bat down over his head

in a downwards arc. It connected with the bulbous skull of the hell hound. With a snarling whine, the beast collapsed sideways into the snow, which immediately begun to melt around it. Jerry swung the bat again, connecting a blow with the beast's hindquarters, causing it to yowl in agony. Before he had chance to swing it again, the beast rose to its feet and fled.

Jerry held the bat above his head and shouted triumphantly. "Flawless victory, motherfucker. Yeah, that's what you get when you mess with the J-Meister."

Harry watched the surreal image of the spotty, teenage boy taking on a pack of hell beasts with a decrepit baseball bat and wondered whether he was stoned. Had his drinking progressed to drug-abuse and he was now lying somewhere, hallucinating the whole thing? It was a thought he would've liked to have held on to very much, but he knew it wasn't true. They were all in great danger and none of this was imaginary. It wasn't a movie.

"Jerry! Get your arse back here, now!"

Harry's warning came too late. The rest of the hell hounds swarmed over Jerry in a never ending wave. Harry was unable to take his eyes away as flesh and fat were shorn from the teenager's bones like meat from a turkey. Razor sharp fangs pierced every inch of Jerry's skin and turned him into a bloody skeleton. Harry thought his ears would explode at the sound of the boy's agonised screams and was grateful that they only lasted a few seconds as the beasts tore out his throat.

Harry sobbed.

"Thank God!" Kath said finally, unlocking the door and pushing it open so hard that she fell to her knees inside. Harry couldn't move, eyes transfixed on the beasts feeding on Jerry's twitching body.

Harry tried to blink, but couldn't. "They're going to kill us all."

"Maybe," said Lucas, yanking him backwards through the open door. "But there's no reason for us to make it easy for them."

Harry took a long hard swallow. Lucas was right. After all the hits life had thrown at him, there was no way he was going to take a beating lying down. "No," he said. "The last thing we're going to do is make it easy for them."

Kath locked the supermarket's door behind them, whilst outside an army of robed demons surrounded them.

29

"Damien...

"Damien, wake up."

Damien opened his eyes, expecting light to stream in and burn his retinas; but there was only darkness. Gradually, he remembered the evening's events. The unending snow, the power cut, and everybody freezing. He could remember no more than that at first, but when he found himself tied to a chair he began to panic as the rest came flooding back.

"Steph!"

"I'm here, Damien. I'm going to untie you, but you've got to stay calm. We need your help."

"That son of a bitch knocked me out. Harry, I'm going to kill you."

"Damien, I can only untie you if you calm down. The only reason Harry hit you was because he thought-"

"I was going to rape you."

"Yes," said Steph. "We got it all wrong. It wasn't you, it was-"

"Nigel!" Damien remembered finding the sick pervert about to stick it in an unconscious woman. Not just any women either: Steph. Damien was a lot of things, but he was no rapist. Sex offenders and nonces were a whole other level of scumbag, sub-human slugs. He wrenched at his wrist restraints, furious when they refused to loosen. "Where the *hell* is that *fucker*? I'm going to kill him."

Nigel appeared from the shadows. There was blood dripping down his face. "I'm here, princess, and guess what? This time you get to watch."

Damien strained against his ropes, unable to see what was happening as Nigel raced past him. He heard the monster taunting the girls, and them crying out in fear, but with his back to the fire place and sofa, he could see nothing more

Damien struggled at the ropes around his wrists. *Come on, come on. Need to put a stop to this before it gets nasty.*

The ropes were tight. So tight that the skin around Damien's wrists was abraded and sore. Still, he began sawing his arms back and forth, trying to create enough slack that he could slip him free.

A wet slapping sound.

Damien flinched as a body fell down in front of him.

Steph lay crumpled on the floor, dazed and barely conscious, blood seeping from a wound on the bridge of her nose. She murmured something to Damien, but it passed him by. It sounded like the word 'poker'.

Damien continued rubbing his wrists back and forth, feeling the ropes loosen a couple of millimetres.

Yes, come on. Come one!

At his feet, Damien could feel Steph squirming on the floor, slowly moving past his legs. At first he thought she was making a run for it, but a tugging sensation at his wrists made him realise she was trying to untie him.

The ropes began to loosen.

With the extra slack Damien shifted in his seat and blinked while his eyes adjusted to the scene in front of him. Nigel had Jess pinned up against the wall beside the fire, struggling back and forth as the girl held onto his wrists and did her best to keep his hands away from her. She was putting up more of a fight than Nigel had obviously expected, if his frus-

trated grunts were anything to go by. Damien almost smiled as he watched Jess spit and bite at
Nigel's face, doing everything she could to defend
herself.

Girl was a fighter for sure.

Damien felt the ropes fall away from his wrists.
A jolt shot from his knees and spread through his
entire body as he leapt out of the chair. He threw
himself at Nigel, landing hard against the man's
broad back. It felt like hitting a brick wall, but the
blow was enough to send Nigel face first into the
wall. Unfortunately, Jess was in the way and got
squashed. The air exploded from her lungs in a
great 'Oooomph!' as she fell to the floor like a puppet
without strings.

Taking advantage of the confusion, Damien
swung his fist.

And missed.

Nigel ducked and countered with a punch of his
own. His large, meaty fist connected with Damien's
ribcage with an echoing thud! The air surged out of
Damien like a whistle on a steam train; a drawn-out,
strangled wheeze that seemed to go on forever. He
fell to his knees in agony.

Nigel stomped towards him like a greasy-haired
rhino, grunting and snorting. There was still too
little air in Damien's winded lungs to launch a de-

fence, and he was about to resign himself to defeat when he spotted something.

The fire poker, lying on the carpet next to his feet.

Damien snatched the poker and held it in front of him. It seemed to glow in the soft light of the fire like a gift from the gods. It was salvation; a tool to knock Nigel back to the hell he came from.

Damien rose up, swinging the poker up and over his head.

The clanging sound of solid iron hitting Nigel's skull was the most beautiful thing Damien had ever heard. It was music.

Head banging music.

Nigel staggered backwards, half-conscious already and legs wobbling like those of a flailing boxer. Damien watched the whites of the man's eyes roll back in his head. Nigel stumbled in a daze, before losing his legs completely and falling backwards. He landed right in the open fire.

With an agonising scream, Nigel's eyes rolled back into their normal position as agony forced his mind back into focus. The top of his head lay in the flames, as if the burning wood inside were a pillow. Immediately his skin blistered and his hair smoked. Like a greyhound out of the starting gates, Nigel leapt upwards, screaming in both pain and fury.

The fire was only embers now and that was the only reason Nigel hadn't been roasted alive. The whole thing happened so quickly that Damien couldn't think fast enough to react to Nigel's hurtling back towards him.

When the knife slid through Damien's ribs, it felt like a bee sting.

Then the pain became unbearable.

"WHAT IN THE hell is happening tonight? I mean FUCK! Fuck fuck fuck." Harry felt like he was going to explode. He'd just watched a teenaged boy get ripped to shreds like minced beef. This on a night where the world was being consumed by a never-ending snow storm and demons stalked the streets. On top of everything, it all seemed to have something to do with *him*. Harry was 'the sinner'.

"Seriously, can anybody tell me what is going on? I just watched Jerry get ripped apart by God-knows what, and now we're trapped in a pitch-black supermarket surrounded by a bunch of homicidal monks."

"I don't think they're monks," said Kath.

"No shit!"

Lucas ambled over to the fire exit and looked

out into the snow. There was movement outside, but for now the creatures outside seemed to be staying away. "I think it would be shrewd if we thought a wee bit less about what those things are out there and a mite more about how to get back to the pub with what we came for. The others need us."

Harry let air flow slowly from his lips, trying to calm his beating heart. It didn't work and only left him feeling more anxious. "We're fucked, do you know that?"

Lucas nodded. "Aye, but better to take a shagging standing up than to bend over and take it."

The remark brought silence.

Harry couldn't help but laugh. "You've obviously spent some time in prison, right?"

Lucas grinned. "You could say that, Harry Boy, and you wouldn't be too far from the truth."

"Okay," said Kath. "Can we just do what we're here to do? It's even colder here than it was outside."

Harry nodded and started moving. "Okay. Let's get the coal, painkillers, and some food. Anything we need to take back, let's get it all piled up over here."

Kath and Lucas nodded and got to work. Before Lucas ran off into the darkness he saluted Harry and said, "Right away, Major Jobson."

It was then that Harry realised something important; something he'd overlooked earlier, not once but twice. He'd never told Lucas his surname, or anybody else, so how did the man know it?

Harry looked over at Lucas and wondered if he'd been played from the beginning. Lucas knew more about Harry then he'd let on. But how?

And why?

30

J ess finally managed to take a breath but it only made her nauseous. She'd watched helplessly as a badly-burned Nigel slid a knife into Damien's stomach, and she was powerless now to intervene as Nigel heaved Steph's groggy body onto a chair.

She scanned the floor for a weapon, looking for a solution, but the only thing she could see was the trusty fire poker, several feet away and out of reach. It lay near where Damien writhed on the floor, gritting his teeth against his pain. He'd tried to save her.

Jess need to reach the poker without being seen by Nigel. Even worse, she had to do it in such awful cold that her body had begun to shiver and spasm.

She would just love for Jerry and the others to

come barging through the door right now and save her from this wretched nightmare. But, if tonight had taught her anything, it was not to hope for the best because things had a habit of just getting worse.

Jess started to move, crawling along awkwardly on her numb hands and trembling knees. She shivered constantly. The chill was bad enough that even the fibres of the carpet had begun to freeze. They were sharp and brittle like tiny needles digging into her palms.

"Rise and shine, sleepyhead," Nigel said as he shook Steph by the shoulders. "I want you to be awake for this. No fun if you sleep through all the good stuff."

Steph opened her eyes suddenly. She spat at Nigel. "Screw you!" But as soon as it arrived, the fight seemed to leave Steph. She was obviously too bruised and broken to keep it up. Nigel slapped her so hard, the sound bounced off the walls.

Jess stayed down in the shadows and winced. She continued crawling for the poker, just a few feet away now.

Nigel slapped Steph again, this time a backhand. "Spitting is very unladylike," he shouted, "and anything unbecoming a lady will not be tolerated. If I wanted a bloke for entertainment then I would have tied Damien back up in the chair. Speaking of which, how are you big man?" Nigel turned to Damien who was still moaning on the floor. "Not such a hard man now, huh?" He took a run up and booted Damien in the chest, making him explode with fresh agony and gasp for air. Jess winced again, glad she wasn't on the receiving end.

She carried on shuffling towards the poker. It was nearly at arm's length now.

Almost there.

Almost...

Jess cried out as a heavy work shoe crunched down on her hand. She knew right away that she'd been too slow and that she would most likely pay for it with her life. Nigel twisted his heel and pushed down harder, cracking and bruising the delicate bones in Jess' hand. She wailed in agony and struggled to get free.

Nigel laughed sadistically.

Jess's screams increased as a rough hand tangled itself into her hair and yanked. The pressure on her hand was released as she was violently hoisted to her feet. She found herself face to face with Nigel. She tried to pull away.

"Not so fast, sweetheart. Now that Steph is nice and comfortable, you and me have some time on our hands."

Jess fought to twist herself free, but it was like being held in a vice. "The others will be back at any minute," she warned him. "You're going to get your arse kicked, you sicko."

Nigel smiled. "By who? Harry, the alcoholic? Jerry, the loser? Or Lucas, the thick Mick? I don't think so, sweetheart. They're probably already dead, and if not then I'll see to them later."

The thought of Nigel killing the others filled Jess with rage. She decided to take a leaf out of Steph's book and spat. Nigel flinched as the saliva hit his cheek and she used this opportunity to try and get free, driving her knee up as hard as she could toward Nigel's groin. The blow missed the intended target but still managed to plant firmly in his mid-section. He staggered backwards, releasing her, as the air escaped from his lungs.

Jess made a grab for the poker, diving to the floor and reaching out with her hand. Her fingers closed around the metal and her heart skipped a beat as she realised she'd actually succeeded in getting the weapon. Now she just had to use it.

Jess leapt to her feet, poker in hand, ready to let Nigel have it.

But Nigel was gone.

Jess did a double take of the room. She knew Nigel was hiding somewhere, waiting to pounce.

But from where? With the poker held out in front of her, she took a tentative step forward, expecting an attack to come at any moment. Her nerves were tattered and frayed by the constant jolts of fear. Moving past the sofa, she prepared to swing with all her might, sure that Nigel would jump out at her any second. She moved carefully, watchfully, deciding that the most effective hiding place for a killer would be behind the bar. There was only one entrance to the area behind it so, if she was quick enough, she could take Nigel out before he could manage to do anything to her. Jess slowed her pace, not relishing an encounter that was life or death.

The bar loomed closer, lit by a collection of dwindling candles. The struggling light shone on the liqueur bottles that lined the shelves, making them look like rows upon rows of crocodile teeth. The final few steps were nerve-wracking. *Deep breaths, Jess. You're ready for him. Armed and ready.* Jess squeezed the poker in her right hand. *Okay, here goes.*

She took the final steps towards the bar and quickly sidestepped to see behind it. As she suspected, Nigel was crouched and waiting for her. What she hadn't expected was how quick the big man would be – and how much it would hurt having a vodka bottle smashed over her head.

Jess felt the blood cascade from the top of her head in an instant. It ran into her eyes and into her mouth. She teetered backwards, legs folding as she hit the floor. Her ears picked up the heavy *clunk* of the poker skittering across the floor. Nigel was on her like a shot, pinning her arms down with his knees and straddling her chest. Held to her throat was the broken remnants of the Vodka bottle.

"Time to die, bitch."

"See you in hell, you small prick mummy's boy!"

The comment seemed to hurt Nigel and Jess started to laugh. Right now, the over-sized, sexual predator looked like an insecure little boy and she would take that satisfying image to her grave happily. Even as the jagged bottle descended towards her throat, Jess continued to cackle out loud, closing her eyes and waiting for it all to be over.

Jess had expected pain, but instead was jolted by a heavy force hitting her. She opened her eyes tentatively, and at first could not understand what had happened. Nigel had collapsed forward. Her face now buried in his fat belly. She punched and prodded at his lumpy body, trying to shove it off of her, but it wouldn't budge. Nigel was unconscious.

What the hell had happened?

Jess finally managed to slump Nigel over to one side and slide out from underneath him. She still didn't understand what happened, not until she saw...

"Peter! You're okay?"

Her friend was standing over her, gripping a thick length of firewood which dripped gobbets of blood onto the floor. He smiled at her, although his ruined face made the expression look ghoulish and grim. He released the length of wood and dropped to his knees. From the floor he spoke to her. "You okay...Jess?"

"Yes, yes, I'm fine. Thanks to you, that is."

Peter nodded and his smile widened. Then he lost consciousness, pitching forward and hitting the floor. Jess felt like doing the same.

31

When Harry found a pile of children's sledges, he thought that things were looking up, but only a little. Sure it would make getting the coal and other supplies back to the pub easier, but it didn't change the fact that the supermarket was surrounded by monsters. To make matters worse, Harry had realised that Lucas was not who he said he was, but he decided to complete the task at hand before he confronted the man. Between the three of them they had managed to pile up more than enough coal to keep the pub fires going for a week, along with a bag full of over-the-counter painkillers. They'd even found a couple of torches and two dozen packets of batteries. Now that they were done and ready to leave,

Harry was ready to confront Lucas about the secrets he was keeping.

"Lucas?"

"Yes, Harry Boy?"

"How do you know my surname?"

Lucas turned to Harry, confusion on his face. "What's that now?"

"I said how do you know my surname? I didn't tell you."

Kath huffed. "Do we really have time for this, Harry? We need to get going."

Lucas shrugged. "I didn't realise it was such a secret, fella."

"It's not," Harry admitted, "but I never told it to you."

"The demon monks outside said it, didn't they? They said, HARRY JOBSON YOU ARE THE SINNER. Or something like that."

Harry thought for a moment. "No, Lucas, you knew before. You called me Major Jobson earlier at the pub."

Kath looked pissed off, but at the same time seemed interested also. It appeared she wanted to see what Lucas's answer would be.

But he gave none.

Harry took a quick breath, trying to stay calm. "Lucas, I asked you a question. Answer it, please."

"Do you really want to do this now, Harry Boy?"

Harry's stomach churned as he wondered whether he really *did* want to do this now. He had no idea who Lucas was, what he was planning, or what he was capable of.

Harry swallowed. "Yeah, I want to do this right now. Who the hell are you and how do you know me?"

Lucas walked over to the cash register and hopped up onto the desk. He took a long, deep breath. "Who I am is something we really don't have time to get into right now, but how I know you is a little easier to explain."

"Get started then," Harry demanded.

Lucas shrugged. "I know you, Harry Jobson, because you're the sinner. Same reason them outside know you – who, might I add, have nothing to do with me."

"You expect me to believe that?"

"Not really, but you have my word, for what it's worth. What happened tonight was going to happen whether I turned up or not."

Kath stepped towards Lucas. "Who *are* you? What's going on?"

Lucas looked tired of the questions already, but he still gave answers, despite sounding like he was doing them a favour. "Both are questions we don't have time for. All I can say is that the fellas outside came for Harry. Does the 'what' or the 'why' really matter?"

"It fucking does to me," said Harry. It felt like his stomach was going to burst open and spill his organs onto the floor. The scar on the back of his hand throbbed. It always did when he was losing control. It reminded him to keep his temper. "Why me? Why do they want me?"

"B'Jaysus, we're going around in circles here, man. Because you're the sinner."

Kath shook her head. "Why is Harry 'the sinner'?"

Harry sighed. "Because I murdered a man."

Lucas acted as though he knew it all along – perhaps he did – but Kath recoiled in horror.

"Calm down, lass," Lucas told her. "I'm sure he's not intending to kill *you*." He looked at Harry. "Are you?"

"No, of course not! The man I killed destroyed my life. It was revenge. There're far worse people in the world than me,"

"I agree," said Lucas. "In the grand scale of things, you're pretty low down on the sin scale, but murder is murder."

"But why did *my* sin cause all this? If that's what

you're suggesting?" Harry felt dizzy. This morning he'd woken up expecting the day to end in a drunken stupor just like the 365 days preceding it. He'd never expected it to end like this.

Lucas stared at Harry intensely. His blue eyes seemed to light the darkness around him. "Because yours was the final sin. The sin what tipped the scales."

Harry was about to demand what the hell that meant, but before he could grab Lucas around the throat and force him to speak sense, the doors blew inwards. Not a gust of wind swinging them open, but a concussive force that ripped them from their hinges and flung them across the room. The wind and snow flew in through the gap like the breath of a dragon.

Harry grabbed Lucas by the arm. "What the hell is happening?"

Lucas had to shout to be heard above the howling wind. "They're coming to get you, Harry."

Something didn't make sense. "But we were safe inside the pub, they left us alone. Why?"

"They couldn't enter the pub, but they can get at you in here. Don't worry, though. I'm going to help you out."

"I'm listening."

Lucas raised an eyebrow and smiled. "Go and get all of the skin mags."

"What?" Kath joined them over at the cash desk. The wind had blown her dark hair into a freakish mess of tangles. "This is no time for perversions."

"Just go and get all the smutty magazines," Lucas reiterated. "You'll see why."

The monsters would be inside any minute. Harry almost slipped on a Gardening Annual as he raced over to the magazine display. On the top shelf was a long row of bikini clad women stacked three deep. Harry saw little choice but to do what Lucas had asked. He grabbed a copy of *Nipples*, then quickly gathered up several more rags of ill-repute, clutching the pile to his chest.

"Set the pornos down on the counter, fella," Lucas yelled, "and pass me that broom."

Harry did as asked. "Okay, now what?"

Lucas took the broom and placed it on the counter along with the pile of magazines. He began tearing out the pages, piling up shiny images of naked men and women.

Kath had her hands on her hips. "What are you doing? We need to hurry. I can hear them out there. They'll be in any second."

Lucas ignored her and continued tearing pages.

Eventually he stopped and grabbed a roll of Sellotape from a display. To everyone's confusion, he then began to wrap the broom with the naked pictures before fastening them with tape.

Harry couldn't take it anymore. "Okay, Lucas, I'm all for arts and crafts, but how is this helping?"

Lucas shoved the porn-wrapped broom into Harry arms. "You'll see. Right, that sorts out the choir. Now something for their lapdogs."

Harry raised an eyebrow. "The choir?"

"Aye, the choir. Somebody get me some salt."

"Salt?" said Kath.

"It'll deal with the growly fellas, trust me. Stop asking questions and get me some."

Kath returned ten seconds later with a plastic tube of salt. She tried to offer it to Lucas, but he told her to keep it. "You'll know what to do when the time comes," was all he would tell her.

The sound of howling wind merged with the sound of growling.

Harry clutched the broom tightly. "Let's just get out of here while there's still chance."

"Too late." Lucas pointed over to the doorway as one of the hell hounds padded inside. Its ears flattened against its skull as it stalked towards them, snarling.

"What should I do?" Kath was holding the salt tube in front of her with a shaking hand.

"Give us a pinch," said Lucas. He offered his open palm and waited while Kath sprinkled a pile of salt into his hand. Then he closed his fist and strolled, almost casually, towards the snarling hell hound.

The beast lowered his head, its rippling muscles tensing. Lucas carried on approaching.

Harry swallowed in anticipation. *Insane. The man's insane.*

Lucas glanced back at them and nodded, as if to say 'watch this', then he flicked the salt from his hands, letting loose an arching stream of granules.

The beast howled like a beaten puppy.

The smell of burning filled the air, like sausages on a barbeque, along with something else...

Eggs?

No, something else.

It was sulphur.

The hound bolted, turning and running back out into the snow. It left behind a cloying puddle of dissolving flesh, sizzling like bacon on the grill.

"Now we can go," said Lucas. "We have a window."

"What about the choir?" Harry asked.

"That's what the broom is for. Make sure you use it when the time is right."

"And how do I know when that is?"

"It'll be when something starts trying to kill you."

"Okay," said Harry, looking out into the freezing dark night. "Let's do this."

32

Jess held Peter in her arms, amazed he was awake. Steph was looking after Damien, who was doing okay, considering he'd been stabbed. The blade had lodged between his ribs but hadn't gone in more than an inch or so. Damien said it hurt like hell but that he'd be okay. He was acting too macho to let anyone take a closer look, but he had bled an awful lot to begin with. Still, he was up and about.

Nigel was out cold in the middle of the floor. They would tie him up once they'd caught their breath. For the time being she, Steph, and Damien were ready to beat him down if he dared make the slightest move. Damien was currently standing over him with the fire poker in hand.

After having saved her and losing consciousness, Peter had eventually stirred back awake, semi-
lucid again. Lying across Jess's lap, his body-warmth
pulsed through her clothing. He was burning up
badly and she worried about his temperature being
high.

"Did the bad man...hurt you...Jessica?"

"No, Peter. You saved me. You're my hero."

Peter smiled a grim, broken-toothed smile. "I
am...sorry I let you go out alone. I...looked for you."

"I know you did. It wasn't your fault. No one
could know what was going to happen tonight. I
think it's the end of the world. Nobody is saying it,
but I don't think the snow is going to ever stop."

Peter closed his eyes for a few seconds and Jess
worried that he would not open them again. His
breathing was uneven and shallow. Jess shook him
gently. "Peter, are you okay?"

He opened his eyes again. "I am...fine. The
world is not ending, Jessica."

"No?"

"No. As long as there are still beautiful things,
we will be...okay." He was looking at Jess and she
realised that he meant her. "Can I...ask
you...something?"

"Yes," said Jess. "Of course you can."

"Can I...kiss you?"

Jess was taken aback. After all Peter had been through tonight, the only thing he wanted was a kiss. *And from me?* Had he had feelings for her before all of this? Or was he just delirious?

"Yes, Peter," she said, "you can kiss me."

She leant forward but then stopped.

"Peter?"

Jess looked down at her friend and realised that he was dead. She leant down the rest of the way and placed her lips against his soft, delicate mouth. "Goodbye," she said.

Damien noticed her tears and came over and asked if she was alright.

Steph was the one who noticed Peter lying dead on the floor. She shook her head solemnly. "I'm sorry."

Jess nodded. "It's okay. At least I got to say goodbye...in a way."

Steph sighed. "Can we do anything?"

"No it's...Shit, Nigel's up."

Nigel leapt from the chair, staggering about like a wounded animal. His skin was blackened, making him look like some nightmarish monster as he headed for the door.

"He's trying to do one," said Damien.

"Let him," Jess said. "He can go outside and freeze."

Nigel barged past the sofa and headed for the door. Then he was gone, disappearing into the night. Jess prayed never to see him again.

Jess snarled. "Good riddance!"

Steph put an arm around Jess. "Come on, sweetheart. We should get ourselves downstairs in front of the fire. The fire here's about to go out and that broken window is going to freeze us to stone. Old Graham will be wondering what's going on. I'm surprised we haven't heard him shouting."

"Probably still passed out drunk," said Damien in a laboured voice.

"We'd best get down there," Jess said. She took two steps when Damien doubled over against the bar, taking in long, laboured breaths.

"You're still bleeding?" Jess said, spotting the blood dripping on the floor.

Damien waved a hand dismissively and Jess saw that it was soaked with blood. "Just a flesh wound," he said and then laughed. "I always wanted to say that."

"It's not a joke, Damien. Are you okay?"

"I'll live."

Steph didn't seem convinced. Jess wasn't either, but what could they do? Jess suspected the wound was worse than Damien was letting on. "Let's go downstairs," she said finally, deciding there was nothing she could do.

They gathered candles from the bar and entered the rear corridor. The air seemed no warmer there, even though it had been filled with a warm air current flowing up from the stairs for most of the night. Now it felt as cold as the rest of the pub.

Steph led the way down. They reached the bottom and darkness greeted them. Both the fire and the room's candles had gone out. Steph quickly re-lit them with her lighter.

Old Graham's body shone into view. Even in the poor light, the waxy blue tinge that travelled the lines of the old man's face were clearly visible. His eyes were dull like stones.

Steph fell to her knees, dropping her candle on the cement floor where it quickly extinguished. In the darkness, Jess and Damien had no choice but to listen to her scream.

OUTSIDE IT WAS as Harry had feared. They were surrounded. In all directions, the robed figures loomed over them, standing motionless, shoulder to shoulder, a towering wall of bodies. Their hounds sat in front of them obediently.

"What do we do?" asked Harry.

Lucas shoved him forward. "Just swing at the first bastard that gets near. Kath and I will handle the mutts."

Harry willed his legs to take him forward. After several false starts, he got going. The monsters remained in place but watched him with great interest. He felt like a lowly ant beneath their stares. A low growl emanated from the hounds but they made no attempts to attack, held at heel by their robed masters.

Did Lucas really expect to take on this army with only a broom and a salt shaker? They were going to die; any other outcome seemed impossible. Still, Harry wasn't going down without a fight. If they wanted him, they would have to take him, kicking and screaming.

Once Harry was within a dozen metres of the robed figures, the hounds at their feet became agitated, their hackles rising as they paced back and forth.

Harry glanced back at Kath. "Ready with the salt?"

Her face was as white as the snow, but she nodded.

"Bring it on," said Lucas. He grabbed a handful of salt from Kath's shaker and flung it into the air.

The granules caught on the wind and dispersed in a thousand directions, disappearing into the blizzard.

Nothing happened.

Then the hell hounds squealed. Their skin smoked and burned, sloughing off into the snow. They hustled backwards, colliding with their robed masters, before fleeing completely into the night.

"Your turn, Harry," said Lucas. "You need to take on the big fellas."

Harry raised the broom like a pike. Images of naked men and women fluttered in his eye line, making him think again about how absurd this was.

The robed figure stood like giant monoliths. When one of them finally made a move, Harry's bowels almost loosed. The very air itself seemed to shake.

The tallest of the robed figures – almost ten feet tall – approached Harry and held out a hand. Curiously, Harry noted the creature's outstretched arm was human, yet twisted and bird-like. It pointed a finger at Lucas and hissed. "*WORMWOOD.*"

Lucas was grinning ear-to-ear, but not out of good nature. The expression was more of a malignant grimace. "How you doing there, Mickey? Been a while?"

Kath's eyes went unnaturally wide. "Y-You know this...this thing?"

"Aye. We go back a ways. It's complicated."

"It always is with you," said Harry.

"Now would be a good time to sweep up the trash, if you get my meaning."

Harry looked at the broom in his hands and took a gulp of air. *Here goes nothing*. He stabbed the broom forwards like a lance, aiming for the robed figure's torso. The blow got nowhere near and that seemed impossible. Harry's target had dodged aside with an unearthly blur of speed; a glowing wisp of light that didn't actually seem to move so much as simply disappear and reappear somewhere else.

Harry cursed out loud. "Damn it! I missed."

"No, you didn't," said Lucas. "Get your bloody arse moving!"

Harry realised that his attack had left a gap in the wall of bodies. The three of them hurried, stumbling through the deep snow, clawing themselves along. Before leaving, Harry had filled his pockets with lumps of coal, and he wished he could toss them aside, but he could not.

Despite their earlier lack of movement, the robed figures gave chase. They screeched and wailed as they drifted through the snow. Harry swung out with his broom as one drew closer. Like its friend, it blinked out of existence and reappeared somewhere else.

"What the hell are they, Lucas?"

Lucas looked back at Harry and smiled. "They're angels, Harry Boy."

"Angels?"

"Aye, Angels, with great feathery wings, but now's not the time. Keep on moving."

The three of them continued making their way through the snow. The 'Angels' continued to screech and wail but they kept a distance. They seemed in little hurry to catch up.

"Something's up ahead," said Kath.

Harry saw the shadow looming ahead. "Ready with the salt?"

"Yes. Ready with the broom?"

They slowed down as the shadow became clearer. It was a person, heading towards them quickly.

Kath stated the obvious. "It's coming right at us."

"I think it's...a person."

"Nigel!" Kath shouted the word gleefully. "Are we glad to see you!"

Nigel staggered through the snow, huffing and puffing and wheezing. The man had dried blood on his clothes and terrible burns on the left side of his face.

"Are you okay?" Harry asked him. "You're hurt."

Nigel acted feral, like an injured fox. His words

were erratic and slurred. "Fwine! I'm fwine. Jush hash an asshident."

Lucas stepped forward and placed a hand on Nigel's shoulder. "You don't look fine to me, fella. In fact, you look and sound worse than a chorus of drunks. What have you been up to, lad?"

Nigel lashed out, shrugging free of Lucas's grasp. "Get sh'fuck offsh me."

Harry didn't like the way Nigel was acting. "What happened to you? Is Steph okay?" Nigel's face scrunched up in a snarl at the very mention of her name. Harry spotted the bloody knife in the man's hand. "What did you do? Did you hurt her?"

Nigel raised the knife towards Harry.

Lucas made a gesture for calm "Whoa, whoa, there, fella. We just want to know the lass is safe. Is Steph okay?"

Nigel spat blood into the snow. "You tell that bitch I'll be back to finish what I started. I'll slice her fucking fingers off one by one and add them to my collection. I'll hang them from the rear view mirror of my lorry. You think she's the first bitch to fight back. I've killed a hundred whores just like her."

Harry snarled. He made a move towards Nigel, but Lucas stopped him. "No need, Harry Boy. Look!"

Beyond Nigel, the shadows seemed to come

alive and cut through the snow. Nigel backed away, unaware that he was heading directly towards them. The shadows enveloped him, coming at him from both sides. He flinched at the sight of the hell hounds and tried to move away, but by then it was too late.

Nigel swiped impotently with his bloody flick knife. He took a chunk of flesh from one hound, but failed to keep away the other dozen that fell upon him.

It was hard to see past the writhing mass of matted fur, but Harry saw Nigel's intestines being fought over in a macabre tug of war. Once the grim satisfaction of seeing Nigel get what he deserved faded, he felt only sick.

Harry turned away and continued on into the snow, back towards The Trumpet.

Back towards Steph.

33

Jess felt no warmer. Damien had managed to get the cellar fire going again, but it wouldn't burn for long. Steph was confident that Harry would return soon, but the truth was there was no way of knowing. Now the three of them lay shivering beneath a dozen sheets and blankets, trying to hold on to as much warmth as possible.

"Poor Old Graham," said Steph, still upset but past the worse of it now that she'd had time to calm down. She'd wailed for almost twenty minutes and Jess knew that Steph felt responsible for leaving the old guy alone. The truth was that Nigel was the one to blame.

Pervert. Hope he's frozen to death out there or being eaten alive by one of those monsters.

Jess thought about the things she'd seen with Jerry and found it hard to imagine them clearly now. With the hours that had passed, it all felt like some weird hallucination. Monsters in the snow surely did not exist, but she couldn't deny the death and bloodshed she'd witnessed. Ben. Peter. Old Graham. They were all good guys. She prayed that the others would make it back safely. She'd do anything, right now, to sit and listen to Jerry's inane film references.

She decided to turn her mind to the present. "How long have you known Old Graham?" she asked Steph.

Steph let out a huff that was almost a laugh. "Whole time I've worked here. Eighteen months, I guess. He could bore you to death something awful, but he didn't have a bad bone in his body. Complained a lot, but never about anyone or anything in particular. I think he was lonely. He just wanted to be around people."

"Least he lived a long life," Damien chimed in, his voice jittery from the chill that affected everyone's lungs.

"He didn't deserve to go like this though. He survived a war and this is how he dies?"

"I think he went the way he would have liked," Jess pondered. "Drunk as a skunk and the centre of attention."

Steph and Damien both chuckled. The sound was jittery as they fought to control their shivering. Jess too was beginning to shake.

"S-so, Damien," Jess moved on, "are you really as much of a b-bastard as you like to make people think?"

Damien was silent for a moment, but eventually answered. "Who says I want people to think that?"

"J-Just the impression you give off. It confuses me though because, after tonight, I'm starting to think you're not s-s-so bad."

Damien cleared his throat. "You reckon?"

"I actually think you might be a nice guy under the hard man act. You just don't want people to know it."

"I agree," said Steph. "I've seen a different side of you tonight."

Damien was silent again. Jess could feel him rustling beneath the duvet. When he finally spoke up, he sounded as tired as he did cold. "M-Maybe the reason I'm not a nice guy is because p-people think bad of me no matter w-what I do."

Jess frowned. "But you make people think like

that. You choose to make people think you're a t-t-thug."

Damien laughed. "You think I...made people see me this...this way? I h-had no chance of ever being anything *other* than a t-thug."

Jess sighed. "Is this the part where you say your daddy never hugged you enough?"

"No. This is the p-part where I tell you my dad had me selling drugs for him at e-eight years old. No one would ever expect a kid, huh? Or how about how my dad put a lad in a coma a couple years b-back and m-m-made me take credit for it around the...the local estate. You're right, my dad never hugged me, because that's not what monsters like him do."

"Are you s-s-shitting me?" Steph asked.

"No, Steph. I'm not shitting you. Truth is, the day he was sent down I was glad. Thought it would s-set me f-free from his fu-fu-fucked-up demands. B-B-But I was just wishing on a fucking star. He calls me at least once a day, making sure I'm running his empire for him till he g-gets back."

"You can't blame everything on your dad," Jess told him. "I s-saw you cause enough trouble to see that you enjoyed being the big man."

"Of course I did. The only l-love and respect I got was from the boys I hung with. If people on t-the estate don't f-fear me then I'm nothing. I'm alone with nothing."

"Why didn't you get out?" asked Steph. "You could have done something, I'm s-sure."

Damien was quiet once more, but the sound of his breathing was heavy and distinct, laboured. "I was getting out tonight. I had a bunch of m-money stashed and I was going to st-stay with an old girl-friend in Edinburgh. I just had one last thing to do tonight and then I was out of here."

"One last thing?" asked Steph.

"Warn someone."

"Who?"

"The guy who gave evidence on my old man and sent him down. Took over a year but the boys finally managed to find out who it was. I was supposed to kill the guy tonight; take him outside and stick a knife in him. Guess my dad was beginning t-to d-d-doubt my loyalty."

"Jesus," said Jess, not believing her ears. "You weren't going to do it though, w-were you?"

"That's what I'm telling you." Damien raised his voice and it seemed to cause him pain. "I was... going to warn him...tell him to get the hell out of... town. Soon as the snow stopped...I was going to get on a train and never come back. Maybe even do something with my life."

No one spoke for a while. It was a revelation, and not one Jess had expected. She felt sad that Damien might not get the chance to fulfil his plans for atonement. She closed her eyes, feeling more tired than she'd ever felt in her life. The cold was no longer bothering her as much as it had. In fact, she was starting to feel numb. Maybe she could finally rest for a while.

So tired...

HARRY WASN'T sure how much further his aching legs would take him. He didn't know whether the pub was two yards away or two thousand. All he could see was snow. His feet were like blocks of ice and it felt like he was walking on nerveless stumps. Kath was suffering too. She hadn't spoken since they'd watched Nigel die. Lucas, however, seemed perfectly fine and entirely unaffected by the cold.

Was the man any more human than the robed figures?

Harry needed to know more. "If those giants are Angels, what are the dogs with them?"

Lucas continued looking forward as he walked, but answered the question promptly. "Hell Hounds."

Harry scratched his chin. "But don't Angels come from Heaven?"

"Aye, they do, Harry Boy, but Angels have dominion over Heaven and Earth, and also Hell in certain circumstances."

Harry felt himself confused already. "Circumstances such as what?"

"You know, family reunions, birthdays, The Apocalypse."

Harry spluttered. "The Apocalypse?"

"Aye, you know, Armageddon and all that, but it's not as dramatic as you might think. There're no horsemen, none of that fire and brimstone nonsense. The old man upstairs likes to do things a bit more efficiently. Biblical floods and such are more His style."

"Or biblical snow storms," Kath added glumly.

Lucas smiled. "Indeed, lass."

Harry was trying to follow, but things still didn't add up in his mind. If this really was the end of the world, and God intended to simply freeze the world to death, then why did he need...?

"The angels," said Harry. "Why are they here?"

"Call them overseers if you will. God can't just make the snow fall unendingly without having a presence on Earth. He needs vessels to channel his power – conduits. That's why the Angels have come down here, to exercise His will on Earth."

Harry nodded, an idea forming in his head. "So if we take out the angels, we can stop this?"

Lucas laughed, loud and hearty. "Do you know how many of them there are? We're talking tens of thousands, and they don't play nice. You can't kill an angel anyway."

Harry sagged. "I still don't understand why they are doing this. It can't be because of me?"

"I already told you, Harry Boy, it's not *just* because of you, strictly speaking. It's because of *everyone*, really. God gave Noah a second chance, but that's all the big man had in his pocket of goodwill. He vowed that if the human race threw it in His face again then there would be no more forgiveness. But that's what you all went and did anyway, with your sinful ways and what not. Fucking, murdering, raping, stealing, cheating, Facebook. You name it, you people have over indulged in it. Over time, you all tipped the scales way past the point of no return."

"But not everyone is like that. And even if I believed what you're saying, why doesn't God just punish the bad?"

Kath sighed. "Because there were probably too few to make it worthwhile."

Lucas nodded. "There are a few decent souls, admittedly, and He took that into consideration, which is why He allowed man to pass judgement on man."

"What do you mean?"

"I *mean*, that He decided to judge mankind by its own values. Harry, after your wife and son were killed you made that choice for everyone, with your actions."

Harry ground his teeth. "I had no choice. The guy had already lost his license for drink driving, but got behind the wheel again anyway. He was a lousy, fucking drunk and could've mowed down a dozen more children before he killed my son. He was an alcoholic. No good to anyone."

"Sounds like you, Harry," said Kath.

Harry snarled, but what was the use in arguing? "Maybe it is like me," he conceded. "But what would you have done after losing your family to a man like me?"

"That's the point," said Lucas. "You had a choice. Did you get on with your life and make the memory of your family proud, or did you give in to sin? Did you know that the reason Thomas was a drunk was because he also lost a son? Kid died in the first days of the Afghanistan mess. Thomas was just like you,

Harry. Ironic, no? Have you really behaved any differently to him?"

"No," said Harry. "But I never drove drunk. I never let my problems endanger anybody else."

"No, you just got hammered one night and murdered the fella. Understandable, I guess, but definitely not the right path. God decided to judge humanity by your actions, and your choice was vengeance. Now vengeance has been reaped upon you all. You committed man's final sin – the last one that counted anyway – and you picked a gem: *Thou shall not kill.*"

Harry thought about the night he'd murdered Thomas Morris. The night he crept into the hospital ward where he'd been admitted for a simple hernia operation. Harry knew all about it thanks to the local newspaper: *Birmingham car killer hospitalised on private ward.*

Getting past the lone prison guard turned out to be easy. It wasn't as if they were going to place a highly-paid special detachment outside the door. It was just one guard, who obviously didn't want to be stuck at a hospital at 3:00AM on a Friday night. Harry walked right by him and entered Thomas's room as soon as the coast was clear.

Thomas Morris had been in a deep sleep. Even after Harry shoved the plastic bag over his head.

It took several moments for him to wake up and realise what was happening. The last thing the man saw through plastic smothering his face was Harry's maniacal grin as he suffocated the life out of him.

Once it had all been over, Harry vomited in the en suite, then hurried out of the room. As he fled down the corridor, he snagged the back of his hand on the sharp edge of an unused trolley bed in the corridor. Blood had gone everywhere. A nurse in a nearby ward had sat him down and stitched the wound for him, remarking on how much it resembled the shape of a star. Harry had been silent the entire time, staring into space like a zombie.

Somehow he managed to walk out of the hospital without incident. He'd just killed a man and no one noticed a thing.

Harry went home and drank for seven days straight. Later he sold his furniture business, as well as his house and car. The sales left him with just over half-a-million-pounds with which to drink himself to death.

A year later, he was responsible for the extinction of mankind.

"Bullshit!" he said finally. "This is bullshit."

Lucas put his hands up. "Hey, I don't disagree, fella. I don't want the world to end any more than you do. I like it here. I like crispy duck pancakes and ice cream sundaes. I like Manchester Utd and *Strictly Come Dancing*. I like a lot of stuff down here, but it's not my call. And it's not yours."

"There's nothing we can do?" Kath pleaded.

Lucas shook his head. "Unless you can convince the big man to change his mind – but I don't think he's listening. You can hold the choir off for a while with objects of depravity like the porno mags. Same reason they can't enter the pub: it's a den of iniquity and they can't set their holy toes in it."

"How do you know so much?" Harry demanded. The snow was sapping his strength and he needed more answers before he was too tired to ask for anymore. "How do you know so much about angels?

"Because I used to be one, laddie. Long time ago."

"What? You used to be...." Harry suddenly understood. It came to him in a flash of inspiration. "They called you Wormwood."

"That they did, but I prefer my rightful name, the name given to me by my lord."

"And what's that?" Kath asked, obviously not yet understanding what Harry had come to realise.

Lucas turned to Kath and grinned, his pointy teeth shining. "Please allow me to introduce myself. I am Lucifer, the Prince of Hell. Pleased to make your acquaintance."

Harry should have been shouting the word 'bullshit', but somehow he knew it was true. The reality of the situation just could not be denied. He was trudging through the snow with the Devil, pursued by murderous angels. There was just one more thing that didn't make sense. "Why the whole Irish jig then, Lucas Fergus?"

"Would you prefer I had horns and a red suit? Let's just say that Ireland is close to my heart. Good, fun-loving, people that know a good time. I can take many forms, and appear however I wish, but Irish is my favourite. Plus, ladies like the accent."

"Why are you here? Are you helping the angels?"

Lucas shook his head vehemently, snow falling from his hair. "Those righteous do-gooders? They may be my brothers, but we parted ways long ago, and for good reason. A few members of the choir, the ones who were any fun, joined me in Hell. It's *the* place to be, as long as you haven't been sent there for, you know...*treatment*, as it were."

"So, we're all going to Heaven or Hell after this?" Kath sounded hopeful. She obviously thought she was destined for Heaven.

"Afraid not, luv. After the final sin was committed, He gave up on you all. You're all coming downstairs with me to whichever level you deserve."

"Level we deserve?" Kath sounded worried.

Lucas seemed to be getting a bit impatient now as they continued through the snow. "The different levels dish out appropriate punishment. A murderer gets murdered. Over and over. Forever. A rapist gets raped. A bully gets beaten. You get the general idea, right?"

"Yeah, I get it." Kath shut up and stayed that way, seemingly lost in disturbing thoughts.

"That just leaves you," said Harry. "You still haven't told us what part you have to play in all this. You're the Devil, which means you're evil and can't be trusted...doesn't it?"

Before Lucas had chance to reply, Harry realised that, once again, they were surrounded.

34

"They're not going to give up are they?"

"No," Lucas confirmed. "Not until they have you."

Harry raised the broom in front of him, hoping it would work as well as last time. "What will they do to me?"

"Send you to Hell."

Harry nodded. "Thought so." He eyed up the line of angels, wondering which one he should go for first. He decided to do as he did last time and aim for the middle of the crowd.

Before he had the chance, a pillar of fire zigzagged towards him, sending him into a sideways dive. The snow cushioned his fall but was still jarring enough to knock the broom from his grasp.

Harry looked up just in time to see another wall of flames rising in his direction. He rolled over, barely managing to dodge the burning death, but found himself even further away from his only weapon. "Lucas," he shouted. "The broom."

Lucas nodded, located the broom, and then went for it. He was too slow though and Kath got to it first.

"Great," said Harry. "Throw it here, Kath."

Kath drew her arm back and looked as though she was going to hurl the broom in his direction, but she didn't release it. Instead she held it in front of herself and examined it. "Without this, you have no way of defending yourself, right?"

"Yes," said Harry. "That's why I need it."

Kath walked away from him and started making her way over to the choir of angels. She approached the tallest in the centre. "You just want Harry, right? What will you do for me if I give him to you?"

She waited for an answer, but received none.

The monolithic remained still and silent beneath its robes.

Kath jabbed and wiggled the broom in the angel's face, not getting close enough to make contact, but making her willingness to do so clear enough. "I asked you a question, so have some manners. Remove your hood and answer me!"

Incredibly, the angel obliged. He reached up and lowered his hood.

Beneath the old, grey cloth was something unexpected. The angel's golden hair spilled over his shoulders beneath a beautiful face with an exquisite complexion. His sparkling eyes were breathtaking cyan, and they were studying Kath curiously.

Lucas moved up beside Harry and whispered. "That would be Lord Michael himself."

Harry considered for a moment. "You mean from the bible?"

"No, I mean from real life. That is God's Field General himself, Archangel Michael. My brother, the Angel of death."

"If he's your brother can't you make him stop? Talk to him?"

"You really don't understand family do you, Harry boy? One thing about Michael is that the only person he listens to is his dear daddy. That's why he was always favourite. Bloody eejit!"

Something was happening up ahead. The angel standing in front of Kath – *the Archangel Michael. Jeez!* – produced something from within his cloak. Something long and metallic that ignited in flames as soon as it hit the air.

"There she is," said Lucas. "The beauty herself. You know, back in the day, that sword belonged to me. Michael took it from me during the Holy War. It looks better on him, anyway."

Harry shook his head. "What the bloody hell are you talking about?"

"The fiery sword of damnation. The sword that turned Sodom and Gomorrah to ashes."

Harry rubbed at his face with ice-cold fingers. This was really it. The end of the world. God had called last orders on mankind and there was only enough time to get one last drink in.

Michael raised his fiery sword, singeing the cold air and creating acrid smoke. Kath stood before him, mesmerised. All of her earlier bluster had evaporated and she was nothing more than a puny human standing before a giant.

Michael brought down his flaming sword with a brutal slash. The blade hissed and spat as Kath's blood instantly congealed on its shaft, turning to black powder and peppering the snow. It had cut through her like a scalpel through cheese.

Kath turned around and faced Harry and Lucas. For a moment it looked like she was okay. Then her head started to tilt forward, independent of the rest of her body. Harry winced as Kath's headless body fell forward into the snow, turning it red.

Harry ran, leaving Lucas behind; not seeing any reason to ask him to follow. He ploughed through the snow with all his energy, kicking and clawing with only one thing on his mind: *Steph!* He had no idea where he was going and only hoped that it was towards The Trumpet. With the apocalyptic freeze, as well as an army of flawless Angels trying to send him to Hell, Harry knew that the rest of his life was measured in minutes rather than hours or days. For so long he had wanted nothing but to die, to leave the world and all its pain behind him, but, right now, staying alive long enough to reach Steph was his only motivation.

The snowfall seemed to increase with every second. It was up to Harry's waist now and still rising. Before long, there would be no world left. No buildings, no roads, no rivers. Nothing. Just unending snow, rising. Rising. Rising.

Harry struggled onwards, each step seizing up his calves, stabbing the tender muscle with icy daggers. If only he could go back and do the right thing. He'd known killing Thomas Morris was wrong. Had known it for sure when he saw the regret and the sorrow in the man's eyes just before he died. Thomas Morris had killed Harry's family, but at the moment of his death, he had been deeply sorry. Harry knew that because Thomas never struggled.

Now the whole world was accepting punishment for what Harry had done. He imagined the billions of people who had already frozen to death. He wondered how many people were still alive, trying to convince their children that the snow would stop soon and that everything would be okay, that it was just bad weather. Harry started to weep, but wiped the tears away before they froze. He had to keep going, didn't deserve time to stop and cry. When the angels finally sent him to Hell he would welcome it, because that was where he belonged. But not now. Not yet.

Ahead, Harry saw the dark rectangle of a building up on a hill. It had to be The Trumpet. With renewed vigour, he began to dive and leap through the snow, sinking and climbing with every step. He was moving at a snail's pace, but gradually, slowly, the building came into view. And it was indeed a pub.

"Thank God. Actually...screw that. Fuck God."

He reached the bottom of the hill and looked up. The pub was dark, deserted. Lifeless. A dead building in a dead world.

As he climbed the hill, Harry felt the angels nearby. "Damn you," he shouted back at them. They stood at the bottom of the hill, each of them now with their hoods down, exposing their beautiful faces and gossamer hair. Harry knew they brought only death and misery. "Damn you," he shouted again. "Just let me see her."

Lucas had said that angels could not set foot inside a den of iniquity. That meant Steph might still be safe inside.

He was nearly there, only a few more metres to the doorway.

Harry stopped in his tracks, falling into the snow and looking up at the figure blocking his way. He'd been so close. "Okay, you got me. Just get it over with."

"Get what over with, Harry Boy?"

Harry looked up. "Lucas!"

"Aye," Lucas offered out his hand and helped Harry to his feet. "I thought you were never going to get here, fella. Took your sweet time."

Harry smiled, happy to see the Devil. But he wasted no time in pushing passed and barging at the pub's door.

It was frozen shut.

Harry was about to howl out in defeat when Lucas strolled up beside him.

"Keep your hair on, lad." He placed a hand on the door. Steam came from his touch and the frost began to melt. Lucas banged his fist once, twice, and the door swung open slowly. He looked at Harry and grinned. "Three millennium in the Hellzone Boy Scouts."

"No shit?" Harry made his way inside and headed straight for the bar, the sudden feeling of an even, solid floor disorientating his weary legs. The room was in darkness with the flickering flame of only a single candle left, but Harry had been there enough times to know where he was going blind. He made it to the bar in six memorised steps and was shocked to find Peter's dead body on the floor. There was no time to fret about it now, though.

Grabbing the remaining candle, Harry made his way behind the bar and into the corridor. Immediately, the freezing temperature told him something was wrong. Earlier the corridor had acted as a flume for the warm air of the fire in the cellar below, but now the air was frigid. That meant the fire was out.

"Shit, shit, shit!" Harry took the steps two at a time, lucky to make it down to the bottom without tripping. As his feet planted on the cellar floor, he moved the candle in a quick semi-circle. The room smelt heavily of smoke, but the dustbin fire was unlit. Next to it was the unmoving form of Old Graham. Harry felt his gorge rise, the fear and sickness taking a hold of him as his mind screamed out with grief. He turned around slowly, illuminating the dark corners of the cellar, searching desperately...

He found Damien first. The lad was slumped in the corner. Harry knelt down to feel the lad's cheek and quickly realised he was dead. Damien's mid-section was covered in blood from some kind of deep wound. Was it the work of Nigel? Despite the freezing cold, Damien was without his thick puffer jacket.

Harry found it nearby, wrapped around Jess. She was dead too. Harry shone the candle light over her face and saw her lips and frosted eyelids. She had finally succumbed to the cold. Had she taken Damien's jacket after he had died? Or had he offered it to her before?

The third body wrapped beneath the blankets made Harry feel faint, paralysed with fear.

Steph lay, swaddled up to the eyeballs by layer upon layer of sheets and blankets. She looked as delicate and as beautiful as Harry had ever seen her and he finally allowed himself to cry. He reached out and touched her face. Like the other's it was ice cold. "I'm sorry," he said. "I'm sorry that I caused all this and that I never got to say goodbye. I used to think I came here every night to get drunk and forget about the past, but tonight I've realised I kept coming back to see you. You were the only person who allowed me to see tomorrow and know that it would be easier than today. It was you that took away my pain, not the booze."

"...Harry?"

The word was barely a whisper. A few moments passed and Harry started to think that his crippled mind was playing tricks on him.

"Harry," Steph whispered again, louder this time.

"Steph! Steph, yes it's me, Harry?"

It didn't seem like she could, but she knew he was there. It was obvious by the look in her eyes. "Harry...I was worried about you."

"I'm sorry I didn't make it back sooner."

"It's...okay. I knew you'd come back. You're a good man, Harry."

Harry bit his lip so hard that he tasted blood in his mouth. "I wish that were true, but I let everyone down. This is all my fault."

Steph shook her head, eyes still closed as though she were reciting a dream. "No, Harry. The only person you ever let down was y-yourself. It's not your fault what happened...what happened...to you."

Harry wiped tears and snot from his face. "You know what I wish, Steph?"

"No, Harry. What do you...wish?"

"I wish that instead of killing Thomas Morris

that night, I'd have met you instead. Maybe you could have saved me. If God is going to judge us all, then he should have tested someone like you, not a loser like me. God stacked the deck against us all when he took my family and left me to be the judge."

Steph's face lit up in a smile that stuck for a moment before falling away. She went very still and did not reply.

"Steph," Harry said softly, but it was no use. She was gone.

Harry moved forward and kissed Steph on her lips. He wanted nothing more than for her to be alive a moment longer so that she could kiss him back, but was thankful that he at least got to say goodbye.

Harry left the cellar and went back upstairs into the pub. He lit the way with the last dying candle. Lucas was already waiting for him, propped up at the bar with a beer in his hand.

"Harry Boy, how about one for the road." He offered Harry a bottle, who took it from him silently. His sobriety didn't matter much anymore. There would be no opportunity for him to clean himself up and make amends.

"It's time isn't it?" he said after sipping down some of the beer.

Lucas nodded. "Up to you, lad. To be honest I'm only here tonight because I'm duty-bound. The apocalypse and all that, you know? It's kind of traditional that I be here. It would be like having a party without cake if the Devil didn't turn up at the End."

Harry took another sip of beer, before disagreeing. "That can't be the only reason. You didn't have to turn up at the pub tonight. You didn't have to try and help."

Lucas laughed his charming Irishman laugh. "Aye, that much is true. Michael summoned me here to watch the destruction of mankind as a kind of punishment. I suppose he thinks I had a hand in bringing down the ceiling – leading men astray and all that hokum."

Harry shrugged. "Didn't you?"

Lucas swigged his beer down to the bottom third. "Well, yes and no. When I fell from Heaven I hated you all with a fury unrivalled – God's most prized creation and the keepers of freewill, yada yada yada. I sought to corrupt you all, to bring you down into the dirt so that God would see how lowly you little fellas were. You know what I learned, though?"

"What?"

"I realised that I was wasting my time. Man was doing a fine thing of fucking things up on their own.

I had a hand, here and there, sure; but Hitler, Bin Laden, that plucky fella Ted Bundy, the nuclear-feckin-bomb? All that wickedness was on you. The worst, most corrupt men who ever lived are mostly men I've never met. I may be the Devil, but you lot are evil."

"Then why does Heaven blame you? Why have they brought you here to watch us die?"

"Because I fell in love with humanity. I rebelled against God because I wanted to live by my own rules. After a few hundred years I realised that humanity was no different. I realised that man wasn't in God's image, but in mine. Men have spent hundreds of years fighting for their freedom, the same way I did in Heaven. Eventually I stopped trying to destroy you and started living amongst you. I buried my anger with God and stopped being the bogeyman you write books about. The only reason I'm here is so that Michael can make a point."

"What point?"

"That anyone who goes against God's will are destined to fall."

Harry laughed.

"Why do you laugh, Harry Boy?"

"Nothing. I just find it amusing that the Devil is benevolent and God is wrathful."

Lucas laughed too. "Well, I hope it teaches you

not to believe what the media says. Especially the ancient Aramaic right-wing media. The bible got me all wrong, I tell you."

The two of them shared a laugh and finished their beers. After a few moments, Harry put his empty bottle on the bar. "Time to go, I guess, but before I do, can I ask you a question?"

Lucas shrugged. "You've done little else for the past few hours. Why stop now?"

Harry took that to mean 'yes', so he asked his question: "You mentioned the levels of Hell, earlier?"

"Aye, I did."

"Which is the worst?"

Lucas didn't seem comfortable at the question. "Well...it's all relative, really. The punishment fits the crime."

"I know that." Harry could feel his body shutting down under the constant attack of the cold. He had to finish this before he gave in to hyperthermia. "But surely some layers are worse than others. Where do the very worst go, like Hitler? People like that?"

"Well, if you listen to Dante Alighieri then there are just seven levels, but in truth the regions of Hell are never ending and infinitely wide. Time and space is eternal and there are an unfathomable number of planes of existence, but the deepest deepest level is reserved only for pure, irredeemable evil. Light doesn't exist there and neither does hope of any kind. It is suffering and despair without beginning or end, a place where agony reigns and flays the skin of any soul unfortunate to end up there. It is a Hell beyond human understanding, and no human, not even the vilest, has ever committed sin harsh enough to be sent there. It is deserving of no man. It was created to hold one being: me."

Harry raised an eyebrow. "A Hell so bad that it was made to torture the Devil himself?"

Lucas nodded and seemed upset by the thought of it. "Aye, they call it...The Abyss."

Harry took that information in and held onto it. The Abyss. The darkest, most desperate level of hell that is fit only for the Devil himself. A place of torture beyond anything a man could imagine.

"Lucas," Harry said. "It's been a pleasure meeting you and I sincerely hope that the Abyss never claims you. Sounds strange to say, but I think you might actually be one of the good guys."

Lucas laughed. "I have many names, but that's a first."

Harry shook the Devil's hand and walked away, leaving his candle on the bar and entering the darkness outside.

35

T he blizzard had finally begun to die down, its job almost completed. The world had been rendered featureless. Everywhere Harry looked was buried beneath giant snow banks. Across the street, the tops of buildings were just about visible, but their doorways were covered up past their lintels. Lucas might have had something to do with the fact the Trumpet was not yet being buried.

At the bottom of the hill stood the angels, forming a line that seemed to stretch on forever.

Harry hailed them. "I'm coming down. I give up, okay?"

Archangel Michael nodded. He raised his arms out in front of him and shot fire.

"Hey!" Harry protested. "I said I'm coming down."

But burning him wasn't Michael's intention. The stone steps leading down from the pub appeared beneath the rapidly melting snow as the fires quickly burned out.

Harry cleared his throat. "Oh, eh...cheers."

He took the newly uncovered steps slowly, in no rush to test out the theory brewing in his head.

Michael was patient. Time probably meant little when you were eternal

When Harry eventually reached the bottom of the steps, he saw that Michael was smiling at him reassuringly, like a Dentist about to perform a root canal.

"Welcome, Sinner," said Michael in a voice far milder than he'd used in previous instances. His presence was no less awesome because of it.

"It's Harry."

"As you wish, Harry Jobson."

"Just Harry is fine...you know what, don't even worry about it."

"Are you ready? It is time."

"I just have a couple of questions first."

Harry thought he saw irritation stream through the archangel's eyes. Obviously, The Angel of Death didn't appreciate being delayed by a mere mortal. He probably found it 'impertinent'.

"Ask your questions quickly, Sinner."

There's that word again. Fucker!

Harry decided not to let it bother him. He would have far worse to endure.

"After what I did, after I committed the....final sin, or whatever it is; it condemned everyone to Hell, right?"

Michael nodded.

"Do you think that's fair?"

"It is His will."

Harry nodded. "Right, right, didn't think appealing to your better nature would work, so I guess I should skip straight to plan B."

"Plan B?" Michael repeated without feeling.

"Yeah, I want to make a deal."

Michael exploded, but managed to do so without moving an inch. He seemed to oppress the air around him. "YOU DO NOT MAKE DEALS WITH AN AGENT OF HEAVEN. YOUR WILL IS INCONSEQUENTIAL TO HIS DECISIONS. YOU WILL OBEY, SINNER."

Harry swallowed, tried to gather himself, and continued. "Okay, okay, but my final wish is that you hear me out. If He ignores my offer then so be it. I will take what comes to me. Just, please, allow me to at least amuse you. I have given myself up willingly, after all."

"Speak your deal. Amuse us."

Okay, here goes.

"Send me to the Abyss."

Michael actually seemed to flinch at the suggestion and Harry hoped that it was a good sign.

"Don't send me to whatever Hell I deserve, send me to the Hell that no man deserves. Send me there and leave me there forever."

Michael seemed to soften, no longer angry. It almost seemed like he was suddenly in awe of Harry. His sparkly eyes were wide and fixed. "You speak of things you can never hope to understand, Harry Jobson. The Abyss is a punishment befitting no man. Why would you ask for such endless suffering?"

"I'll tell you, but first let me know, can it be done? Can you send me there?"

Michael nodded. "Yes."

"Then my offer is that you send me to the Abyss in exchange for all of the souls that have been damned to Hell since I murdered Thomas Morris. Save Steph, Jess, Jerry, and all the others who don't deserve Hell. Send me to the Abyss to pay for humanity's sin. Will my torture there outweigh the debt needed to spare these people?"

Michael shook his head and began to be sob. The sight of it was almost heart-wrenching – the very act of an angel crying seemed to be the embodiment of the word 'tragedy'. "The debt of suffering would be a thousand times more than that which is owed. You cannot imagine such suffering. You should not make such frivolous suggestions without knowing the full consequences."

Harry stepped forward and was amazed to see Michael wince. Apparently, talk of the Abyss was enough to make the archangel anxious. "Then show me. Show me and let me decide. If I can still make the same decision afterwards, then you can decide if you will honour my proposal."

"So be it," said Michael, placing both of his hands upon Harry's head.

What happened next was indescribable. Images and feelings shot through Harry's very soul, showing him inhuman tortures at the hands of even more inhuman creatures. It was a place of endless and unimaginable pain and suffering. A place where every second lasted centuries and was enough to break a man's mind into a million agonised pieces. It was the heart and soul of Hell itself.

Harry reeled backwards from Michael's grip, falling onto his back and panting in the snow. Tears fell from his eyes and already his soul felt damaged just from seeing mere fleeting images of the Abyss. His soul was bleeding.

Yet, Harry forced himself back to his feet, weak, broken, and terrified. Taking a breath was hard, almost impossible, but he made himself speak. He had to speak.

"Spare their souls," he said. "Send me to...send me...send me to the Abyss."

Michael seemed sad, in fact the archangel's very being seemed to turn melancholy. "So be it, Harry Jobson."

God's Angel of Death reached forward to place his hands on Harry's forehead, but before he made contact, Michael took a step backwards and looked up at the sky. All the other angels did too. All of them gazed upwards in a never ending line. Harry looked upwards too, but saw nothing but empty, black sky.

Michael began to smile. In fact, joy itself seemed to cascade from the archangel's body in bright, incandescent waves. He looked at Harry and nodded, as if he knew something that he did not. "Goodbye, Harry Jobson."

Michael placed his hands on Harry's skull.

The pain of his soul being ripped from his body was exquisite. Like having a thousand fish hooks dragged through the insides of his veins. Harry's final thought was about how much worse it could possibly get.

EPILOGUE

A news reporter came onscreen. She was enveloped by an over-sized pink ski-jacket. "Good evening, I'm Jane Hamilton, reporting for Midland-UK News. Fortunately, after nearly 19-inches of snow, the weather in Britain finally seems to be improving. Temperatures have begun to rise and the snow is predicted to end soon. Roads are in the process of being reopened while train links are expected to resume within the next few d-"

Harry found himself at the bar of The Trumpet. It didn't happen instantly and it felt as though he had flowed back into his body like gravy through a sieve. At first he remembered nothing...

Until the person next to him spoke.

"How you feeling there, Harry Boy?"

Harry almost choked.

"Calm down there, fella. You made it. All is well for now. The big guy gave you lot another chance."

Harry was stunned. "He...he did?"

Lucas sipped the pint in front of him. "It's what you planned, isn't it?"

"Well...yeah, but I didn't expect to be back at the bar. I thought I really would go to the Abyss, or maybe, best-case-scenario, God would let me into Heaven for my good deed. I didn't expect...this."

"Well, as it turns out the man-upstairs loves a little sacrifice, here and there, and yours was a biggy. Reminds me of another fella who died for humanity's sins once upon a time. The big guy decided your final deed was enough to convince him that maybe humanity still has a fighting chance. Good on ya, lad! Though you're the only one that can remember any of it, so don't expect a fanfare."

Harry shook his head, blinking like he'd just awoken from a dream. "So why are you here? Here now, I mean?"

"I wanted to say goodbye. I like this crazy, fecked-up world as much as anyone, and without it I wouldn't have a thing to do but sit around in an overcrowded Hell. Truth is I knew there was a chance you might turn things around."

"That's why you were here wasn't it? To help me?"

Lucas hushed him and looked left and right shiftily. "Keep your voice down. If Michael and his choir of pansies hear that, they'll come after me with their self-righteous wings all in a flap. I didn't come to help you. I just wanted to make sure you were...properly informed of all the options."

"Thank you."

Lucas nodded. "Just enjoy your life while you can. You may have gotten a reprieve, but there're are dark times coming. Just because God isn't going to destroy you all, doesn't mean you won't somehow manage to do it yourself."

"What do you mean?"

"Just don't plan on any cruises."

Harry didn't understand. He looked around the brightly-lit bar and still struggled to believe it. Everything was as it should be. The lights were on, the room was warm. "Well, Lucas," he said, turning back around, "if you don't fill me in on what's going to happen, how can I know what to expect? Lucas?"

The Prince of Hell had departed, disappearing without Harry or anybody else in the bar noticing. Old Graham sat at the end of the counter, drinking by himself and staring into space. Harry found it ironic to be so happy to see the old codger. He made his way over to say hello.

"Hey, Harry," Old Graham said when he saw Harry approach.

"Hey, Graham. You're into History and all that, aren't you? Weren't you in the army?"

The old man beamed proudly. "That I was, twenty long years. Royal Signals I was. Hit the Falklands a full hour before the SAS did. Yet they got all the glory."

"Brilliant," said Harry. "I wanted to find out more about the past, and about brave men like you. I was thinking about going to the Imperial War museum this weekend. Would you come with me and be my guide? I'll pay, of course. You'd be doing me a favour."

For a moment, Harry thought the old man was going to fall off his stool, but he gathered himself and nodded enthusiastically. "You know, I haven't been out of this bloody town in eight years. I would love to come, Harry. Thank you, I mean it."

Harry patted him on the back. "Good. We'll have to make a regular thing of it. Right now, though, I've got to go, so I'll come by tomorrow night to see you. You'll be here right?"

Old Graham laughed. "Does the Devil have horns?"

"I think you'd be surprised."

Old Graham obviously didn't understand and Harry was glad about that. Knowledge of the night's previous events was a burden he was more than happy to shoulder alone. He walked over to the centre of the bar. On the other side was someone he wanted to talk to very much.

Steph smiled when she saw him. Harry couldn't forgive himself for ever ignoring how beautiful she was.

"Harry," she said to him. "Another drink?"

Harry shook his head. "No thanks, I've given up."

Steph looked at him in bewilderment. "What since five minutes ago?"

"It seems like longer, but, yes, I have. Time to start living my life in better ways. Who knows when it will end?"

"Good for you, Harry. Does that mean you won't be coming in here anymore? Cus that would make me sad."

"Maybe," said Harry. "Which is why I wanted to know if you'd come to dinner with me on your next night off."

Steph's seemed confused at first, but then she smiled. "I'm free Thursday night."

"It's a date then. You can tell me all about this

pet grooming business you're going to start up. I used to have a business myself. Perhaps I can help."

Steph was surprised. "How did you know about that?"

"I don't know, but I want to hear all about it, and about you. Right now I have to go, so I'll be back tomorrow night to arrange with you."

Harry left Steph in a fluster behind the bar and moved towards the exit. Damien was lying across the sofa, hogging the fire

"The fuck you looking at?"

Harry smiled. Finally he could see through Damien's hard man disguise and see the lost boy beneath. "I just wanted to ask you something, Damien."

"What?"

"I was thinking of starting up a carpentry business, like the one I used to have, but I need a partner – someone young and smart. An apprentice, really. I don't have a son to teach what I know. I used to but he died just over a year ago. His name was Toby. You would have liked him."

Damien's eyes flickered back and forth, as if he expected a sneak attack to come at any moment.

Harry continued, not giving the lad too long to think. "I know you're a busy guy, Damien, but I don't think you enjoy selling drugs. You're better than that and I'd really like to help you be successful in a less dangerous way. I need someone like you. I think we can make a lot of good honest money together. If your dad tries to make your life hard, he'll have me to answer to."

For a while it seemed like Damien was going to strike out and hit Harry, but then his eyes moistened and his lower lip trembled. "Y-You're serious?"

"Extremely." Harry went for a handshake. "Do we have a deal? A new start for both of us."

Damien smiled and shook Harry's hand vigorously. "Yeah, man. Yeah, deal."

"Great, I'll speak to you about it soon." Harry walked away, but Damien stopped him.

"Harry?"

"Yeah?"

"Thanks. You know, for the opportunity and everything. Most people just think I'm a thug."

"You and I are going to change their opinion."

Harry headed over to the exit and prepared to leave. There was a lot to do in order to get his life back on track, but first he needed to find a phone. He had a call to make to the Police about a sicko named Nigel who liked to keep women's fingers in his lorry.

Harry was going to start living his life again, putting the world right and making things better, one thing at a time. For the first time in a long time, he was finally looking forward instead of back.

The only thing to worry about was whatever Lucas's final warning had meant. *Dark times are coming. Don't plan on any cruises.*

Harry shook the warnings from his mind and smiled. Whether humanity had one day left or one million, he had at least bought himself some time to die with dignity and pride. He had time to get his life back. Whatever happened next was up to God.

When Harry left the pub, the snow had stopped and the sun was shining.

CLICK HERE TO GET 5 IAIN ROB WRIGHT BOOKS FOR FREE!

SPECIAL EDITION BONUS CONTENT

TALES FROM THE FINAL WINTER

CHANCE OF SNOW

"I can't believe this!" Richard turned away from the window and faced his family, each of them huddled beneath a blanket. "I know it's winter, and everything, but this is *Florida*."

Richard's family, daughter and wife, said nothing. They knew better than to converse with him in the state he was in. He wasn't angry at them, of course – wasn't angry at anyone in fact – but he'd built the vacation home in Florida purely to get away from home during the winter months. He expected snow like this in England, but not here.

Richard looked back out of the window and stared out over the lake that edged his second home. The water was starting to freeze over and snow banks had built up around its edges. If there were any alligators currently in there then he held little hope for their survival.

Least I'm not them, thought Richard.

"Why don't you come and sit down, honey," said his wife. "I'm sure there'll be a weather forecast soon. They'll tell us what to expect."

Richard huffed. "Well, they didn't bloody-well tell us to expect this, did they? Would have stayed in England if I knew there was going to be all this snow."

"Miriam said it's the same back home," his wife stated. "I called her this afternoon. They're completely snowed in."

"It's like this everywhere," Richard's daughter chimed in. "They said on the Internet that every country in the world is covered in snow. There's a group on Facebook that say it's all down to aliens."

"Don't be so stupid, Charlotte." Richard went and took a seat beside his wife and wrestled the television remote from her hands."

"Don't snatch," she said meekly.

Richard ignored her and flicked through the TV stations. He hated American channels; they were filled with so much dross. How he longed to flip on BBC One and get some straight-forward news. Eventually he found a station that seemed to be discussing the weather and he settled on it, resting back into the sofa."

"...temperatures expected to drop further in the coming hours and are likely to remain there," the weather report informed. "Be sure to wrap up warm, Florida, and enjoy the snow while we have it. It's once in a lifetime."

"Enjoy the snow," Richard grimaced. "Who comes to Florida to enjoy the snow? They certainly don't spend half-a-million building a house here to *enjoy the snow.*"

Richard's wife stood up from the sofa and headed off. "I'll go make a pot of tea and turn the heating up. I wish you'd stop stressing. We're still on holiday and together, aren't we?"

Richard let out a sigh and rubbed at his cold forearms. He turned to Charlotte who was sat on the armchair beside the sofa. "Am I being a bit of an ogre?"

Charlotte raised an eyebrow. "Little bit. Just chill out, dad. You're upsetting mom."

She was right of course. Richard was not unaware of how tightly-wound he could be. That was why he'd built the holiday home sixty miles north of Miami. It was supposed to be their place to relax and spend some quality time together.

Good job you're making of it!

Richard stood up from the sofa and made for the kitchen.

"Where are you going?" Charlotte asked him.

"To apologise to your mother." He headed through a door that bordered the lounge and entered the family kitchen area. It was a large, modern room with a breakfast bar at its tiled centre. It was his wife's favourite part of the house. Currently, she stood up against the oversized ceramic sink, filling up the kettle beneath one of the chrome taps. He went up behind her and placed his hands on her shoulders. She did not jump so she must have expected his arrival.

"You calmed down yet?"

Richard squeezed her shoulders gently and began rubbing. "When do I ever calm down? The best you can hope for is that I realise when I'm being insufferable."

"And have you?"

"Have I what?"

"Realised that you're being insufferable?"

Richard turned his wife around to face him and planted a soft kiss on her cheek. "Yes, I realise, sweetheart. I'm sorry, okay?"

She kissed him back. "You're forgiven. Let's just enjoy ourselves for the rest of the week. There'll be plenty of sun next time, I'm sure."

Richard nodded glumly. "Hope you're right."

His wife was about to reply to him, when Charlotte's voice carried from the other room. "Hey, mom, dad, I think you better come look at this."

Richard and his wife looked at each other and frowned. Together they exited the kitchen and walked back through to the carpeted lounge. Charlotte was stood up against the window where Richard had earlier been looking out at the lake.

"What is it?" Richard asked her.

Charlotte turned around and faced him. Her expression was mostly one of curiosity, but Richard could see a hint of anxiety there as well. "Come look."

Richard walked up beside his daughter and leant forward to look through the double-glazed glass window. Outside was the same, semi-frozen lake that he'd already seen, snow piling up all around it as fresh powder continued to fall. "Everything seems normal to me, sweetheart."

Charlotte nudged him on the arm. "Look closer, at the far end of the lake."

Richard focused his eyes further afield. If it were not for the outdoor lighting then he would have seen nothing at all, but thanks to the illuminating glare of the high-watt bulbs, Richard could see what his daughter was trying to point out to him. "Gators?"

"Yeah," Charlotte replied. "What are they doing?"

Richard's best guess was that they were migrating. They were common visitors to the lake and they always seemed happy to bask and feed in a group, so seeing them all bunch together now was not all that interesting. What was a little more unordinary, though, was the fact that they were currently fighting their way from the lake, pushing and burrowing through the snow banks that towered over them. "Looks like they're leaving the lake," Richard guessed. "I'm not surprised with the water as cold as it is."

"But where would they go?" Charlotte asked. "Surely they wouldn't be any better off in the snow?"

Richard shrugged. "I expect they're just as confused as everyone else is in Florida right now." His wife was nearby and he smiled at her so she knew there was nothing to worry about. "Go get that tea on, sweetheart. We can settle down and try to watch a film."

His wife smiled back and quickly departed, leaving him alone with his daughter. Charlotte was still looking out of the window, enthralled with the alligator's behaviour.

"There must be at least fifty of them out there, all in a group," she said.

"Will you just get away from that window? I want to close the curtains and keep the heat in."

Charlotte sighed and turned away from the window. Richard took her place and prepared to close the curtains. He took one last look outside at the departing alligators and let out a chuckle. It really was something to behold. He stretched out sideward and grasped the curtain and started sliding it across the window, but, before he got it all the way across, something made him stop.

"What the...?"

Charlotte came back over to the window and looked out through the small gap that still remained through the curtain. "What?"

Richard didn't turn to face his daughter. His eyes were too transfixed on what he was seeing. "There's someone out there in the snow."

"You're joking," said Charlotte. "They must be mad. It's freezing.

"Mad or not," said Richard, "they're there."

Richard left the window and marched across the lounge towards the French doors at the rear of the house. They led out to a veranda which doubled as a smoking shelter for his wife's habit. As soon as he pulled open one of the doors, the cold hit him like a punch in the face. His nose started burning almost immediately as the chill bit at his extremities.

He stepped out into the snow nevertheless, but wishing he was wearing something more substantial than trainers – snowfall was not something he'd packed for. The growing wind also made him wish hard for a winter coat.

"Who's out here?" he shouted into the floodlit night. "This is private property. I'm afraid you'll have to leave."

There was no answer and Richard took it as a threatening sign. He stepped cautiously as he approached the front of the house where he had seen the stranger. He couldn't be sure, but it had looked to be a man; a tall one wrapped in a billowing coat – or maybe a cloak.

When Richard reached the side of the house that faced the lake, he was surprised to find the stranger was still standing there, quite assumedly. The man seemed to care little about his trespass.

"I said you need to leave," he reiterated. "You're worrying my family."

"Their worry is well-founded," came the stranger suddenly with a baritone voice.

Richard took a step towards the man. "Is that a threat?"

"A threat would imply uncertainty. There is none of that here."

Richard examined the stranger with suspicion that was beginning to border on concern. The figure towered above the snow and was tall enough that Richard would not fancy his chances if the stranger attacked him. Unsettling too was the unusual cloak covering the man from head to feet – it was not something an ordinary person would wear in the 21st Century.

"Look," said Richard. "What do you want?"

The stranger seemed to move very slightly to face him as he replied. "I desire nothing. His will is my will and I do only as requested."

Richard didn't understand. He was cold and extremely confused. "Who is he? What are you talking about?"

"You ask of Him? You should know your Lord and revere him with the love and respect he demands. Perhaps if you had, your fate would be less perilous."

Richard had had enough. He took the final few clumsy steps towards the stranger and pointed a finger right at his face. "You get out of here, right now. I love America, I really do, but you don't half have some bloody nutcases here. Leave, or I will call the police."

The figure let out a laugh that rattled Richard's very bones. "You demand nothing of me, mortal. Your threats are puny. Your insolence, maddening."

Richard was lost for words. This person was obviously a madman, just by the way he spoke, but so too was he huge and menacing. *What the hell should I do?* Richard decided that lowering his tone would be best. Steering away from any animosity seemed far safer than inciting any. "I'm sorry to offend you. Could you just tell me who you are, please?"

The stranger lowered his head as if to focus on Richard more clearly. The cowl was too tightly wrapped to give anything away about the man's face; not even the eyes could be seen. To Richard's surprise, the cloaked stranger raised both hands and began to pull away the hood. Slowly the cloth fell away to reveal a face of utter beauty and a head full of mahogany-streaked hair.

Richard took a breath and struggled to let it back out again. "Jesus!"

The beautiful man shook his head and seemed angry at the word. "You do not speak of The Son without reason. I am not Jesus."

Richard was in awe. "Then who are you?"

The stranger's face was without emotion as he answered. "I am Mika'eel. I am the first Harbinger of this world's demise."

"I-I'm sorry? Demise?"

Mika'eel nodded. "Your time of decadence has ceased. This world is to be no more."

Richard shook his head. "Are you...are you a terrorist?"

The man showed no expression – in fact he seemed incapable – but he did shake his head. "I am no terrorist. I spread not terror, but extinction. I bring snow and ice to freeze further the cold hearts of man. It is an honour for you to meet me, an Angel of the highest order."

Richard choked. "An Angel? Are you crazy?"

"Crazy is a state of mind beneath me – as are you, Richard Pointer."

"How do you know my name?"

"I know all names, all fates, all journeys. Yours is a particularly interesting one. Your true mother abandoned you, but this you do not know. Yet that nagging feeling of rejection has spurred your every decision. You are a callous businessman, a competitive being, and a domineering husband. Your wife dreads you."

Richard's heart throbbed at the accusation, causing him actual pain. Perhaps the reason it hurt so much was because, deep down, he knew it was true. He was a control-freak and always had been. The fact that he allowed himself to control his lovely wife made him feel wretched.

"Do not fret, Richard Pointer. There are many men worse than you. Despite their dread, your family loves you. Go to them now. Comfort them as the end draws near. You have an opportunity that many will not. You know that the end is coming; you can say the things that need saying and die with an unburdened soul."

Richard looked at the...*Angel*... and knew that it was all true. The world was truly ending and this being before him was its deliverer. Life was an inconsequential mess and it was now coming to an abrupt finish. Despite the fear that knowledge brought, Richard was indeed grateful for the gift of knowing. He would enjoy his final evening with his family; enjoy the final winter of man's existence. Richard turned around and headed for the house, to be with his family and wait for the end of the world.

COLD SHOULDER

"Any more wine?" asked Amanda.

John turned to his wife and sighed. "Haven't you had enough tonight?"

"Just go get another bottle and stop giving me grief. It's not like I have work tomorrow. Maybe not all week if it keeps snowing like this – Whoop!"

John shook his head. He knew his wife was drunk because he was too. They'd polished off a bottle of red each and the heavy feeling it left him was dragging him towards sleep. Amanda was different though – she never quit while the night was still young. There was no point arguing with her, so John diligently went and got another bottle of Shiraz from the kitchen cabinet. There was another three bottles after this one and he worried. His wife would never drink them all – nowhere near in fact – but she may well keep going until she passed out.

Or turns nasty.

John re-entered the living room and unscrewed the bottle cap. He leant over Amanda's glass and started pouring until the glass was almost full. He then topped up his own glass halfway.

"Sit down, honey. *Never Mind The Buzzcocks* is coming on. You like that."

He did and was grateful that his wife was in an accommodating mood. He sat down beside her and put a hand on her lap. It was a struggle to focus on the television, however, because something was on his mind. "You think Jess is going to make it home from work okay?"

"Yeah," slurred Amanda. "Why wouldn't she?"

John shrugged. "The snow's gotten pretty bad. Have you seen it recently?"

"Couple hours ago. Wasn't that bad."

"It is now. I'm starting to get a bit worried. You think I should try and walk down and meet her at the supermarket. Her shift finishes in ten minutes."

Amanda turned the TV up slightly and frowned. "She'll be fine. If you leave now you'd only end up missing her."

John thought she was probably right. The weather was close to a full-blown blizzard now and it was difficult to see beyond a couple of feet. Unless he knew the exact path that his daughter took home, they would miss each other. He didn't fancy going out in the cold pointlessly.

On the television, the programme began and John and his wife watched it. It was funny, but John couldn't find it in him to laugh. The same wasn't true of Amanda who was cackling at every joke, even if it was only mildly funny.

How the hell did we end up like this, he thought to himself secretly. Amanda hadn't always been like this. The underlying edge of aggression she now possessed seemed to grow more volatile each year, and her drinking was becoming more common-place. His own drinking had gotten much worse than it used to be too. After twenty years of marriage, an unspoken resentment had begun to take control of their relationship. John didn't know how to stop it and was unsure if he even wanted to. It felt like something *needed* to change.

He wouldn't change the past though. Most of those twenty married years had been joyous, moving down to contentedness in the latter half. And of course they had a beautiful daughter. Jess being born was the proudest moment of John's life and he never stopped feeling that way about her. She was a strong girl with a character he admired.

In fact she seemed to have many of her mother's good points – he just hoped that she lacked some of the worst.

"You paying attention?" Amanda asked him, breaking him away from his thoughts.

He nodded to her. "Just tired. Think I might go to bed soon."

Amanda huffed. "God, when did you become such a fuddy duddy? It's not even ten yet."

"I just can't hold my wine like some people."

Amanda scowled at him and leant away on the sofa. "What is *that* supposed to mean?"

John sighed and got up from the sofa. "Nothing. Nothing at all. You just do whatever you want, while I go to bed. Think that would suit both of us."

"Would suit me better if your bed was somewhere else."

Amanda often said nasty things when she was drunk, but that one was uncalled for. He turned around and faced her. "You keep saying things like that and you may just get your wish."

Amanda stood up and came at him. "Don't you threaten me."

He took a step away from her. "You're the one who bloody said it! Just sit back down. I'm not in the mood."

He tried to walk away, but Amanda followed. "What's your problem, John?"

He carried on walking. "What's my problem? I'm fine. I just want to go to bed."

"No," said Amanda. "I want to know what your problem is."

John hadn't been aware that he had voiced a problem, but rationality was never a key component of one of Amanda's arguments. He was starting to feel angry, but he had to keep a lid on it. The last thing the situation needed was two drunken people going at each other.

"Stop walking away," Amanda shouted after him.

He did so, turning to look at her. He tried to stay calm. "Look, honey, I'm sorry if I upset you. I don't want to fight. I'm just worried about Jess."

Amanda huffed. "You needn't be."

Something about the way she had just said that raised the hackles on John's neck. He felt a sudden stone of dread in his guts. "What do you mean by that?"

Amanda laughed and walked away. "Nothing. Don't worry about it."

"No," said John, following back after her. "What are you talking about? Why would I not worry about my own goddamn daughter?"

Amanda spun around and looked at him with a hatred that John hadn't realised she'd had for him. Their marriage really was over, he realised. The suffocating sadness that he felt was lessened slightly by the relief that also took root inside of him. He didn't care about any of that right now though. He wanted to know what Amanda had meant. She told him.

"She's not even your daughter," she shouted at him. "She never has been. I was shagging one of the neighbours when we lived in Burnley."

They'd lived in Burnley at the start of their marriage, almost twenty years ago and left five years later. Jess was seventeen. Amanda sat back down on the sofa and stared at the television as though she hadn't said anything. John felt a loathing for his wife now that was almost boundless.

He stood in front of her, blocking the television. "Say that again, and if you're lying..."

Amanda scowled upwards at him. "If I'm lying, what? What you going to do about it? Just get out of this house and don't come back. Jess isn't your daughter so you've got no reason to be here."

Rage took ahold of John as if his entire body was merely a marionette on a flimsy set of strings. Without thinking about it, or even realising he was about to do it, John picked up the half-full bottle of red wine and walloped it over his wife's head.

Amanda fell back, stunned, blood already seeping from a crack on her forehead. The bottle had not broken, so John swung it again, hitting her in the temple. The shock left Amanda's face and was replaced by a look of bewilderment. Still the bottle did not break. Infected with an unbridled rage, down to his very soul, John swung one last time with all his might. This time the bottle shattered, smashing off Amanda's forehead with an almighty *crack!*

John had never seen a dead body before, but he knew he was looking at one right now. He was glad. Now his wife would not become the full-blown monster she was threatening to become. The decaying rot of her spirit had been halted by death and she would pass on with her memory intact. A tear escaped John's eye as he realised he would get to remember his wife as the woman he had loved for so long.

John picked up the wine-soaked dead body from the sofa and started dragging it to the front door. The plan was to dump her somewhere, close by, on the estate. Later he'd call the police and claim she hadn't come home. Until then, he would dump the body and return, sit back and wait for his daughter to get home. He looked forward to raising Jess alone.

WHEN HELL FREEZES OVER

The snow was really falling now. A nervous person might even say that the weather had become unnatural. With every minute that passed, the temperature dropped and water froze. The cold was enough to kill a man stone dead – but not the man that currently stood beneath a blinking streetlight on a desolate council estate.

Although, in all honesty, he wasn't really a man.

Lucas looked up at the moon and saw that it was full. There was something happening tonight, that much was clear. He just hoped it wasn't the thing he was starting to suspect. Four-thousand years of existence was a long time, but Lucas wasn't ready for it to end yet.

I haven't watched the latest series of Dexter, for one.

Lucas walked forward, feet resting on the surface of the snow as if he were weightless. He'd never visited this particular town, it was without any notable history, but there was a lot of supernatural energy suddenly leaked into the world and he had traced it to here. Now he just needed to find out the source.

It wasn't long before he found it. Lucas stopped walking across the snow and turned around. Behind him was an old friend, from long long ago.

"Gabriel?" Lucas raised an eyebrow. "I take your being here to be a bad sign."

The Angel Gabriel stepped forward to approach Lucas and shook his head. "On the contrary, Lucifer. I would say that my presence is an extremely good sign. It signals the end of the decadent cesspool of this humanity. The Lord's patience has worn thin and He has sent forth his armies to-"

"Still towing the company line, huh?" Lucas interrupted without his Irish accent. It was unnecessary in the current company. "You don't seriously buy into the whole apocalypse thingy-majig, do you?"

"It is His will."

Lucas sighed. "So it's really happening then? I'd worried as much."

"The scales have tipped. A sinner was chosen and failed to redeem himself...and therefore his species."

Lucas took another step towards Gabriel. It wasn't confrontational – the war between Angels was a one-time event never to be repeated – he just wanted to read the other Angel's expression. "I always hated that contingency – from the very day Michael dreamt it up. It's perverse to pin the world's hopes on a single individual. So who is it anyway?"

Gabriel took in a breath that he didn't need. "The sinner? Harry Jobson."

Lucas closed his eyes and summoned knowledge – one of the few talents he still retained from his days in Heaven. Harry Jobson was a good man turned bad by events beyond his control, not from any taint of his soul. "That's not fair!" Lucas said, and was aware of how whiny he sounded, but carried on anyway. "If anything, the revenge he took on the man that killed his family only proves the capacity of love he had for them in the first place. If man wasn't capable of great compassion and loyalty, then revenge would be of no interest to them. That's how He made them, so why should they suffer?"

Gabriel was silent and for a moment and almost performed a gesture approaching a shrug. There was a sadness to the Angel that Lucas could sense; like fumes from a petrol can.

"You don't agree with this either," Lucas stated.

Gabriel shook his head futilely. "My opinion is of no consequence."

"No being should accept slavery as a birth right, neither Angel nor Man. To be created is not an obligation to servitude. We have the right to our own opinions. You should have joined me long ago, brother."

Gabriel swiped a hand through the air and fried the falling snowflakes that were unlucky enough to touch him. "Blasphemy! Your unrighteous war sought to enslave man. Now you speak to me of such things as free will?"

Lucas shrugged and resumed his Irish accent. He no longer felt like showing reverence of respect. He was more human than Angel. "Well, a fella can change his mind now, can't he? In fact the almighty father changes his own every five minutes so it seems."

"He is your father too and you will speak ill of him no more. The time for wrath has arrived and you are summoned to be its witness. Your hand in Armageddon is such that you deserve a front row seat."

Lucas wasn't about to accept any more of this pious nonsense. "Look, Gabriel. I know you spend your weekends at Vegas, counting cards and downing Amaretto cocktails like you're trying to put out a fire in your belly, so why don't you cut the bull and start speaking a wee bit of the truth. How can I stop this?"

Gabriel seemed to think for a moment before letting out a sigh that seemed to signal his walls coming down slightly. "Brother, you cannot. While my own fondness of humanity, and its vices, is something I admit to, I will not defy my Lord. Not all can have your strength of rebellion – and not all would even want it. It is done. A concordant has been met and at this very moment a plague of Angels descends to the Earth like you once did – thousands of falling stars ready for retribution. All life will be extinguished."

Lucas couldn't believe what he was hearing. It was this lack of rational compromise that turned him against Heaven in the first place. He didn't miss it. "There are...loop holes?"

"Perhaps," said Gabriel, already turning to walk away. "But can you remember them?"

Lucas shook his head. "I can't, it was too long ago. Gabriel stop, I need answers."

Gabriel turned back around. "I cannot remain

here, Lucifer. I have...duties. If you need answers, perhaps you will find them in there."

The Angel pointed and Lucas spun around. Behind him, on that hill, was a pub called The Trumpet. Lucas smiled to himself.

A drink sounds like a bloody good idea right about now.

NEWS AND WEATHER

"**This** is Jane Hamilton, signing off for Midlands-UK News." Jane handed her microphone to a production assistant and let out a shiver. She was wearing a huge pink ski-jacket but the cold was still getting through. "Was that okay, Steve?"

Her cameraman, Steve, gave her a thumbs up. "Perfect. There might have been a slight issue with snow on the lens, but nothing we could do with things the way they are. "

"I know, it's crazy, right?" Jane looked down from the motorway bridge and examined the tipped-over transit van. She had no idea what the contents were, spilled all over the snow, and each second only shrouded them further in layers of fine white powder. As a professional news reporter, Rule One was always to remain unaffected by the stories she was reporting, but this one gave her the willies. All of the meteorologists back at the studio were flummoxed by the recent weather – a few went so far as to say it was impossible. She took their expert opinions very seriously and had some serious anxiety about what the coming days would bring. People had already started dying and she couldn't help but worry that the toll would continue to rise substantially.

"You okay, Jane?"

She let out a breath and watched it steam in front of her face. "Yeah, Steve. Thanks. I just don't like this cold."

"You want me to get one of the guys to fetch you a coffee from the van? There's still a bit left in the Thermos."

Jane cringed at the thought of the stale taste of lukewarm coffee from a flask. "No, thanks, that's okay. I just want to get back to the studio. There's going to be other things to report before the night is through, I can feel it."

"You're probably right," agreed Steve. "We'll get going in a few minutes. Mike and Tony are just trying to dig the van loose."

Jane's eyes widened. "What?"

Steve tutted. "Hard to believe, but in the short

time you were reporting, the snow was heavy enough to cover the wheels."

"Oh, hell!"

Steve waved a hand. "Don't worry about it, Kitten. We'll be gone in a jiffy."

Jane narrowed her eyes. "I told you to stop calling me that. We're not together anymore."

"Pity," said Steve. "You look hot in that ski-jacket."

Jane laughed and decided to head for the van. The snow was beginning to melt through her boots and her thick socks were becoming soaked. It was hard to walk and, after only a few steps, her calves began to ache. She wanted nothing more than to wrap up warm at home with a DVD and her cat, Thompson, but she knew the night would be long. At times like this it was all hands on deck. The freak weather conditions would keep every news channel in the world busy until its cause was known.

"Hey, Mike, how's it going?"

Mike was kneeling next to the van, mini-shovel in hand. "My hands are so numb you could put them on a pair of tits and I wouldn't even know."

"Charming," said Jane, laughing. "I guess I should stay out of the van until you're done. My weight would probably make it harder to get the van free?"

"Dunno," said Mike, "but don't worry about it. I'll manage."

"You're a dear," said Jane. She patted him on the head and stepped into the van via the side door, then slid it shut after her. The van was slightly warmer than outside, but was still uncomfortably chilly. A bank of blinking monitors lined one side and she sat on the stool in front of them. The monitor on the left showed the studio feed that was currently going out live to the nation. The monitor on the right showed the feed from Steve's camera outside – the images were still streaming but were not being recorded. Back at the studio, one of her colleagues was interviewing an ecology expert. He was currently refuting claims that a damaged Ozone layer could be the cause of all the snow.

Something caught her attention on the other monitor. The camera mounted on a tripod outside had picked up the image of Tony, the other production assistant. He was currently taking a piss off the top of the bridge to the deserted road below.

"Nice," Jane commented, shaking her head. Steve was in the picture too, speaking on his phone. He was probably checking in with the studio to confirm it was okay to come in. Beyond both men was something else: a dark shape in the background, partly out of focus and obscured by the snowfall.

What is that?

The shape seemed to be coming closer, heading towards Steve and Mike at the centre of the bridge. Jane leant closer to the screen to try and make out some further details. The dark shadow didn't seem like another person. It was closer to a small vehicle than anything else – perhaps a motorcycle.

As Jane continued watching, the shadow continued getting closer. Inch by inch, the shape revealed itself. When it became clearer, Jane was even more confused.

"What the...?"

It appeared to be an animal of some kind; a huge dog maybe – but too big and too hairy. It was creeping up slowly behind Tony, who was still taking a leak.

Jesus, is that guy part-camel or what?

Jane kept waiting for Tony or Steve to notice the creature, but they did not. She tried urging them through the monitor to look around, but of course she knew it was hopeless – she wasn't telepathic. Just when she was about to lean out of the van and shout for their attention, the creature made itself known to the two men outside.

The over-sized hound pounced at Tony from behind, crushing him up against the bridge's railings. The monitor didn't give out sound but Jane could hear his startled cries from inside the van anyway. The bloodcurdling screams that followed were unpleasant enough, but twinned with the disturbing images on the feed monitor they were horrifying. The beast outside had pinned Tony to the ground and was ripping and tearing at his back. The snow turned red all around.

Steve realised the situation and made a run for it, most likely heading for the van. He exited the view of the camera and Jane was left wondering how close by he was. A second later her stomach turned as she watched the hound-beast leaving the mutilated corpse of Tony behind to give chase to Steve.

Jane stared at the monitor and tried to control her breathing. Steve's screams were coming closer and it wasn't long before she heard Mike's join them. Outside of the van the two men were being attacked by something she couldn't describe – something unnatural.

Banging at the van door.

"Jane, let me in. Open the door." It was Steve.

Jane stared at the door handle and found herself unable to move from her seat. Every part of her mind screamed at her to let Steve in, but every fibre of her nerve-endings refused to let her move. Steve continued to scream as ripping sounds began.

Whatever was out there was ripping him to shreds. Mike was probably already dead, and here she was, hiding like a coward while it all happened only inches away from her.

I just report the news. I don't take part in it.

Steve's screams finally stopped and Jane sat in silence, listening only to the sounds of her own panting breath. She turned back around to face the monitors. The live feed from the studio had gone black, but the camera outside was still recording. On it she could see the snarling face of a jagged-toothed demon appear from off-camera. Then she saw its jaws gape wide and the video feed was no more.

Jane waited in terror for what seemed like an eternity, hoping against all hope that the beast would go away. But it didn't.

The van began to rock as the creature attacked it, trying to get at the prize inside. Jane Hamilton cowered in the rear of the vehicle, knowing it was only a matter of minutes until she joined the recent death toll.

CLOUD COVER

Quinton Barstow was worried. Flying an airliner was nothing new to him; he was more nervous driving a car in actual fact. In a car you have to trust in the driving skills of other people, and trust that people are even paying attention, but in a plane it's just you and the clouds; nothing to crash into and nothing that could go wrong in the engines – there were just far too many ground checks to miss anything. Piloting an airliner was almost fully-automated and pretty plain sailing – *or flying to be more accurate, and excuse the pun.* Yet he was worried all the same.

All of the above only applied, however, when the aircraft's electrical systems were responding correctly. This evening they were not, and Quinton could think of no reason why. Any errors with the plane's on-board computers should have been rectified by a quick reset, but he had tried that several times now to no avail. He needed those systems to compensate for what his eyes could not see. The current weather was making his natural vision near-useless.

"I can't believe they cleared us to fly in this," said Quinton's co-pilot, James.

"They didn't see it coming," replied Quinton. "The weather reports for the week ahead were mostly clear. All of this cloud cover doesn't make any sense."

"You think we should bring her down at the nearest airport?"

Quinton looked at his dials and meters. The spindles spun and flickered without any sense of reason. They were flying blind. "I'm beginning to think so."

"Okay," said James. "I'll try and contact ground support at Paris. They should be able to receive us."

Quinton nodded his agreement and continued to examine his controls. The autopilot navigation system was displaying random error codes in sequence, as if it could not decide what its problem was. The dials continued to spin and the altitude indicator seemed to think that the plane had banked to the left 90-degrees. In twenty years of fly-ing, Quinton had not witnessed such a catastrophic failure of instrumentation.

"I can't reach anyone," said James without any sign of exaggeration.

Quinton looked at him. "What?"

James thumbed at buttons and switches on the console but gave up with a concerned sigh. "I'm get-ting nothing but static."

"That's nonsense. De Gaulle is only thirty-miles away.

"They're not responding. I'm not even sure they're reading us."

Quinton did not like this at all. "Okay, we'll hold position in the area for thirty minutes. Keep trying to reach someone. Try Heathrow."

James nodded uncertainly and went back to twisting dials and flicking switches. Quinton would have liked to have inputted some commands into the guidance system and gone and stretched his legs, but the way things were, meant that he had to remain at the plane's manual controls. He steered in a steady curve, planning to circle until they spoke to someone on the ground.

As was natural to an airline pilot in the 21st Cen-tury, Quinton began to worry about the bogeyman of all frequent flyers. He wondered whether his air-

craft had been the target of terrorists. Had the on-
board systems been tampered with in the effort to
bring the plane down? Was this just step one of 9/11
part two?

No. Something told Quinton that his concerns
were misplaced. For all the effort and planning it
would take to disable a plane's systems so entirely, it
would be just as easy to plant a bomb on board or
hijack the cockpit. Whatever was going on here had
to be down to some other cause. Quinton couldn't
understand why, but he felt that it had something to
do with the weather.

A knock at the cockpit's door startled Quinton
and he spun around on his cabin chair. After a
hostess identified herself, he pressed the lock release and a red light above the door turned green.
Samantha entered with a mug of coffee for both
him and James. Coffee was as necessary to a pilot's
job as aircraft fuel and he couldn't have welcomed
anything more at that moment. He took one of the
steaming mugs from the hostess and thanked her.
She looked back at him with a scrunched up expression that he supposed meant she had an issue
to raise with him.

"What is it?" he asked her.

She took in a breath as though she had many
words to get out. "It's really bizarre. I don't even

know how to explain it really. At first it was just one or two passengers but then more and more people started to complain, and now I think it's everyone."

"Spit it out," Quinton told her.

"Okay, okay. Well, it would appear that anything electrical has gone a bit haywire. The passenger's phones, ipads, mp3 players, et cetera have all gone a bit...funny."

Quinton raised an eyebrow. "Funny?"

Samantha nodded. "All the displays have gone squiggly as if something is interfering with them."

Quinton turned around and looked at his own malfunctioning gadgets. Something wasn't adding up here, and anything unknown aboard a plane could be extremely dangerous. He leant forward and pressed the intercom button. The normal *ding!* sound did not occur. In fact nothing happened at all.

"Damn it! The intercom is down. Samantha could you inform the passengers to turn off all electrical devices. Tell them that...we're passing through an electrical storm and leaving them on could permanently damage them. Also, please inform them that we will be performing an unscheduled landing due to adverse weather conditions."

Samantha nodded, but didn't seem comforted by his suggestions. Quinton couldn't blame her, he wasn't either. He turned to his co-pilot. "You got anything, James?"

James' bleak expression told him the answer was no.

Quinton bit at his lip. There were no protocols for this. In the event of system failure, the plane needed to land, without question, but the danger of coming down unguided in the thick snow blizzard that hid beneath the cloud cover would be a near suicide-mission. The situation was dire, and as Captain it was his responsibility to decide what to do next.

"Okay, James, enough. We're going to bring her down."

The co-pilot's eyes went wide. "We're going to land blind?"

"What choice do we have? I would rather that then run the risk of falling out of the sky if the engines fail."

James nodded. Quinton knew the other man thought he was right. It just didn't make the decision any easier.

"Okay," said James. "Reducing speed. Descending to 20,000 feet."

Quinton prayed that the plane's landing gear would deploy when approaching the runway. Being mechanical, he hoped they would. After all, the flaps and rudders were all responding.

Many tense minutes of ensuing silence were eventually broken when James spoke again. "Cruising at 20,000 feet. Runway is approximately twenty miles out."

"Reduce altitude to 10,000 feet."

James did as he was instructed and Quinton looked at his dials out of habit despite the fact they were currently useless. Once he reminded himself of this, he instead chose to look out of the cockpit's wide, glass window. Now that the plane was descending, he could see the bulbous clouds below more clearly. They seemed unending, letting no light from below make it through. Which was why Quinton thought it inordinately strange when he saw several bright lights coming from above the plane.

He craned his neck to get a better viewing angle and saw that more than a dozen glowing spheres had appeared in the sky. They seemed to be falling, like meteorites, but Quinton knew that wasn't what they were. He knew that, because they were falling too slowly, not free-plummeting the way a lump of space debris would.

"What the hell is that," asked James, suddenly noticing.

Quinton stared out at the descending lights and wondered that himself. The way they moved was almost gentle, as if they had some great purpose that could not be rushed. It was then that a blinding light also filled the cabin.

The two pilots cried out and shielded their eyes, holding onto their chairs as they fought to stay seated. Mere seconds later, the light had gone again, and Quinton opened his eyes. The lights outside were still falling, but something inside the cabin had been altered. Something unexplainable.

Quinton looked down at his instruments with horror as he realised that they were no longer there. All that remained was a blackened husk of metal where dials and equipment used to be. The smell of ash lingered in the air, and Quinton felt dizzy as he realised something else.

His dizziness turned to panic.

The engines had stopped. They were going down.

Outside, the bright lights continued falling like stars, Angels from heaven. The plane fell faster.

JACK

It was funny how people found religion in times of crisis. People that hadn't seen the insides of a church for years would suddenly get down on their knees and pray, whenever they were out of any other options. As much as Father Pitt enjoyed seeing his pews full of parishioners, he knew they were all hypocrites.

He considered giving another sermon, but then decided against it. Nobody was listening. His parishioners were huddled together in small groups and families, seeking only the shelter and community that the church provided, nothing else. They were not looking for tales of morality. As soon as the snow cleared, they would be gone again, returning to their mundane and selfish lives. In many ways the drastic snowfall was a blessing. Perhaps it was God's way to send these lambs to Father Pitt, so that he may attempt to capture their spirits and return them to the Lord's path. But he could no longer be bothered.

The church had been full for almost twelve hours now as the snow outside continued to fall so deeply that people had started turning up for fear that the world was ending. No one stated such absurdities, but their presence at the church spoke of a collective fear unspoken. At first, Father Pitt had served his calling well; had sought to help them with their anxieties and teach them about God's plan for them. Within a few hours, however, he saw the futility of such pursuits.

Then they found the first body.

～

Mary found the body in the church's sole toilet. It was a small, recently-built cubicle set inside the entrance corridor that led inside the church. Mary had been fighting the urge to urinate for a while, too chilly to unwrap herself from her seat, but she could hold it no longer.

The toilet's door had been unlocked when she

tried it and she hurriedly stepped inside without thinking about it.

The dead man staring back at her made her yelp.

She had noticed the overweight man earlier in the evening, alone and praying. Now he was sat upright on the toilet with his pants around his ankles, guts spilling from his bulbous stomach which peeked out beneath his ill-fitting sweater.

Mary slipped on the bloody tiles and fell against the wall.

She screamed.

~

Dr Wallace came out of the toilet wiping his bloody hands on his shirt. In all his years of being a Doctor he had not seen such a grotesque wound. The man's stomach had been torn in two, his large intestine severed and leaking out onto the floor. The smell was overpowering and would soon invade the interior of the church and make them all gag.

"What happened to him?" asked the woman who had found him.

"Mary, is it?" he asked. She nodded. "Well, my answer is that I have no idea, except to say that he was clearly murdered."

Everyone in the church gasped. Some of the women began to cry. The church's priest stepped forward, a look of utter despair on his face. "I don't understand. How could he have been murdered with all of us here?"

"Yeah," said a ginger-headed man wearing a green cardigan. "He was sat in the corner praying only twenty minutes ago. I saw him."

Wallace shrugged. "All I'm telling you is that he didn't die of natural causes. He was gutted like an animal. Also, I found this..." He offered out his hand so that everyone could see. It was a playing card: the Jack of Hearts. "It was forced into his mouth," Wallace explained.

"Oh God," said a young blonde of perhaps twenty. She had her hand to her mouth.

"What is it?" Father Pitt asked her.

"It's Jack the Raper."

Wallace huffed. "You mean that killer in the papers?"

The girl nodded. She wore a supermarket uniform and a name tag that read: *Kelly*. "That's his thing," she said. "His calling card or whatever."

"How do you know that?" someone asked.

"Because I like reading about serial killers and stuff. I've googled this guy like a hundred times."

"That's sick."

The girl rolled her eyes. "*Whatever!* Doesn't change the fact that this is him. He's already killed seven people, and every time he leaves a playing card stuffed in their mouths – always the Jack of Hearts. The papers say it represents sin because of its link to gambling and the heart is supposed to show lust. There was a whole article on it from some professor guy."

"Are you serious?" Wallace asked.

"Yes. The guy breaks into people's homes, kills any husbands or men in the house, and then rapes and kills the wife. That's why the papers have called him Jack the Raper."

"I feel sick," said a woman in the back of the assembled group.

Wallace shook his head. He was feeling rather nauseous himself. "I have to report this," he said.

"Well, no one has a mobile that works," Kelly said. "I think the snow is interfering or something."

"I'll have to go find someone, then," said Wallace.

"You can't go out there," said the man in the green cardigan. "The snow is three feet deep. We're all stuck here. With a goddamn killer in the room no less. Jesus Christ." Father Pitt cringed at the blasphemy and the man seemed embarrassed. "Sorry," he quickly added.

Wallace wasn't in the mood for a debate, so he headed towards the church's exit corridor. He tried to ignore the fecal scent of the dead man in the toilet as he passed. Up ahead was the old, wooden door of the church. He grasped the large brass hoop that constituted the handle and turned and pulled. The door fell open with force, knocking Wallace back onto his ass. Snow flooded in from outside, piling up on the ancient carpet.

"I can't believe it," Wallace said as he scurried back to his feet. "The snow must be six feet now. How long have we been in here?"

"Last time we checked outside was about six hours ago," said the ginger man in the cardigan. "It was nowhere near that high then."

"It's the end of the world," said a woman in the crowd. She was the first one to finally say it. The first one to say what they were all thinking.

"We have to get out of here," Bradley whimpered, reaching into the pocket of his cardigan and pulling out his phone. The LCD display still read NO SIGNAL and he sighed as he put it back away.

"Calm down," Dr Wallace told him. "The more

we panic, the less rational we will be, and that's the last thing we need right now."

"So what do we do?" Mary asked. "Are we in danger?"

"I'm sure we're fine," said Father Pitt. "We just need to stay calm."

Kelly began flapping her arms. "*Calm?* Calm? How the heck can we stay calm with Jack the Raper around?"

Bradley was getting annoyed at the girl's wild assertions of a serial killer being amongst them. Life was a pretty shitty place, for sure, but he wasn't about to believe that this 'Jack the Rapist' was currently standing in the same church that he was. "Stop making assumptions," he said. "We don't know what happened to that man in the toilet."

"We know he was murdered," said Wallace. "And with the snow the way it is outside, we know that it was one of us that did it. No one else could have gotten in."

"We know no such thing," said Father Pitt. "Anything could have happened."

Bradley had heard enough. He just wanted to sit down and wait for things to blow over. He went over to one of the pews and sat down. As soon as he did, the church's lighting went out.

~

Kelly shook her head. This was bad. Snowed-in inside a church with Jack the Raper, and the lights had just gone out.

"Everybody hold on a minute and I'll get some candles," said Father Pitt. "It's not a problem."

Everyone mumbled anxiously in the dark and all Kelly could see was the soft, flickering shadows of their movement.

"This is so screwed up," said a voice. Kelly thought it was the man in the cardigan, sitting on one of the pews.

Maybe he's the killer. He is *a bit of an oddball.*

Jeez, I can't wait to get out of here. I'm freezing my tits off and I don't want to get raped and butchered.

Now that the quiet buzz of electricity had halted, the whistle and howl of the wind outside was the only sound.

When Father Pitt returned with an arm full of candles, which they lit one by one, they all found another body.

It was the cardigan man.

~

"We were just talking to the guy," Kelly shouted. "Like two minutes ago. What happened?"

Dr Wallace leant over the man's body, pulling up his ripped and bloody cardigan that was no longer green but red. Then he opened the dead man's mouth. He pulled out another playing card and held it to the group. "It's another Jack of Hearts."

"I want to get out of here. Somebody get me out of here." It was Mary. Apparently two dead bodies in one night was too much for her. She began fluttering about, shoving people at random and begging for their help. Her panic was infecting the other half-dozen people in the group. They were all starting to lose it.

"Should we slap her or something?" Kelly asked.

"No," said the Doctor, who quickly grabbed the woman in a calm embrace. "Calm down, dear. We're all here with you. Nothing bad will happen to you."

Yeah, right, thought Kelly. *Two down already.*

"This is the Devil's work," said Father Pitt. "Someone capable of such deeds has no place in my church."

"We need to find out who it is," said Kelly. "We need to check for...I don't know; clues or something."

"The playing cards," said a nearby woman. "We

should check everyone to see if they have any of those cards on them."

"Good idea," said Wallace, "But without resorting to a strip search, it would be very easy to hide such a thing."

"No one is looking in *my* knickers," said Kelly.

"Maybe that's because you have something to hide," said Mary, suddenly back in control of herself.

"Yeah, right," said Kelly. "Little old me has been travelling around England raping and killing people. Are you on drugs, you daft cow?"

"How dare you call me that."

"Ladies, ladies," said the Doctor. "We can't assume anything right now."

"It's probably you," said Kelly. "There are lots of killers that worked in the medical profession. It's even thought that Jack the Ripper was a surgeon. Then there's Harold Shipman, the Angel of Death killings, and Marcel Petiot in France."

"It's you," said Mary again, pointing her finger at Kelly. "You're a freak. Who knows all that stuff you're talking about?"

"It's just an interest," said Kelly. "It doesn't make me a freak. I just like to read. You should try it sometime, you dumb bitch."

Mary lunged through the candle-lit shadows and went for Kelly's throat. Kelly jumped aside, up the steps that housed the church's altar and lectern. Her foot struck something and she went hurtling to the floor.

"What the fuck is that?" she cried out as she fumbled about on her hands and knees. When she felt the soft, slick flesh of another dead body, she screamed.

It was crazy, but Mary was certain that the little blonde bitch had something to do with what was happening. She kept going on about serial killers, like they were some sort of heroes or something. The girl was small, sure, but that didn't mean she couldn't stab someone to death.

And maybe she has an accomplice. Maybe I'm surrounded by bloody killers.

"That's three people dead," said Wallace.

"We're dropping like flies," said Kelly.

"God help us," said Father Pitt. "Let me head into the vestry and try to get a call through to 999. The police need to get here right away."

"I'll come with you," said Mary. "I don't want to stay out here."

"Fair enough," said Father Pitt. "Come along then."

The two of them disappeared into the shadows, their candles bobbing along through the darkness. A shiver rushed along Mary's spine as she realised she was now more alone than she had been. There was still a handful of people gathered in the church, but how could she trust any of them?

She gathered a candle in each of her hands and then went and followed Father Pitt. Inside her little cocoon of flickering light, she felt as if she might just make it. She just wished it was not so cold. It was as if the snow was never going stop falling and they would be trapped there forever.

Father Pitt had been gone for several minutes and Wallace was getting anxious. As a Doctor he was expected to be one of society's wardens, in the same way as a teacher or police officer. It would not do for him to show his fear at the situation. People would be looking to him as some sort of authority. The priest, too – which was making him wonder where Father Pitt had gotten to.

"Is everybody okay?" he asked the group. "I'm just going to find out what Father Pitt is doing."

No one said anything so Wallace felt it safe to sneak away for a few moments. He headed down towards the altar and then turned right into a small side door. Through it was a small antechamber that had been turned into an office of some kind. Lying on the floor, dead, was the older woman, Mary. A few feet away from her body an old swivel chair lay. Slumped over it, and also dead, was Father Pitt.

Wallace raced back out into the church. "They're dead," he shouted. "The priest and the woman are both dead. We need to get out of here right now."

It was finally too much and the group lost it completely. Everyone began swarming around, heading for the nearest windows and doors. Wallace headed back to the church's front entrance and pulled open the door again. Just like before, the snow piled in and covered the carpet; only this time it was higher than the doorway. He was faced with a sheer face of packed snow. Against all rationality, he lunged forwards anyway. He shoved both arms into the snow and succeeded only in getting his hands and wrists through before it compacted and became utterly solid. It would take a tonne of pressure to clear the doorway.

They were trapped.

And to make matters worse, someone back inside the church was screaming loudly. And then the scream suddenly stopped.

~

Kelly was about to shit a brick. Another person was dead; gutted just like the others. Even with a group of people huddled together, someone was managing to pick them off one by one. If only it wasn't for the dark.

The latest dead person was an older gentleman who had kept to himself since entering the church. His wife had found him propped up against a large wooden cross at the side of the church. A playing card hung from his lips: a Jack of Hearts.

Now there were only a handful of the group left and Kelly wasn't about to trust any of them. The main suspect in her eyes was the Doctor, but it could have been anyone. She had to keep her distance.

The wife of the dead man had now joined forces with a teenage boy in trying to smash through one of the stained glass windows. It held strong, braced by the snow against its other side.

The Doctor was sitting by the front door, slumped on the floor. It seemed like he had finally lost it, too, but it could have been an act. Then there was a middle-aged man and another woman who was likely his wife. That was all that was left of the group of strangers.

To think we all came here for safety. What's the worst that could happen in a church?

Kelly wanted to be alone until she knew it was safe. There were bodies everywhere, which is why she decided that the church's small side office would be as good as anywhere. At least it had a door she could close. She quickly headed there before the killer attacked anybody else.

Inside the office, the smell of blood and guts was strong, but she would have to bare it. She turned around and started to close the door. The pain she felt when the knife went into her guts was excruciating.

∼

Wallace sat on the floor and shook his head. He stared into the flickering flame of his candle and asked himself over and over if he was dreaming. Half a dozen people murdered in less than an hour, and there was no escape. No way to find help.

As he sat there, Wallace's mind began turning to maudlin thoughts; regrets of not having a family and instead choosing to be a slave to his work. What did any of it matter really? Curing people was a worthwhile pursuit for one's lifetime, but it was a selfless task that brought a man no true happiness – not in the way a family did. Wallace had only come here tonight because he had nowhere else.

Why am I thinking things like that? I still have decades left. I am not going to die in this godforsaken church.

Wallace hopped up from the floor and headed out of the church's exit corridor. The church's interior was quiet. There were only a few people still alive inside, but right now they were making no noise and he could not see their candle-light.

"Hello!" Wallace spoke out, not knowing what else to say. "Where is everybody?"

"They are all dead," said a voice from the front of the church."

Wallace gulped and tried to force down an air bubble trapped in his throat. He knew who was speaking to him. Could hardly believe it, but he knew. "Jack the Raper?"

"That is what they call me. The unwashed, sinners. They read their papers, enjoy their trash, and scurry about their rancid little lives with utter disdain for the gifts they were given."

Wallace took slow steps forward. "By God?"

"Of course," the voice almost spat the words.

"Who else? All of you came here tonight for selfish reasons. You seek his comfort when it suits you, but when do you give back anything of yourselves."

Wallace stepped up before the altar and was surprised by who he saw. He shook his head. "But, you were *dead*."

"Did you check my body?" Father Pitt asked. "Perhaps you should have. Now everybody is dead. And you will follow. The Lord has rained down an icy death upon us all, but you are not worthy to die by his majestic hand. I will do his bidding until my time is nigh. I will slice out your life like I have so many before. I will violate your sinful orifices and revel as your soul descends to Hell."

"You're a fruitcake."

"No," said Father Pitt, leaping forward like a man half his age. He drove a long thin blade into Wallace's guts and looked him right in the eyes, smiling. "I am God's will. And soon I will join him in the Kingdom of Heaven. Goodbye Doctor. Give my regard to the serpent king."

Dr Wallace hit the floor, dead. The final victim of the man they called *Jack the Raper*.

WINTER BEFORE LAST

The drive had been a long one. Bristol was a long way from Stoke and the Boxing Day journey had been slow and cautious, the roads slippery with ice and slushed snow. Harry hated winter, hated the cold. In the summer, people came together – BBQs, festivals, zoos, and theme parks – but in the winter people stayed away from each other, wrapped up warm and ignored the outside world. Winter was the season of isolation and loneliness. Yet, out of all the dreary winters of Harry's life, this one had been the best. Sure it was damp, icy, and grey; sure he had spent the last week with his wife's condescending parents; and sure he was itching to get back to work, but this winter was great for one reason: Toby.

Of course he had spent several Christmases

with his son already, but those had been interspersed with work and commitments. This year his furniture business was successful enough that he had been able to leave the running of it to his cousin and take a massive ten days off to spend with Toby and his wife, Julie. It had been total bliss to watch his son open his presents on Christmas morning, ripping open the packaging on his new bike and then moving on to the wrapped-up Nintendo DS beneath Julie's parent's tree. He'd never seen his son so happy, and he had never been so happy himself. What Julie had gone on to tell him that night had only made the day even more special.

He still couldn't believe she was pregnant.

"You paying attention?" asked Julie, sitting on the passenger seat beside him.

Harry turned to her and smiled. "Yeah, sorry. I'm just so happy. Life is pretty good, huh?"

Julie smirked and shook her head at him. "I think you had a better Christmas than little man."

Harry glanced back at his sleeping son on the back seat and agreed. In fact, he may have had a better Christmas than anyone.

"Anyway," said Julie, "you should have come off at junction 16. You just missed it."

Harry shook his head, annoyed with himself. "Bugger it. Okay, I'll come off at the next one."

Julie mumbled something under her breath and Harry just about heard her.

"Did you just call me a fish head?"

Julie shrugged. "Dunno what you're talking about."

Harry huffed. "Oh, really? Well it sounded like you called me a fish head."

"Maybe I did, maybe I didn't."

"Well, that's rich, coming from a dog head."

Julie hit Harry in the arm, causing him to swerve slightly. "Cheeky sod."

"Whoa! Watch it, woman, you'll have me in a ditch."

Julie laughed. "Sorry. I didn't mean to endanger your perfect driving record."

"Always pays to be safe. Baby on-board."

Julie looked back at her son and smiled. She was so beautiful as a mother. There was something about her now, that Harry loved, which had not been there before Toby's birth. It was something un-explainable to anyone without a child of their own.

Harry was just about to say, I love you, when something caught his attention from the corner of his eye. The sight was followed by a lot of chaotic noise.

"Shit!" Harry saw the vehicle on the opposite side of the motorway swerve. It careened across several lanes and came crashing up against the central reservation several yards ahead. His stomach fluttered and he thanked God for the near-escape, but then the speeding vehicle cartwheeled into the air, flipping the balustrade upon impact and hurtling, end over end, down the other side of the motorway; the lane that Harry was occupying. Harry would have liked more time to react, but before he even thought to swerve out of the vehicle's path, his entire being seemed to shudder as his consciousness was battered from his body.

Harry opened his eyes and then closed them again. A light had burned his eyes and he had to flutter his eyelids until the dull aching went away. He found himself staring at a blank white ceiling with a small, tinted window looking out at star-filled sky. It was a vehicle; the back of a van perhaps. When a paramedic appeared in his field of view, Harry realised he was lay in the back of an ambulance.

The woman's name badge read: Penelope. "Hey there," she said. "Everything is okay. You've just been in an accident."

Harry shot up on the stretcher. "My son...my wife?"

The paramedic tried to ease him back down but he resisted. "There are people trying to help them right now."

"Help them? What do you mean?"

The woman looked him in the eye for a moment but could not hold the gaze. Something seemed to trouble her. Harry didn't feel like getting information about his family second hand from someone else. He pushed the woman aside forcefully and stumbled off of the bed. His legs felt like jelly as he hit the tarmac outside the ambulance. His breathing was painful too, but none of that mattered. He needed to find his family.

There were flashing lights all around him and fluorescent white jackets flitting to and fro. The motorway had been closed off, probably by sideways police cars at the entrance to each junction. Harry staggered forward. There was a huge fire truck up ahead and it blocked his view any further down the road. People seemed to be congregating in that area and he headed towards them, as fast as his confused feet would take him.

"Excuse me, sir?" A police officer walked up to Harry with a palm raised. "You shouldn't be here."

"Harry swiped at the hand in his face and snarled. "Where is my family?"

The officer stepped towards Harry, but backed

off when he saw that there was no chance of his authority holding any weight. The man tried a different tact. "They're being rescued now."

"Rescued from what?"

The police officer sighed. "My name is Officer Tonks. Why don't you come and sit down with me and we'll have a chat about what is going on."

Harry looked at the man and saw genuine compassion, but that didn't change the fact that Harry didn't want a conversation with anyone but his wife. He turned away from the officer and hurried towards the fire truck. The man did not give chase.

Once Harry reached the bright red vehicle, he saw the wreckage beyond. His brand new Mercedes was a ball of twisted steel and a mangled truck seemed to be entwined with it. Before he knew it, Harry was vomiting all over the floor. Maybe he had a concussion, but he was pretty sure it was purely because of what he was seeing.

Despite his injuries, Harry ran forward, dodging past anybody that tried to stand in his way. Over at the pile of compacted vehicles, two firemen worked at the steel with heavy cutters. When they saw Harry coming at them, wild-eyed, they stepped aside with concern.

It was then that Harry saw what was left of his family. He could make out Julie's crushed face, squashed beneath the Mercedes window strut. One of her eyes seemed to bulge from her socket. Harry fell to his knees and tried to reach out to her, but he could not. As he tried to crawl his way into the car, he saw the mess that had been his son. Toby's body no longer resembled human form. If it were not for bloody scraps of clothing and puckered flesh and protruding bones, Harry would not have even known it was his son.

Harry screamed out, loud enough to reach the moon. Someone pulled him back by the armpits and he kicked out and struggled. The person turned out to be Tonks and the officer was no longer willing to stand by. He controlled Harry's body with a well-trained grasp of how joints and pressure points worked. Harry was forced by his twisted elbow to walk away from the scene.

"Why?" Harry cried out. "Why are they dead and not me. Why am I fine?"

"I'd say because you're lucky," said Tonks, "but I think you'd probably hit me. You were thrown free from the car upon impact. So was the driver of the other car. Your family...well they didn't have the luck that you did. I'm sorry, Harry, I really am."

Harry felt weak and struggled to keep his legs from folding like accordions. "How do you know my name?"

"Paramedics found your driver's license in your wallet. Would you like me to contact anyone?"

Harry shook his head. "...No. I-I will do it later. I want to see my family. I want them out of there."

Tonks nodded. "I know you do. They're working on it. Let's just get you to the hospital for now. There's no way to deal with something as terrible as this, so don't try."

Any fight Harry might ever have possessed was gone from him now. He allowed the officer to take him by the arm towards the ambulance and he would also let them take him to the hospital too. There was no reason to resist now, no reason to fight...no reason to care. Harry's life was without purpose and always would be from now on.

As he neared the ambulance, Harry noticed something up ahead. There were two other police officers standing with a weary-looking man. They were breathalysing him. Harry's own breath caught in his chest and the only way he could let it out again was by talking. "Is that the other driver?"

Tonks seemed to stiffen then and started leading Harry at a slightly different angle, putting distance between them and the other officers. "Yes," he said. "He says he doesn't know what happened. He'll be taken in for questioning once the paramedics clear him."

"Why are they breathalysing him?"

"Standard procedure," said Tonks without missing a beat.

Harry nodded and let the officer think he was satisfied with the answer. Really, he was taking one last, long look at the man that had just murdered his family, and committing his face to memory. Harry realised that, in actual fact, his life still did have a purpose: to take the life of the man that took his.

Enjoy what's left of your life, whoever you are, thought Harry, *because I promise that this will be your Final Winter.*

WANT FREE BOOKS?

Don't miss out on your FREE Iain Rob Wright horror starter pack. Five free bestselling horror novels sent straight to your inbox. No strings attached.

Just visit iainrobwright.com

PLEA FROM THE AUTHOR

Hey, Reader. So you got to the end of my book. I hope that means you enjoyed it. Whether or not you did, I would just like to thank you for giving me your valuable time to try and entertain you. I am truly blessed to have such a fulfilling job, but I only have that job because of people like you; people kind enough to give my books a chance and spend their hard-earned money buying them. For that I am eternally grateful.

If you would like to find out more about my other books then please visit my website for full details. You can find it at:

www.iainrobwright.com.

Also feel free to contact me on Facebook, Twitter, or email (all details on the website), as I would love to hear from you.

If you enjoyed this book and would like to help, then you could think about leaving a review on Amazon, Goodreads, or anywhere else that readers visit. The most important part of how well a book sells is how many positive reviews it has, so if you leave me one then you are directly helping me to continue on this journey as a fulltime writer. Thanks in advance to anyone who does. It means a lot.

Iain Rob Wright is one of the UK's most successful horror and suspense writers, with novels including the critically acclaimed, THE FINAL WINTER; the disturbing bestseller, ASBO; and the wicked screamfest, THE HOUSEMATES.

His work is currently being adapted for graphic novels, audio books, and foreign audiences. He is an active member of the Horror Writer Association and a massive animal lover.

www.iainrobwright.com
FEAR ON EVERY PAGE

For more information
www.iainrobwright.com
iain.robert.wright@hotmail.co.uk

OTHER HORROR BY IAIN ROB WRIGHT

- Animal Kingdom
- AZ of Horror
- 2389
- Holes in the Ground (with J.A.Konrath)
- Sam
- ASBO
- Dark Ride
- The Housemates
- Sea Sick
- Ravage
- Savage
- The Picture Frame
- Wings of Sorrow
- The Gates
- Legion
- Extinction
- Defiance
- TAR
- House Beneath the Bridge
- The Peeling
- Blood on the bar
- Escape!
- 12 Steps

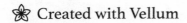